AND THIS IS TRUE

EMILY MACKIE

SCEPTRE

First published in Great Britain in 2010 by Sceptre
An imprint of Hodder & Stoughton
An Hachette UK company

First published in paperback in 2010

1

A CIP catalogue record for this title is available from the British Library.

ISBN 978 0 340 99251 7

Typeset in Sabon MT by Palimpsest Book Production Limited,
Grangemouth, Stirlingshire

Printed and bound by
Clays Ltd, St Ives plc

Hodder & Stoughton policy is to use papers that are natural, renewable and
recyclable products and made from wood grown in sustainable forests.
The logging and manufacturing processes are expected to conform to
the environmental regulations of the country of origin.

Hodder & Stoughton Ltd
338 Euston Road
London NW1 3BH

www.hodder.co.uk

For my mum

1

You have to start with a bang, he said. He clapped his hands together when he said it. BANG, like that. You've got to make people want to read what you have to say, otherwise they're not going to stay interested. They'll put you down and go make themselves a cup of tea and then they'll never come back. No chance. If you want to be a writer, boy – he said – you've got to grip people by the throat and shake them in those first few seconds. Shake them hard like you're never going to let them go. Then they'll be so dazed they'll have to read on. There'll be no time for tea. No thoughts of anything except reading your story.

I kissed my father once; when he was sleeping. It happened in the van. He'd been lying with his head cocked back and his mouth slightly open. Out for the count. I called his name softly and then more loudly and then louder still, but nothing. It was funny. I guess I thought it was some kind of a game to see what it would take to wake him up. I crawled across the van and poked him in the side.

'Marshall.'

He didn't even flinch. With thumb and forefinger I separated a couple of hairs from his head and tweaked hard. The hairs came away but Marshall slept on. I touched his face. Nothing. I stroked his nose. Nothing. I kissed him. An experiment. He didn't even move or grunt or attempt to roll over. I kissed him again. Nothing. I could smell the pea soup we'd eaten only an hour or two before still on his breath and in his beard. I could taste the salt from his lips. I closed my eyes and held our mouths together. I'm drinking you, I thought. When I opened my eyes again Marshall was still asleep. His breath was slow and deep, unwavering.

'Marshall?'

He didn't move.

When my father wrote, he sat hunched over his jotter, continually frowning while he scribbled out his fits of inspiration. My father always frowned with great intensity whenever he wrote. He leaned into the page as though waiting for it to grow teeth and bite off his head; when eventually he did come up for air, to straighten his back or stretch out his legs, his face certainly seemed chewed somehow. My father would be chewed and then spat back out by his own writing. He did not devour the words so much as let the words devour him. But perhaps that is the making of a good writer.

When my father wrote, he squeezed the pen so tightly his hand cramped up. A painful knotted ache, he said. He had to stop for a while, shake it out, massage his knuckles. There is a hardened wart-like lump on his middle finger where the pen pressed in. When I think of my father writing, all tense and bent up over his paper, I think of that lump. It contains every word he's ever written. I can see them all squeezed up in there, jam-packed, tight. It's waiting to burst, I think, explode and spill out over the paper, onto the floor. Those words want to take over. I imagine them filling up the van like water. They're in my mouth, my nostrils. We're breathing them in.

I didn't just kiss him once. That was a lie. I kissed him several times. But only once when he was awake.

2

I lived in the van with Marshall for eleven years. Not a camper van. Not one of those old hippy brightly coloured things with fold-away beds and a mini kitchen all nicely fitted in. It was a Ford Transit and it was white. The only *hippy* thing about it was the curtain Marshall put up to make the driving space separate from the sleeping space. I used to wonder if that curtain had been salvaged from the house. A thick greying-white material, like cord, with delicate thin flowers sewn into it. I tried to picture it in a living room or bedroom, imagined Marshall pulling it back in the morning to let in the sun. But I knew it was more likely he found the material in a skip somewhere. There was nothing in the van from the house, not even a photo.

The house: I don't remember it, not really. It was just a house. Big square thing with windows and doors. Red brick probably. England not Scotland. Was there a driveway? I don't remember. Let's give it a driveway, a small gravelled space at the front where a couple of cars could park. A garage maybe? Why not? Let's give it a garage. And let's throw in a bird table and water feature, round the back with the overgrown gazebo and creeping ivy. The unattended rock garden. The annual weeds. That's how I like to remember the house, slowly deteriorating, getting eaten away by all that hungry vegetation.

Inside there was a red carpet. It was on the landing at the top of the stairs. It's the only thing I remember about the house because I used to play there. I had a plastic washing-up bowl filled with little metal cars and a floor mat with roads and buildings and traffic lights printed all over it. Those little metal cars were my favourite toys. In particular, I remember a brown car made to look all chipped and rusty. There was some kind of trigger built in so that when something hit its side the bottom half of the door flipped round to look as though a dent had been made. I used to make that car crash all the time. Flip, the dent went round. Off to the garage to get it fixed: flip, the door was as good as new again.

I do not remember the day my father brought home the van, but I like to pretend I do. Me in an empty house, on tiptoes, peeking out through one of the windows as my dad pulls into the driveway. I see him wave at me to join him – and as I go the front door of the house closes behind me, and it locks. 'We're leaving,' I make him say.

Or, 'Nevis boy, I'd like you to meet your new home.' And I feel happy and excited, fit to burst.

We'd left because she'd left. She'd left because she'd found somebody else. A friend of a friend whom they'd both met at a party. An artist, a stone sculptor; renowned for chipping out grotesque images of women with penises and two men's heads for breasts. Apparently she couldn't get enough of it; and couldn't get enough of him either – her wide eyes glued to his with such interest when he spoke. She laughed at his dumb jokes, flicked her hair and flirted when she thought Marshall wasn't looking. She'd been all over him 'like a fly over shit'. And then she left. Abandoned us both. And so Marshall hit the road with his son at his side and pen in his pocket.

My father was always drunk when he told me anything about her. I remember how he'd squeeze my shoulder and breathe his whisky breath into my face, 'But we're all right, 'int we, boy, me an' you. Make a good team. We got each other. Don't nee . . . don't need . . .' and I waited for him to say her name, but he just kept squeezing my shoulder. 'We don't need anybody else.'

My mother: I don't remember her, not at all. Let's make her blonde. My father and I have dark hair. Let's make her have blue eyes because my eyes are brown. She can be tall in heels, smart in her fresh-pressed power suit. Why not? It doesn't make any difference to me. When I think of her now it is only another false memory:

a face I barely recognise looking out from a house I can't picture while my father and I drive away. And neither of us waves.

I only ever asked about her once. In later years when I was old enough to understand what was what, I asked my father this: 'Did you love her?'

And he looked at me blankly. He didn't answer.

'Do you love me?' I asked.

'Of course, Nevis,' he whispered.

And I promised him then, made a silent oath, that I would never leave. I would never abandon him like she did.

The practicalities: that's what they wanted to know about at the farm. 'So how do you go about living in a van for eleven years?' The questions mostly came from Ailsa and were mostly answered by Elspeth, her mother. Where did we sleep? What did we eat? How did we cook?

'They probably had a wee portable stove, Ailsa. Like the one we used campin' in Wales that time. Do ye mind? Rained solid fer five days. Never seen rain like it. An' that's sayin' somethin' comin' from the Highlan's, Mr Gow. Yev driven quite a bit aroon' Scotland, I expect. Eleven years, yev probably explored all the nooks and crannies of Great Britain.'

'But how do ye wash?' Ailsa was obsessed. 'God,

7

there's no WAY I could live without a bath. I have to wash and straighten my hair every day, ye know.'

On that first day in the kitchen; Ailsa was on one side, Elspeth on the other, going on about baths and washing and general hygiene, with Duckman sitting opposite, scratching himself and staring at me; the kettle boiling; the dogs outside barking. I wanted to close my eyes, cover my ears and scream. Instead I stared at the table in front of me. I studied the deep scratch that cut into the wood where I sat. I studied it so hard it seemed to stretch slightly, twist at the corners into an unnerving smile. I kept my mouth shut.

A hand rested on my shoulder. Marshall. I remember how I wanted to turn and bury my face in his jumper, have him close to hide behind.

'Nevis,' he said, 'I've run a bath for you.'

I was shocked to see he'd cut his hair. He'd brushed and cut it back uneven and close to his head. The length that had tangled and knotted into clumps around his shoulders only an hour or so before had gone. And he'd shaved. His cheeks were pinkish clean, his jawline, chin and upper lip free from the wiry hair he'd let grow in the van. His lips seemed thicker, more red without it. He looked different. He wasn't even wearing his own clothes. He was wearing a brown V-neck jumper I'd never seen before and underneath that a white shirt with red and yellow checks. He had clean jeans on, slightly too short in the leg. They must have belonged to Duckman or perhaps Nigel Kerr – the farmer I hadn't met yet.

'My . . . look at you, Mr Gow!' said Elspeth. 'What a handsome man underneath all that hair.' And I saw her shoot a wink at her daughter across the table. I looked up at Marshall and saw him smiling politely.

He moved his hand and touched the back of my neck lightly. 'Follow me, Nevis,' he said.

The bathroom was hot with the steam rising from the bathtub. Marshall walked in first.

'Here.' He pointed to a bright yellow towel draped over the radiator. 'And here,' he said, showing me a pile of clothes on the toilet seat. A pair of jeans and a shirt similar to the one Marshall was wearing. 'They're being very good to us,' he said then. 'They said we could stay a while in their caravan out back.'

'A while?'

'That's right.'

'Until the van's fixed?'

Marshall didn't answer. I looked at his face. Without the beard and long hair he looked thin and his eyes and nose and mouth so much bigger. It'd been a long time since I last saw Marshall without facial hair. I was sure his face had been fuller than that, rounder. He must have been wasting away behind that hair and I never even noticed.

'You look different,' I said.

He nodded.

'Younger,' I said.

He frowned. 'Don't forget to lock the door behind you, Nevis,' he replied. 'We don't want people walking in on you when you're in the bath.'

The practicalities: we slept on sofa cushions in sleeping bags and in the winter, or just when it was cold, we slept close together under heavy blankets. In the cities we washed in public toilets, in the country there were often streams. If nothing else there were always baby wipes, although as I grew older Marshall stopped insisting I wiped my face or cleaned myself properly 'down there'. At night – or when there was no other choice – we shat in bagged buckets, pissed in pint glasses or bottles. For our meals we cooked on a propane gas stove, outside or with the back doors wide open. We never cooked where lots of people could see us, we didn't like attracting unwanted attention. Marshall changed the back door windows to a black tint so nobody could see in. Not just to prevent theft. Travellers are unpopular. We didn't want people knowing we lived there.

Drinking water: a five-gallon container with twist tap at the bottom. Food: a chest full of instant edibles. Tins and jars, packets of noodles and pasta, porridge oats, cereals and cup-a-soups. Things that didn't go off quickly, things that didn't need to be refrigerated. Fruit was good. Potatoes great. Marshall drank black tea and coffee, I used dried milk, one sugar.

Money: I was never really very aware of it. I knew it existed. I understood its necessity. We couldn't have food without money and we couldn't buy fuel. Marshall used to keep a wad of notes and coins in a biscuit tin underneath the driver's seat – and in his inside jacket pocket he kept a black leather wallet full of plastic cards. I knew he had a bank account, although I didn't know how or why or where he got his money from. He was an English teacher before the van. He told me that much. And we lived in London. Maybe he had savings? Maybe the house sold for a lot of money? It just didn't seem very important. I don't remember Marshall ever being short of cash, even though he never sold his stories.

All those written words and not one of them published. I used to imagine my father as an overprotective hen, roosting on his unfinished work, waiting for stories to hatch, perfectly formed, all by themselves.

'Marshall, what are you writing?'

'Shh . . .'

'Can I read it?'

'No, boy.'

'Why not?'

'It's not finished.'

And yet there were thousands of notebooks and journals and illegible paper-clipped scribbles all over the

11

van. I remember waking up one morning covered in these papers.

'Don't move,' Marshall said. 'I'm organising.'

So I lay there for well over an hour in silence, watching my father's eyes scanning those sheets, his hands placing them into piles, shuffling them into some kind of order.

'Are any of them finished?'

'No. Now promise me you'll never read my writing? Not until they're finished.'

So I promised.

Within days of organising his stories, the papers and jotters were scattered everywhere again. We could never keep the van clear. In the end we decided to dedicate the corner behind the driver's seat to his manuscript mountain. Marshall attached thin sheets of wood to the van's sides so we could nail in hooks and hang things from them. Marshall hung up his stories, all the jotters and papers he was working on clamped in bulldog clips and kept neatly on individual hooks so they were easy to find. Our one pot and frying pan were hung on the opposite side, along with our jackets. This freed up floor space for the sofa cushions, blankets, sleeping bags and clothes, which we heaped up under our heads at night for pillows. And then, of course there were the books.

'Every good writer is an avid reader,' said Marshall.

Down the sides of the van were books stacked in towers that toppled over the sofa cushions when we drove. Behind the food chest yet more books were piled and more still on the floor underneath the glove compartment and a selection on the dashboard. Marshall insisted he knew where every book was.

'Cluttered chaos,' Marshall said. 'But organised cluttered chaos.'

Alone in the bathroom I locked the door and turned to the bath of hot steaming water. I studied the taps and the narrow tiled shelf behind it, the bottles of soaps and shampoo and conditioner and body gels. I touched the transparent plastic curtain, covered in colourful fish, that hung limp from a metal bar above; and then moved my hand, slow and dreamlike, onto the shower attached to the wall, its long hose twisting around itself and its showerhead pointing out at an odd angle. I thought then of the public washrooms my father used to take me to when I was much younger: the steam and the soap and the warm, wet smell of bodies washing; the way the men's cocks hung, limp and long and fatter than my own, a thick triangle of hair surrounding them. 'Do as I do,' Marshall used to say and with a flannel we would scrub at our arms, across our chests and around our necks. He used to lather the soap into the short black curly hair around his crotch and wash his penis and balls.

I turned to the toilet, pushed the neat pile of folded

clothes to the floor and sat down. This is my fault, I thought. All my fault. But thinking and feeling guilty doesn't stop the blood pumping around my body and into my cock. It doesn't stop the erections. 'Leave me alone.' I leaned my elbows onto my knees and gripped the roots of my long hair between fingers. 'Just go away. Leave me alone.'

3

It doesn't start at the farm, but I'll start at the farm because sense of place is important and the farm is where everything happens.

A narrow dirt track with deep ruts and potholes leads up to the house through two fenced-off grazing fields. I say 'grazing fields' because that is what they used to be. When we arrived at the farm there was nothing grazing there. The fields were empty except for one row of plastic-covered hay bales left to rot. I was told a week or so later that there used to be cattle, pigs, hens, but the livestock had all been sold after the death of a woman – Catherine Kerr.

There is a feeling of foreboding that comes with approaching a farm consumed by a death. It may sound dramatic, but you know it before you even step onto its mud. It seeps from the earth in puddles, creeps like rising damp into all the walls, it evaporates into the air so that when you breathe you're inhaling the stuffy death into your lungs. And then after spending any amount of time breathing in this dead air, you begin to ooze the death yourself. It infects you. Nigel Kerr, Duckman, they breathed the air longest and moved around the farm as though ghosts of themselves.

'Grief' was the word my father used. 'The Kerrs are grieving,' he said. But that feeling of foreboding doesn't come from grief. It comes from the feeling of 'farm'. I know I'm not wrong. I used to play in fields when I was little, losing myself in wheat crops that were taller than me or digging in the dirt among potatoes and carrots or lying down in grazing fields, absolutely still, so the hares would come out of their burrows and box around me. I know what the feeling of 'farm' is like. Springy with life. Even at harvest time when the farmers are all out picking or cutting their crops with those big combine harvesters, or taking their livestock to be auctioned at market, even then there is life, because you know, don't you? You know it's all part of a living cycle. Take life away and you upset the ebb and flow of everything essential about a farm. I know I'm not wrong. I *know* how I felt when we drove up that track and I am not wrong in saying I felt a most definite sinking sense of foreboding.

The house is a small rectangular block of grey granite stone, two storeys. On its front face there are the twisting brown branches of ivy weaving their way into the walls and the painted white wooden frames of the windows.

The gutters are blocked, overloaded with leaves and meaty earth and twigs from old birds' nests. The roof is tiled with slate, mottled with weather, splotched with circlets of grey and black and green. The slanting porch roof above the front door is similarly tiled. Underneath it on either side of the door there are two bush-like plants sharing their potted soil with weeds and small sproutings of grass. On the step there is a brown mat and next to it, actually cemented into the ground, is a piece of metal which, I was told, is used to scrape the mud from your boots.

The house sits in the basin of a valley. Green and yellow and brown squares of land lead all the way to the bare hills in the distance, the peaks of which touch the clouds or in cold weather gather mist to breathe down into the fields. On a winter morning you will often see this mist leeching close to the land and in the distance the brown body of the hills emerging from its thin veils like a chain of islands. Although on a truly grey day these hills will disappear completely. It is only in clear skies they come out and let the vast, almost empty, space between you and them be known.

Circling the house there is a narrow paved path that leads from the front door round both sides of the building. I will walk it on paper. It's important to remember everything correctly. So, turning right, ignoring the windows on either side of the front door (as they simply look into a furniture-cluttered reception area), the first window of any interest shows the kitchen. A square table in its centre; a maple dresser with crockery and cutlery and ornamentals next to the door on the left; a cherry unit with knife-scarred surface along the furthermost wall, with both a modern oven and a traditional aga fitted into it; another window above the sink looking out into the yard round the back; matching cherry cupboards hanging from the wall on the right and underneath it more unit space for kettle, toaster and other electrical appliances (not to mention scrap paper and magazines, pens and pencil sharpenings, unopened letters, matches, nails, screwdrivers and other such paraphernalia). This room is large and square but with every seat filled around the centre table there is only a narrow walkway left that circles it.

I have broken one of my father's writing rules already: when writing about a room there is no need to focus on everything inside it. That technique, however honest you feel you're being, will only confuse the reader; it clutters their thoughts with furniture and 'things'. The best way to deal with a room – he used to say – is focus on one or at the very most, three important aspects of it.

'And you should choose these aspects carefully, boy. Remember to write in the knife block if later someone is stabbed – even if the murderer doesn't use a kitchen knife, it plants a seed. Do you see?'

There *is* a knife block in the corner of this kitchen. But let me make it quite clear now that there is no murder and no one is stabbed. I am writing it purely because I want to remember there was a knife block in the corner, just like I want to remember the glass jars on the wooden homemade herb rack, the pot of kitchen utensils next to the hob, the bottle of ketchup and brown sauce always left on the side, with their tops stuck together with dried encrusted red or brown sticky matter. But for the sake of Marshall, or maybe more for the memory of his mini pockets of wisdom, perhaps I should do his bidding and pick three things to focus on. So picture this: there is a table in the middle of the room and lining the walls there are wooden units (you can forget they are made of cherry) on top of which there is everything a kitchen normally has plus extra clutter and mess. Lastly there is the floor – dusty terracotta square tiles. I didn't mention these before but perhaps they are the most important aspect to focus on. I certainly spent a lot of time staring at them when made to sit at the kitchen table with the family at the farm. Elspeth, Ailsa, Duckman and the farmer, Nigel Kerr – those are their names. But I will not introduce them yet, not properly. There are plenty more pages to fill concerning them. And there's no rush. My memories need to be laid out clear and concise. This is important.

So moving on. The next window you can look into

is not part of the house, but part of the shed-like extension on its side. A glorified porch made from painted white wooden panels. Through the window – not even made from glass, but plastic – you can see a long wooden bench with wellies and muddy boots underneath and on brass hooks hang green waxed jackets and waterproofs.

Round the side of the house there is nothing much of note. It leads to the dog kennels and the small muddy yard. Behind these kennels begins the narrow strip of trees that runs down and curves around the back of an overgrown field where an old abandoned caravan is kept. Beyond the caravan field and trees there is a small stream – or burn, as Duckman calls it. To follow that burn you would eventually meet the river and bridge where the road out front takes you, or if you crossed the burn and walked through several potato fields, you'd come to a much deeper forest of pine. I could see the trees in the distance, but I never went there. I was scared that if I walked too far and came back too late my father would no longer be at the farm.

Returning to the house, standing at the back door, you are looking directly across the yard, which in theory is not really a yard; the definition of which, I know, requires the space to be enclosed. But it is somewhat squared off by the combination of the house, the kennels and a granite bothy-like building opposite, long with a low roof, which the Kerrs call 'the tool shed'. It, in turn, is not really a tool shed. But alongside miscellaneous junk and clutter – rusty bike frames, wheels, engine parts, bird feed – it also houses some tools. So by definition it is the tool shed and likewise the yard is the yard.

It was in the tool shed that Duckman used to sit on an upturned bucket, roll his cigarettes and smoke. He never used the door, which was bolted shut with a thick and heavy padlock. Instead, he would climb in and out through one of the gaping square holes where a window used to be. Nobody ever went into the tool shed apart from Duckman. They weren't allowed. There was one time I saw Ailsa dare touch her toe onto the windowsill as though about to climb inside and then Duckman appeared at the back door, arms folded. 'You go in there, Ailsa, an' ah'll break ye in half.' He said it with such sincerity and calm. Aggression would have been far less frightening. Ailsa sheepishly lowered her foot back to the ground and ran off.

Directly behind the tool shed is the aforementioned caravan field. An old wooden crossbar gate leads into it. When we first arrived at the farm the field was so overgrown we had to wade through waist-high grass and weeds and tall purple-headed thistles to get to the caravan door. You couldn't even see its little metal step. In fact, I remember Marshall tripped on it and had to steady himself against the wall of the caravan, swearing at his stubbed toe as he did so. I remember this vividly. I know exactly where I was standing, slightly behind and to the left of my father as he cursed and clenched his eyes shut against the pain. I remember holding back. My instinct was to reach for his elbow, ask him, 'You ok?' But I didn't. There was something between us in those first few days, an awkward, uncomfortable tension – unspoken and growing bigger. I held back because I knew if I reached out to him he would snap at me. I didn't even have to touch him for this to happen; the tips of my fingers could accidentally brush the cuffs of his shirt and he'd turn on me in a rage – 'Don't touch me. Do you hear? I said, *don't* touch me.'

Perhaps I am getting ahead of myself. I need to take this steady – and slow. Everything has to be remembered accurately. I was describing the farmhouse.

Continuing round, there is the other window into the kitchen: centre table, wooden units, terracotta-tiled floor. I will also mention the cork notice board on the far wall, pinned to its maximum capacity with notes and receipts and postcards and pamphlets. This is not a 'knife block'; it is merely something you can't see when looking through the opposite window.

Moving on there is a narrow frosted pane of glass which belongs to the toilet underneath the stairs, and next to it the black drainpipe, which runs straight down from the roof gutter. It is fixed to the wall with iron brackets and can hold a boy's bodyweight. I know because I shimmied down it, or rather slipped ungracefully, scraping my knees against the rough stone all the way. Now this is a knife block.

There are two other rooms worth mentioning, although the thick curtains of one are always drawn and I have never been able to see inside. I know it was Nigel Kerr's study and the only way into it was through the forbidden room. This sounds very exciting. Marshall would be impressed. Now there's a room *primed* to be explored. A study you can't get into! Perhaps there's a magical cupboard inside that acts as a portal to another world. Or perhaps there's a trapdoor underneath an old dusty rug that leads into an underground cavern, where a strange furry creature lives and grants you a wish a day. Or perhaps, on a more sinister note, that is where Nigel Kerr stores all the dead bodies. He eats their flesh and when done uses their bones to fashion together strange and beautiful pieces of furniture.

We will never know. I never went inside his study. Not ever. So it will have to remain a mystery.

The forbidden room, however, I did go into once. But I looked into it more from my viewpoint outside. This was Catherine Kerr's music room. Floor to ceiling cabinets lined the back wall, the doors of which were long and narrow, oak framed with glass centres. Each set of two doors had a little lock and key behind which I could see books – caged books – and some ornaments. On the right side of the room, near the door to the study there was a sofa and two armchairs, all matching with their faded brown fabric and cushions. They were arranged around a coffee table and faced the grand piano opposite.

The forbidden room was haunted. You could feel its ghosts through the single glazed window. Press your fingers onto the glass and you'd be filled with an icy chill. In the beginning, I thought it was possessed by the ghost of Catherine Kerr, but later I began to understand it was the living ghost of Nigel – her husband – who haunted this room. Whenever I passed the window and looked in, I saw him in one of those brown armchairs, looking emptily across at the piano.

I will describe him now. It seems fitting to pencil him in while looking into the music room, as that was where he spent most of his time.

Quite a short man, shorter than my father anyhow – and perhaps even slightly shorter than me. He had a bald head apart from some grey-streaked hair around his ears joining behind at the bottom of his skull; and he had a round face that acted as a sort of temperature gauge, his small button nose, hamster-cheeks and the lobes of his slightly sticky-out ears flushing pinky-red in cold weather. I never got the chance to see him when it was warm, but I like to think now that his face took on a deeper purplish tint, like beetroot, to indicate the heat. His eyes were small and beady – like a hare's. Although not really, because a hare's eyes are full of focus and attention, whereas Nigel Kerr's always seemed glazed over. I will say then that they were like a blind hare's beady eyes. Now imagine this man in a plain jumper and jeans, sitting in the forbidden music room, or driving a Land Rover or walking slowly about the farm with his waxed jacket and rubber boots on, shotgun broken over his arm. But you must imagine him doing all these things in complete silence, because I never heard this man say a word, so utterly consumed was he with the death of his wife.

Apart from once. I did hear him utter a word once. He told the dog to 'sit'. And the dog sat.

There are two dogs at the farm, black and white collies. They're kept chained by their collars to the kennel walls. Their names are Red and Murdoch. It's easy to tell them apart. Red is quiet; when he's excited he bows his head, wags his tail but stiffens up so it looks as though his whole body is wagging. Murdoch jumps and barks and pulls at his chain, chokes himself to get people to fondle him, pushes and licks their hands when they stop. They call him Murdo for short. Murdo and Red.

The dogs weren't there on that first day when Duckman pulled into the yard and parked up next to

Nigel Kerr's Land Rover, but I noticed the empty kennels. I imagined the collies running around in a field somewhere herding sheep, the farmer whistling at them – this way, that way, come by, come by. Of course, that's not what they were doing. I didn't know then that the livestock had all been auctioned off and the farm was also up for sale. So looking back with hindsight, the dogs must have just been out walking with Nigel Kerr, for neither they nor the farmer were at the house the afternoon of our arrival. Day one.

It is now day thirty-eight. And so begins the documentation of all those days in between. The unravelling of events. Here is where it really begins.

4

It was Duckman who picked us up and drove us to the farm. And he did so in complete silence. It was not until we'd parked in the yard, got out wordlessly and followed him to the back door that he finally said something. And this wasn't until he'd inspected his boots and kicked his feet against the wall to flake off the loose mud. He sniffed and rested one hand on the door handle. 'Listen,' he said. He wasn't looking at us, but at the muddy doormat under his feet. 'The woman in there's no ma mother. She's ma auntie.' He scratched his knee through the tear in his jeans. 'Jus' so as ye know.' And then he forced the door open with his shoulder. I tried to catch Marshall's eye, a warning glance. I didn't want to go in there. We should never have left the van. But Marshall's back was turned towards me.

We followed Duckman inside. I could smell rubber boots and waxed jackets and old dirt and fresh air. It was cold in this room. Duckman kicked off his heavy boots under a bench and nodded for us to do the same. Marshall bent down to undo his laces. He looked at me.

'Take off your boots, Nevis,' he said.

So I did. I heaved them off without undoing the laces and placed them next to Marshall's underneath the bench. I felt the cold of the concrete floor seep straight through my socks and up my legs.

Duckman sniffed and scratched his arm awkwardly. He scratched his arm, his neck, his cheek while he waited for us to take off our jackets and hang them on free hooks. Duckman often sniffs and scratches himself like that. As though he's never quite comfortable with his body, awkward inside itchy skin. And he spits, a horrible hawking up of phlegm from his throat.

'It's because he smokes,' Marshall would tell me a week or so later. 'Have you seen his fingers? All yellowed where he holds his cigarette. His lungs must be thick with all that filthy black tar. And he's only two years older than you, Nevis. That's why you should never smoke.'

But I knew it wasn't because Duckman smoked. I could tell he suffered deeper than that. His whole body was brimming with it, about to spill out, and that's why he had to spit. He had to try to get rid of all that suffering like baling water over the side of a sinking ship.

The woman Duckman had warned us about was Elspeth. We heard her before we saw her, behind the closed door. 'Colin? Is that you, Colin?' After which the door swung open and the oven-heat of the kitchen swept through. 'What are ye doin' lingerin' oot here in the cold, Colin? Our guests will catch their death ...' and she looked at us, smiled broadly, hungrily with fat cosmetic-red lips. 'Lovely guests,' she said. 'What perfect timin'. The kettle's jus' boilin'.' And she pressed her big body back against the wall and waved us past. 'Mind yer step there, Mr Gow, an' mind yer head. Ye're ever such a tall one, aren't ye?' She winked at me. 'An' look at you.' She grabbed my arm as I tried to get past and squeezed it roughly. 'Look at this, my nails are almost touchin'.' I stared at the fat fingers and long painted nails gripping my arm. 'No meat on ye at all.' I tried to pull away. She laughed, nostrils flaring, and I felt her breath bellow against my face: chewed food mixed with a sickly sweet perfume. She released me and I hurried away.

'He doesnae speak,' Duckman said. I felt him staring at me from his place at the table. 'He's no said a word since ah picked him up.'

'He *does* speak,' Marshall said. 'He's just shy.' He placed his hand heavily on my shoulder. 'Isn't that right, Nevis?'

My head was spinning.

'Och, if he doesnae want t' speak, let him be,' said Elspeth. 'I'll do enough talkin' fer the pair of us.' She closed the kitchen door. 'Grab a chair, love,' she said to me. 'Ye must be fair beat after everythin' you've been through. What an ordeal, eh?'

An ordeal, yes. This is what happened.

We crashed. Nothing serious. Marshall had been driving all day. He'd been driving with a quiet, intense determination not to stop. It was night time, not late, but dark outside. Marshall had driven for so long he'd drifted into a sort of semi-sleep and when his head nodded forward quite suddenly into the steering wheel he woke with a start, swerved to the right and crashed straight through the rickety fence that had edged along the road beside us. Something blew in the engine. Steam hissed from the bonnet. My father and I sat in a shocked silence, looking out.

'You ok?' I asked.

'Damn it,' he said, not at me.

We were in a field, long and narrow. I couldn't see much; just the broken fence and road behind us and in front the silhouette of trees. Marshall kicked open the van door, torch in hand. I watched him walk round, crank open the bonnet and cough and splutter and wave his arms about at the ensuing blast of hot, thick, white air. He peered through the steam with his torch light on, finger prodding at nothing in particular. I stayed where I was, watching him through the windscreen. Eventually, after what felt like a forever five minutes, I wound down the window.

'Can we fix it?' It was a pointless question. Neither I nor my father knew anything beyond the very basics about engines. I said it more to break the day's long silence between us. Marshall didn't even look at me.

So this was where things really began. This was where everything changed, where the van stopped but Marshall marched on, dragging me behind him. I'm talking metaphorically. We didn't go anywhere that night. It was too cold and too dark and we had no idea where we were. On principle Marshall never looked at his map. He liked to 'follow his nose', taking the more scenic routes and beaten tracks, ignoring road signs. Marshall enjoyed this feeling of 'lost'. He said it inspired him, made him want to write. Although, that evening he wasn't inspired. He didn't pick up a pen once.

We sat in silence on the sofa cushions, in our sleeping bags with blankets around our shoulders and a hot mug of soup cupped in our hands. We sat, unmoving, in amongst the small chaos caused by the crash. Books were haphazard-strewn all around us. The water container had fallen and its twist tap broken, letting the liquid seep out over our clothes and bedding. My father's writing pile had formed a kind of landslide in its corner next to the food chest. Our jackets still hung from their hooks on one side of the van, but the pot had fallen and the hook holding the heavy frying pan was completely torn out. We sat there sipping our soup, not saying a word.

It was my fault. That silence. I knew that. And the crash was my fault. The silence caused the crash. I thought about apologising. I thought about trying to make up an excuse, one that maybe Marshall wanted to hear, but I was too tired and anyway, it was his turn to say something. And after a whole day's quiet driving and more than two hours sitting wordlessly in front of each other, this is what he said:

'I think . . .
  it's best . . .
    if I sleep in the front of the van tonight.'

My father drives with mechanical arms, both hands on the wheel, stiffened back and shoulders, eyes fixed on the road. So slowly. I will not easily forget the following day, the shock of riding with Duckman, the way he leant back into his seat as though sinking into an armchair, revving the engine, flinging the car up and down the gears, the speed. He drove with a quiet aggression, steered one-handed with his elbow half hanging out the window, smoking a rollie, flicking the ash out into the open air. I'll not forget it. If it's possible to gawp through gritted teeth, then that's what I did, pressing my feet down hard into the car floor, gripping onto the side of my seat. I remember glancing across at Marshall then, wondering if he had the fear like me, but he just sat there all stiff and glazed over, oblivious.

I'd woken up that morning with my cheek pressed uncomfortably against the bent spine of a paperback book – open-mouthed and dribbling over its cover. I moved it away from my face and rolled onto my back, holding my hand to my head. I remembered the crash.

My father was already up. When I looked out the back windows I could see him topless and bent over the bucket, lathering soap into his hands. I watched him wet his face and scratch deep into his beard with his nails. I watched him wash the mass of hair underneath his arms and scrub at his chest and neck. He'd tied up his knotted hair into a ponytail so he could clean behind his ears. His body looked thin and pale. His back covered in sore red spots. I could count his ribs. I pressed my hand over my own ribcage as I swung open the door. My father looked up at me – and then straight back into the bucket again. He continued washing.

The field was more of an empty overgrown paddock. The ground was soft and uneven under foot. All down one side there were trees, fenced off, a forest thick with pine and heather. On the opposite side there was the broken fence and the road stretching back the way we came through open farmland. In the far distance I could see the hills, bleak in the grey morning light.

In one corner of the field there was a small wooden-roofed structure stacked with old hay bales that looked damp and greenish-brown. I walked around to the front of the van to see its damage and noticed two or three jumping fences, their white- and red-striped cross-poles collapsed and hiding in the tufts of grass.

The bumper hung lopsided from the van, the lights were smashed, there was a large concave dent where we'd run straight over the fence post.

Marshall had pulled on a jumper and was boiling more water. 'Where are we?' I asked. If he'd been in a good mood he'd have answered, 'Exactly where we're supposed to be: here.' Which is his way of saying, 'We're lost. Isn't it great?' But he was not in a good mood.

'You're to wash yourself,' he said, and as he poured the hot water from the saucepan into the bucket half filled with cold, I noticed my father had even cut and cleaned under his nails. 'It's important you wash properly.'

'Why?'

He threw the towel at me. 'Just do it, Nevis,' he said.

I was expecting him to go back to the van while I washed, but he didn't. He stood over me as I crouched by the bucket. The water was tepid. I splashed my face.

'No, Nevis,' and his hands were around my wrists as he pulled me to my feet. He grabbed the bottom of my t-shirt and lifted it over my head. 'Sit down,' he said. I sat down quickly. I watched him as he tore my t-shirt in two, dipping one half into the water and then splashing it over my body. He rubbed soap into the material and then scoured at my back. He pressed so hard I yelled out.

'Well you do it then,' he said angrily.

'I *was*,' I replied. My father walked back to the van. I took hold of my t-shirt and started rubbing at my arms, my chest, my stomach; the soapy water dribbling down the front of my jeans. I glanced behind me at Marshall who was in the van, picking up clothes and holding them to his nose. I carried on scrubbing. I lifted my arms and worked the soap into the thin strips of underarm hair before washing it out.

'And your neck, Nevis,' I heard Marshall say.

I gathered my long hair round to the side of my face so I could rub at my neck. I started to shiver. The morning air was cold against my wet skin. Marshall came up behind me.

'Here,' he said softly and beckoned for the t-shirt. I handed it over and watched as he rinsed the material in the water and then twisted it out over my back and neck. He washed away the soap. 'Stand up,' he said. I stood up. He handed me the towel and for a moment we just stopped and stared at each other. I tried to break the tension with a smile. Marshall did not smile back.

He went to find help. He left following the road back the way we came. He thought he remembered passing a farm the night before. I was told to wait with the van and not wander off. I couldn't help but think, 'Where else would I go?' I took the propane gas stove and heated up the remainder of the water we'd managed to save from the container spillage. It wouldn't be long, I thought. My father would find a farm and get help.

I made coffee. I sat with the back doors wide open, mug in hand, blanket draped over my shoulders, my legs dangling over the edge of the van. It had cleared into a bright mid-morning and warmed up a little, although the heat of the coffee still curled white from the mug. I remember this moment very clearly. Like a snapshot. And when I think about it now I do pretend it's a photograph. I can see myself framed by the open back of the van. I'm holding the coffee with both hands up to my chin with an exaggerated smile, playfully kicking out my legs as they swing beneath me. I make myself look ridiculously happy in this picture. Here I am, in my van, drinking coffee just . . . like . . . normal.

This was not really where everything began. I'm trying to fool myself.

Before all this: before the farm, before the crash, before the day's long drive in silence, this is what happened.

Marshall was asleep on his back, his arms at his side. He must have drifted off while reading; the book was beside him, thumb still marking his page. He hadn't climbed into his sleeping bag or pulled any blankets over the top of him. It was October. The van would get cold. I was lying inside my sleeping bag, fully clothed with two blankets over me. I watched him breathing. I could hear him inhale, exhale slowly.

He'd freeze, I thought. I shuffled myself up onto my knees, caterpillar-crawled to the front of the van where Marshall had dumped his blankets. He sighed in his sleep. Dead to the world, I thought. I pulled over the blankets into the back of the van. I did everything slowly, careful not to wake him. No chance. When my father slept he slept deeply. He had wild dreams. Sometimes I would sit and watch him. I would see his eyes move and dart behind his eyelids. The next morning he'd wake and rant excitedly about his 'sleep-adventures'. He'd write them in his journal, collect them like a man picking interesting pebbles from a beach, taking them home, polishing them, perfecting them.

I plucked the book from his hand and put it to the side, folding the page corner to mark his place. He didn't stir. My father could sleep through a hurricane, an earthquake, a nuclear war. I pulled the blanket over us both. I put my arm around him. It would be warmer like this, I thought. My father shifted slightly, but didn't wake.

I thought about kissing him. Like I'd done before.

Why not? He could sleep through anything.

My father was wearing his blue woollen jumper. My hand found its way underneath it and underneath his vest, so I touched his skin. I rested it in the middle of his ribcage. My fingers stroked the thin hairs on his chest gently, ever so gently. My father sighed.

I thought about masturbation. I thought about *him* masturbating. I'd seen him once. We'd parked in a disused industrial site where large open barn-like structures housed heavy machinery, rusting and full of cobwebs. A small office building had been boarded up, warnings plastered over the walls. Marshall said it used to be a tree felling business. 'This is where they chopped the wood to make paper,' he said. He seemed pleased with himself. 'A writer in a place where paper was made. How novel!' and he laughed at his own joke and I smiled.

It was later that evening I saw Marshall. He was leaning against one of the long metal half-circle bunkers; his head was resting on his arm, covering his eyes, his free hand around his cock, pumping vigorously. He moved his pelvis back and forward, back and forward, over and over, until at last a soft grunt escaped from his lips and a long shot of white came from the tip of his penis and hit the metal side, dribbled down the ridged surface. Marshall held himself there, breathing into the crook of his elbow. He held himself still for quite a while and then tucked himself away, wiped his hand on the back of his jeans and zipped his fly.

When I touch myself this is what I think about. I think about him jerking off by that bunker. And when I come, it's when he comes and I grunt like he grunts. But that night in the van, with both of us underneath that blanket, instead of touching myself I let my hand move down and rest in between Marshall's legs. I stroked my fingers over him gently, like I'd done with the hairs on his chest. I watched his face. I felt sick with the excitement but I made myself move slowly, so slowly. My father sighed. He was hard underneath my hand. I moved closer so I could feel his breath against my cheek. His lips were parted, I could see his tongue, wet inside his mouth. I felt hot. Held him gently, so gently. I watched his lips, leant forward, kissed him. Held my mouth to his and breathed him in.

Let me lie like this forever, I thought.

And then a hand over my hand. I looked at my father and his eyes were open and staring straight at me.

So that was the beginning.

And then after that came the silence; the next day the crash; then came Duckman in his rusting mud-splattered blue Sierra with his yellowed fingers and brown roll-up cigarettes. 'This is Colin,' said my father.

'. . . Duckman,' corrected Duckman and he sniffed and hacked up some horrible grog from his throat and spat it out the car window.

5

'Bath': a large container for water, used for immersing and washing the body. I pulled my jumper and t-shirt over the top of my head and threw them to the floor. I swished the water with the tips of my fingers. From somewhere an image popped into my head of a woman in a bath full of bubbles, eyes closed and head back, toes tightening around the taps as she placed a square of chocolate to her lips. An advert from a city billboard. *This is heaven,* it said.

When I unzipped my jeans and dropped them to the floor I could smell myself – the sweat and yellow underneath my foreskin. The smell seemed stronger in the stuffy air of the bathroom. It lingered. I kicked away my boxers and pulled off my socks. With one hand steadying myself against the wall I lifted my leg and cautiously dipped my toes into the water and then my foot. Slowly I stepped in.

The water was hot. It was cold water I wanted. I remembered how a couple of years back when I was getting ready to wash in a stream I became hard. This isn't unusual. I get erections all the time. But before I thought I had to masturbate to get rid of them quickly. It wasn't until that day I realised otherwise. Stripping myself naked and sitting in the stream, the cold water bubbling about me, I started to go soft again.

And so there, standing in a tub of hot water half way up my shins; the first time ever in a bath, in a bathroom, in a house in eleven years; standing hopelessly with my cock pointing defiantly into the air, and me, determined not to touch it, refusing to even look at it. I leaned over to the shower and studied the dial. I pressed the ON switch. Nothing happened. I pressed it again. Nothing. I twisted the dial this way and that, but not a single drop of water came out from the showerhead. I didn't know then that I had to pull the white cord that hung from the ceiling next to the shower. This was something I found out days later. So instead, I got to my knees and pointed my dick underneath the taps. And there I knelt, in that tub of water, cold-rinsing my erection and willing it to go away.

I felt dirty. Even though I'd washed earlier that morning I still felt the filth creeping all over me. It was guilt, I thought. Surely not a speck of dirt should be on my skin. So it was guilt.

I took hold of a bottle of body-wash and squeezed the blue gel onto a flannel, and still kneeling, I started scrubbing at my body, harder than ever before. My chest, underneath my arms, my stomach and pubic hair, behind my ears, my neck and shoulders; I scoured at my fore-arms and the backs of my hands and in between my fingers. I picked the black out from under my nails. I rubbed at my face, the soap stinging my eyes and then I cupped water into my palms and splashed it over my cheeks. I sat back, the water spilling over the side of the tub with my sudden movement. I poured more of the blue gel into the flannel and lifted one leg then the other; washing my thighs, knees, shins and feet. My skin was red raw where I rubbed so hard and still I felt dirty.

I closed my eyes and held my wet hands over my face. We could stay a while in the caravan – he'd said.

'A while?'

'That's right.'

'Until the van's fixed?'

No answer.

Through my fingertips I could feel the blood pulsing in my forehead. My skin crawled with all the droplets of water. It must never happen again, he said. Do you understand, Nevis? Do you understand? It must never happen again.

6

SCENE: *The stage is split in two by a panel with a door. On the left side of the panel, the stage is set out like the inside of a caravan. A long-haired scraggily looking boy sits against the door, curled up, holding his head in his hands. The right half of the stage is set out like an overgrown field with a Scottish Highland backdrop. A blonde girl sits on a metal step on the opposite side of the door to the boy. She is talking at him.*

GIRL: Why won't ye let me in, Nevis? *(pause)* I know you're in there. *(pause)* If you don't let me in I'll start t' sing. *(pauses for a little longer then turns to the door and presses her ear against it)* Hellooo . . . anybody home? *(she tries the handle – the door gives a little but the boy on the other side slams it shut again with his back. The girl is affronted)* Well, that's no very nice. *(bangs on the door)* Why won't ye let me in, Nevis? I don't understand. I'm jus' tryin' t' be friendly. *(softening her tone)* I could show ye aroon' the farm, we could go on a walk. I know lots of secret places. *(when still no answer she bangs angrily on the door again)* Nevis, I'll tell on ye if ye don't let me in. You're being very rude! I'll tell my mum and she'll throw ye out and ye'll have t' hit the road again – you and yer tinker father.

7

Marshall did not pick up a pen after our arrival at the farm. He became silent and short-tempered. This wasn't unusual for him; in the van he would often be quiet for hours or snappy if I made a noise while he was working. But it never lasted. Often the next morning he'd be calm again. He'd wake with a fresh mind and talk to me with a cool clear air. A new day, he'd say, is like newly washed and freshly pressed clothes. Dump yesterday's dirty washing in the bin. Funny to think that on the farm we had fresh clothes washed and pressed and folded for us, yet Marshall's mood stuck to the air like heavy thunder.

The farm was not good for us.

In that first week I hardly saw my father. I would hear him get up early in the morning. He would always leave without speaking or seeing if I was awake. Lying in my narrow bunk, I would hear the door clicking shut behind him and that's when I'd get up and go to the window to watch him wade through the waist-high weeds across the field towards the farmhouse. He would return an hour or so later, washed and shaved with some food for me and some tea. He would leave again shortly after.

And I would wait.

On the fifth morning I told Marshall I wasn't sleeping properly. Every night I'd had nightmares and they were getting worse. I'd always dream we were in the van. Sometimes it would be the moment kissing my father, but when I opened my eyes his face had turned into a werewolf, his beard had grown into thick fur covering his cheeks and forehead. He'd open his mouth wide and roar into my face, spittle stretching from his long yellow canines to his bottom lip. Or I'd dream we were in the van together, seconds before the crash. But my father was not drifting into sleep like he had been in real life; he was wide awake, his face fierce and angry. He was aiming for the rickety fence, accelerating towards it.

And every time I'd wake up in the pitch black, frozen stiff. It was so dark I would start thinking, 'I'm dead. I'm dead.' And I'd feel the wood panelling down the side of the narrow bunk and I'd reach up and touch the caravan ceiling so close to my face. I panicked and thought I was in a coffin.

Marshall listened when I told him all this and stared into the heat of his coffee, his hands around the mug for warmth. 'It's the cold,' he said. 'I'll speak to someone about a generator.'

It wasn't what I wanted. Yes, the caravan became bitter

in the middle of the night. I had to sleep in the small, narrow, boxy room with bunk bed and built-in wardrobe. There was a tiny square window in there; Marshall had been pleased about that, as though it was a prize room because of it. But the window wasn't fitted properly. It filtered in a bitter draught. And I knew that Marshall too suffered because at night I would wedge open the flimsy door to the bunkroom with some folded cardboard and I could hear him shifting about uncomfortably, rapidly rubbing his legs against the bed sheets to heat up. The cold was biting into him as much as me. But warming the caravan wouldn't stop the nightmares. I knew that much. His arm around me, however, would.

The kitchen table we'd been sitting at folded down into a double bed. That's where Marshall slept. Every night I told myself to creep out of my bunk and under the duvet next to him. Why not? There was enough room for both of us. And we used to sleep arms around each other in the van, separate sleeping bags but with blankets thrown over the both of us. It's always warmer with two bodies. And it helps keep away the bad dreams. But Marshall needed space. He wanted to sleep alone, that's what he told me. Eleven years living in the back of a Ford Transit together and now he had trouble sharing a caravan.

'It's not just the cold,' I said. 'It's the girl.'

Marshall frowned. 'What girl?'

The night before I'd had a different dream. I was in the front of the van, just dropping off to sleep with my jumper wedged up against the window, when I heard Marshall cooing me from the back, Nevvvis, Nevvvis. But when I pulled back the curtain it was Ailsa kneeling there, naked, pouting and twiddling her hair. And then I noticed my father's face, duplicated and shrunk down, jutting out from where Ailsa's breasts should have been. Nevvvis. And she started to wank. She started to jerk off the giant penis that was growing out from between her legs. 'Don't ye miss yer mum, Nevis? Don't ye miss yer mum?'

'What girl, Nevis?' Marshall asked.

'Ailsa. I don't like her.'

'That's absurd.'

'She follows me around. She picks on me.'

'How?'

'She asks me questions.'

'About what?'

'Me.'

My father raised his eyebrows. 'She's thirteen, Nevis. You're having nightmares because Elspeth's thirteen-year-old daughter is asking you questions about yourself?' I could tell he thought it was ridiculous.

'It's the farm,' I said quietly, looking at my hands. 'It's not good for us.'

'I think that's enough now, Nevis.' And he got up to leave.

'Where are you going?'

'To mend the fence.'

'I can help.'

'No, Nevis,' he said. 'I think it's best if you stay here.' He didn't tell me why.

Through the window above the sink, I watched my father stoop against the morning cold, hands thrust deep into jacket pockets. He walked across the field to where Nigel Kerr was already waiting for him in his Land Rover, the exhaust fumes belting out into the air. My father nodded his greeting to the farmer, opened the door and climbed in. Marshall in the passenger seat. So strange to see him sitting there, being driven. I breathed an 'O' onto the window and wondered how long it would take to fix a fence.

I began to wait.

8

GIRL: I've made ye some lunch, Nevis. A cheese and pickle piece. Ye must be hungry. Ye've been sittin' in there all day. Ye know, it's really unhealthy t' stay inside all the time. Yer body needs sunlight. I learnt about that in Science. Did ye know that, Nevis? Did ye know your body needs sunlight? Otherwise yer skin gets all pasty white an' ill looking – it doesn't get all the nutrients it needs or something. I bet ye didn't know that did you, Nevis? Ye've never been to school, have ye? I can teach ye things if ye like. I can teach ye all aboot Science an' History an' Geography an' things. An' you can teach me aboot livin' in a van. Not that I really need to know, but I've told my friends aboot you and they're really interested. Do ye have any friends, Nevis? I mean . . . do ye know *anyone* apart from yer father? It's a bit weird that, don't ye think? Or maybe ye don't think so. Maybe ye don't think at all. Ye certainly don't say much. *(pause)* Nevis? . . . Nevvvis?

9

We found out the field we crashed into had belonged to the dead Catherine Kerr. Elspeth had informed Marshall and Marshall had informed me. The field was for her horses. Apparently she used to ride all the time. And then she got sick. 'Cancer,' Marshall said. 'Best not say anything about it, Nevis. It's still an open wound.' Who he thought I'd mention it to was unclear. I avoided the Kerrs as best I could. I would've avoided the farmhouse completely if it wasn't for Marshall insisting I washed in their bathroom. Through the day, when my father was away, I only ever went to the farmhouse when I needed to shit. Pissing was done outside behind the caravan. Not into the sink. I had already made that mistake, not realising it wasn't plumbed in. I had to mop up the mess that leaked out into the cupboard underneath. Shitting *could* have been done in the woods. In fact, on my first day at the farm I had every intention of doing just that to avoid the house and the people inside. But I was followed. Moments before pulling down my jeans and boxers to squat, I noticed Ailsa sneaking from tree to tree to get a better look at me.

'What are ye doin', Nevis?'

I ran all the way back to the caravan.

'Are ye afraid of me, Nevis? What's wrong?'

My father didn't understand. She was everywhere. Or at least, everywhere *I* was. She would even sit on the little metal step outside the caravan door and talk and talk and talk if she knew I was hiding inside. She would've come in, only I'd got into the habit of sitting directly on the opposite side so she couldn't push past. 'Nevis,' she'd say, 'why won't ye let me in? This isn't very nice, ye know.'

Going for a walk had nearly become impossible. I'd have to hide out in the caravan and watch and wait until I knew where every Kerr was. Duckman in the tool shed, Elspeth in the kitchen, the farmer in the music room. But Ailsa was like a heat-seeking missile. Even if I saw her moving about in her bedroom or walking down the track towards the outbuildings she'd soon find me when I left the caravan. Within minutes. So I would more often than not sit against the door of the caravan and wait . . . wait . . . wait . . . for Marshall to reappear.

But on that fifth day, not wanting to spend another afternoon barricaded behind the caravan door, annoyed because Marshall refused to take me with him to fix the fence and see the van, I decided to go for a walk.

Duckman had already passed. I saw him go by with a bucket in hand, the bottoms of his ripped jeans wedged into welly boots, his tobacco tin bulging from the breast pocket of a thick cotton shirt. No jacket. Duckman never seemed to feel the cold. It was as though his cigarettes provided him with enough inner warmth. I saw one of the brown papered roll-ups tucked behind his ear. Duckman's ears weren't big, but they stuck out slightly like his father's. One of them was pierced with a small gold stud. When he'd passed earlier that day he'd glanced across at the caravan, watching for me. But I'd been quick and hid from sight.

I tried to choose my moment carefully. Duckman was busy; Elspeth I knew had left for town much earlier that morning with Nigel Kerr and when he returned to pick up Marshall she hadn't been with him. That meant it was only Ailsa who was left unaccounted for. Where was Ailsa? I imagined her lying outside in among all the long grass and thistles, flat like a sniper, hawk-eyed and waiting, wetting her lips with her sharp little tongue. Or maybe she was hiding in the cluster of trees that led right up to the house. She could just skip the fence behind the dog kennels and be safe in the shadows, like a fox creeping down to the caravan field.

But I couldn't bear it any longer. I clicked the door shut behind me. It wasn't so cold outside. The morning frost on the grass and weeds had melted into wet. I walked to the gate, peered into the yard. Nobody around. The dog kennels were empty. Nigel Kerr and Marshall must've taken them with them to the field. I looked down the mud track to where Duckman had disappeared. No sign. I climbed the gate, dropped down to the other side and with fists clenched around thumbs I strode across the yard. I'd go to one of the big grazing fields in front of the farmhouse. Not the empty one, but the one with the long line of hay bales wrapped in black plastic. I could hide behind them for a while. Watch the road and wait for Marshall to come back.

Somehow she spotted me. She must've been hiding somewhere. Didn't follow me straight away but waited another five minutes for me to walk all the way to the hay bales and take off my jacket, sit myself down, get myself comfortable. I was picking at the wet grass, watching the road. I was imagining Marshall and Nigel Kerr working together to fix the fence, the dogs barking and running in circles, the van sitting there all locked up and lonely. I wondered if Marshall would try to have another look at the engine. Maybe Nigel Kerr could help. Wouldn't that be good? Seeing the van driving up to the farm, Marshall behind the wheel, beeping his horn.

'Are you hidin' from me, Nevis?'

Voices have a strange effect on me. I was never aware of this living alone with my father in the van. But when I hear someone talking, someone other than Marshall,

I feel a tightness at the base of my neck. I tense up, clamp my teeth together, my heart beats faster. It makes me feel sick. Physically sick. It makes my head spin. I'm not so bad anymore. Once I get used to a voice the panic subsides. But even now when a stranger says something to me I get that horrible tightness and sick feeling.

'You're always hidin' from me, Nevis. Don't try t' deny it. I see you hiding away from me all the time.'

Once, a long time ago, when I was really young, when I was maybe six or seven – my father took me into a shop with him. He used to do that a lot when I was younger. He didn't like leaving me in the van alone. Or was that me? Did I not like being left in the van alone? It doesn't matter. The point is there was a time I used to go into shops with my father. He'd hold my hand (or would I hold his?) and we'd walk up and down the aisles together. He'd pick food from shelves and put them into baskets. So he must have let go of my hand occasionally, but I don't remember that. I just remember his big palm and fingers and thinking how mine seemed so small in comparison.

This one particular shopping trip there was a woman at the checkout, picking up our items from the basket and blip-blipping them through the machine. This woman was so fat she seemed to fill the tiny till compartment. She was so fat she was sweating from her face, I could see it mottling her make-up. She had thick red-pasted lips and smudged black eyes. Her blonde black-rooted hair pinned so tight into a ponytail her face seemed to bulge forward. I was watching her from behind my father. My fingers were hooked into his back pockets. The woman told Marshall how much it all cost and then her big black eyes locked onto me.

'Oh! Look at you hiding there. I didn't even see you!'

I was petrified.

'Now what's a big boy like you doing hiding behind your father, eh?' The woman chuckled. 'Are you shy, my love?'

I gripped on tighter to Marshall's pockets and bored my eyes into his back. My father handed the woman her money.

'He's shy,' he said. 'But he's a good boy.' And his arm came back and curled around my shoulders. He pulled me round to his side so as I had to hide my face in his t-shirt. I felt the fat woman still staring at me. 'Thank you.' Marshall picked up his bag of shopping.

'Have a good day, sir,' the woman said. 'And you too, young man.'

I wished, I wished, I could've disappeared.

'Have I done something to upset you, Nevis?'

Why did she do that? Tag my name onto the end of every question?

'Nevis? Why won't ye speak to me, Nevis?'

I hated it.

'Ok fine, don't talk to me then. But I think it's very rude.' Ailsa was on the hay bales when she said all this. She'd crept up from behind so I hadn't seen her walking across the field towards me. She'd jumped up on top of the bales and squatted there, snipping her questions. When she moved, specks of wet flicked off the plastic and hit the back of my neck. I had already tensed up. I stared at the laces on my brown leather boots and willed her to go away. She didn't. Instead she dropped down beside me.

'I'm goin' t' sit with you,' she said. 'I'm goin' t' *make* you talk to me, Nevis. God, but I'm filthy now. Look what ye've made me do, grub under ma nails.' From the corner of my eye I could see her pick momentarily at her nails, then brush down her long waxed jacket. She inspected the wet grass next to me. 'But do we have t' sit here, Nevis? It's so cold and wet. We could go t' the house instead?' When I didn't answer she sighed irritably. 'Well fine. We'll stay here.' And she pulled her jacket around her bum and sat down. '*Boys*,' she said. I felt her next to me. I closed my eyes, clenched and unclenched my hands.

'Look at you,' she said. 'What's *wrong* with ye, Nevis? Why are ye so afraid of me? Is it because I'm a girl? Do ye not know how t' talk to girls? Livin' in a van with yer daddy all yer life, I guess not.'

She wasn't going to go away. I could sense it. If I stood up and walked across the field, so would she. She would follow me. I would have to go back to the caravan, sit behind the door so she couldn't get in. But even then there was no escape. She'd just sit outside and fire her questions at me through the thin walls.

'Open yer eyes, Nevis. Why won't ye even look at me?'

I opened my eyes.

'Am I so ugly ye can't stand the sight of me?'

When I was nine I met a girl in a park. I know I was nine because I was half way through a book my father had given me for my ninth birthday about reptiles. I was reading it under the slide when this girl approached.

'What are you reading?' she asked me.

It was a section on chameleons and how they could change colour to merge into their surroundings. I didn't answer the girl, but I looked at her. Although now, no matter how hard I try, I can't see her face. She was blonde – I'm sure of that – and she was wearing a green skirt. I remember particularly the green skirt because she'd taken my hand and put it underneath, pressing my fingers in between her legs and against her pants. I tried to pull away, but couldn't. This girl would not let go of my wrist and the more I struggled, the more she pressed and rubbed my hand against her bits.

'What's wrong with you?' she asked. 'Don't you like it?'

'No,' I said and finally my hand was let go.

'Well most boys do,' she said and snorted at me. 'There must be something wrong with you.'

'There's nothing wrong with me.'

'Yes, there is. You must be gay.'

'I'm not gay.'

'Yes, you are! You prefer fiddling boys!' And she laughed and howled and flicked her hair about gleefully. 'You're a poof. You're a little gay boy.'

'You're ugly,' I told her. 'I don't want to touch you because you're ugly.'

And then she punched me. Punched me real hard, right between the eyes. Busted my nose. Blood everywhere. And then she punched me again, just for good measure.

'So am I ugly, Nevis? Is that it?' Everything about Ailsa was sharp, her thin face and cheekbones, her pointy nose and chin, her cutting eyes. Her hair was mouse-blonde like Elspeth's, but she didn't wear it up like her. She told me, the very first day I met her, about how she spent over an hour each morning washing, drying, straightening and spraying all sorts of products into it and over it and all around to prevent it looking anything less than perfect. It was pointless. She'd leave the house and the cold wind would blow it wild again. She sat there with eyes fixed onto mine, all pinched lips and plucked eyebrows. She was wearing make-up. I could see little lumps of black mascara clinging to her eyelashes.

'See, Nevis, I'm no so bad to look at, am I?'

My throat was so tight and dry I couldn't even swallow. I looked away.

'God, what *is* your problem? Do ye fancy me, Nevis? Is that what it is?'

I closed my eyes. I knew I'd have to say something. She would never leave me alone if I didn't. With my eyes still clamped shut, I opened my mouth. 'I'm just ... waiting ...' I said, '... for Marshall. I'm just waiting for Marshall to get back.'

Marshall and Nigel Kerr didn't get back until evening. It was dark when eventually I saw the headlights of the Land Rover bump up the track towards the farmhouse and then swing into the yard. I was watching them from the caravan window. Elspeth was with them. I heard her laugh before she even opened the door to get out.

'Och, what a hoot!'

The two dogs jumped out after Elspeth and the back door light switched itself on.

'Look at them, eh? Tired puppies goin' straight t' their beds. Ye've had lots of exercise today, boys, haven't ye? Ye'll be hungry and wantin' yer tea. Ah, Colin – get these poor puppies their dinner, would ye? And Marshall, where are ye going? I need yer help carryin' in this shoppin'. Don't *you* hurry off to yer kennel now.' I frowned at her loud laughter and the way she squeezed my father's arm as he stood beside her. 'Big manly muscles,' she said. Marshall waited by the open boot while Elspeth shuffled plastic bag handles into bunches for him. He looked across at the caravan. I raised my hand quickly in a kind of wave, but he didn't see me. It was dark. There were no lights in the caravan, only a big industrial torch that stayed in the corner. I hadn't switched it on. It would only have tempted Ailsa to come over.

Marshall clutched at the bags Elspeth had organised for him and pulled them out of the boot. 'Nigel can grab the rest, can't ye, Nigel?' Elspeth had one bag in each hand. 'Follow me, Marshall, we'll dump them in the kitchen an' then stick the oven on. Colin, do ye know where Ailsa is? In her room I bet avoiding havin' to take in any shoppin', the besom.'

Marshall started to quietly follow Elspeth. I was about to bang on the window to get his attention but stopped myself. I didn't want Elspeth or Nigel to hear me. Instead I ran to the torch and clicked down the switch, on, off, on, off, and then on again. The room lit up. I ran back to the window but it was too late. He hadn't seen me. I heard the faint click of the back door as it shut and

Elspeth's laugh rattle from inside the walls of the farmhouse. He was gone. I pressed my forehead and the tips of my fingers into the cold of the glass. I'd have to wait . . . wait . . . wait some more. And then, from one of the windows on the top floor of the farmhouse, there was a movement. A room in darkness and then a light switching itself on, off, on, off and then on again. I tensed up. Ailsa appeared at the window. She stared down at me, pressing her head and hands against the pane like I was. From the yard light I could just make out her face. She was smiling a thin, tight smile.

LIST 1

- **Wheels** – blackened bolts without hubcaps
- **Bonnet** – rickety, rusty, requires slamming shut
- **Pedals** – clutch, brake, accelerator
- **Dashboard** – littered with crisp packets and bottles and books to be read
- **Indicators** – the tick, tick, tick of turning
- **Rear-view mirror** – the hanging cardboard tree, swinging, sweet-smelling
- **Locks** – raise handle from outside, push lock down on inside, close door
- **Gear stick** – long and thin and bulbous head, vibrates when engine running
- **Ignition** – turn key, press accelerator, rev engine to warm up
- **Side pocket** – where he kept his pens

10

With a biro, I started scoring the days I spent on the farm into little tally marks on the caravan ceiling. They do that in prison. I don't know how I know that. I must have read it somewhere or Marshall must have told me. The prisoners tally up days to keep track of time. It's easy to lose track in prison. One hour feels like the next. Days melt together. It's the same on the farm.

Seven days. One set of tallies and two marks complete. That evening Marshall came over from the farmhouse with my dinner.

'It's been a week,' I told him. He placed the plate of food onto the table in front of me and sat down. He did not answer or even look at me. He rubbed his hands over his face. I picked up the fork and scooped up some of the lukewarm mashed potato. Marshall had already said during the week if I wanted my dinner hot I'd have to eat at the same time as everyone else around the kitchen table. I told him I'd rather have it cold. 'You have a bad attitude, Nevis.' Marshall had got angry.

'You should be grateful. Elspeth doesn't have to cook for us.' No, I thought, she doesn't. And I wish she wouldn't. I missed cooking meals with my father.

'It's been a week,' I repeated.

'Yes, Nevis. It has.' Marshall sounded tired and irritable. I forked one of the sausages and took a bite. 'When you've finished that, you're having a bath.'

'I've already washed today.'

'Don't lie to me, Nevis.'

'I'm not!' My voice sounded high-pitched and indignant. For the last two mornings I'd been washing on the other side of the woods. I'd found the narrow burn that skirted the full length of a potato field. Despite the cold I'd taken off my jumper and t-shirt and washed under my armpits and across my chest. I scratched at my skin to remove dirt. I used one of Duckman's t-shirts that Marshall had given me to dry myself. On the second morning I even kicked off my jeans and boxers to wash myself properly, kneeling on the grass and scooping handfuls of freezing water to my crotch. I'd need soap, I thought. And a flannel. And a proper towel. But even without I was happier washing in the stream than in the stuffy claustrophobic air of the bathroom.

'Elspeth tells me she hasn't seen you for two whole days.' Marshall was fierce, jabbing his finger on the table as he spoke. 'What's more, Ailsa says you've been ignoring her.' I stopped chewing and pushed the plate away. 'Is that true, Nevis?'

I swallowed the lump of sausage meat. 'She follows me around,' I said quietly.

'Well she's back at school tomorrow,' he said. 'So no more nightmares, eh, Nevis? She can't follow you around when she's at school.'

I saw her the next morning at eight fifteen, picking her way on tiptoes through the mud towards the car where Duckman and Marshall were waiting. She was wearing a uniform: a grey pleated skirt and matching grey cardigan, a white shirt and a black and yellow tie. All the girls would be dressed like that, I thought. Different faces, hair and shapes of bodies all wearing the same grey uniform. I stared at the soft bone-white of Ailsa's bare legs; her frilly ankle socks and polished buckle shoes. She scooped her skirt beneath her as she sat, tucked her straightened hair behind her ears. Duckman had revved the engine and started out the yard before Ailsa had even closed the door. She quickly slammed it shut, her face contorting into a swear as they moved off down the track. I watched them disappear.

One set of tallies and three marks. At least, I thought, prisoners have a release date. Something they can count towards.

Marshall had gone with them. He'd left in a bad

mood without saying goodbye. It was my fault, his bad mood. He'd told me to go with him to the farmhouse for breakfast. 'Elspeth asks after you every morning,' he said. 'You need to make more of an effort.'

'I'm not hungry.'

'Then you'll go without.'

I shrugged. He walked off.

Marshall must have clung to that mood all day. When he returned in the evening the first thing he said was that I would be joining everyone for dinner at the farmhouse, no buts. Elspeth had offered to cook for us, he said. It would be rude to refuse. I told him I wasn't feeling well.

'Then a proper meal will do you good,' he said. 'And you can have a bath afterwards. Come on, Nevis. Get your boots on or I'll march you across there in your socks.'

He *actually* said that. I remember it perfectly, word for word. *I'll march you across there in your socks.* 'You need to make more of an effort,' he said. 'You need to speak to Ailsa and Duckman. Make friends. Be polite.' He seemed irritated by me. I pulled on my boots very slowly. Quietly.

'I'm really not feeling very well,' I said. It wasn't a lie. The panic rises in me like a sickness. I get light-headed. Nauseous.

'You haven't eaten all day,' Marshall said. 'You must be starving.'

I shook my head. I hadn't eaten anything all day; that was true. But the thought of something heavy and solid in my empty stomach made me feel worse. 'I don't think I should go,' I told him. 'I think I need to lie down.'

'No, Nevis,' he said, quite plainly. 'You're going.'

And so I went to the farmhouse with my father, not that I had a choice, and allowed myself to be ushered in by the flamboyant Elspeth, who pulled out a chair for me and ruffled my hair as I sat. She was alone. Nigel Kerr wouldn't be joining us, she explained. He preferred eating his meals by himself. 'A bit like you, Nevis,' she said chuckling. 'But it's lovely to have ye. Ye mustn't be shy usin' the house now. Come an' go as ye please. It's your home too.'

Home? I looked at Elspeth, then at Marshall expecting him to correct her. This isn't our home, I thought. Tell her, Marshall. Tell her it's only temporary. But Marshall wasn't looking at me – and Elspeth had already begun to talk about something else. 'Ailsa and Colin are a wee bitty late,' she said. Elspeth always made a point of calling Duckman 'Colin'. 'But no t' worry, the ham isn't quite cooked yet. Do ye like egg an' ham, Nevis? I have t' admit it's one of ma favourites.' I didn't answer. The smell of boiling meat was twisting at my insides. Marshall looked up and glared at me.

'I'm not feeling very well,' I said to him. I said it under my breath so as Elspeth couldn't hear, but she was already talking about something else. I closed my eyes and caught only snapshots of the conversation . . . Colin . . . make friends . . . boys my own age. And then there was a sharp prod in my side.

'Nevis.' Marshall's voice was low, almost a growl. 'Pull yourself together.'

A noise from outside, the dogs started barking and through the semi-steamed-up kitchen window I saw the haze of Duckman's headlights pull to a halt out in the yard. One door opened, slammed shut, followed by another. The backyard light switched on. Duckman, in no hurry to get out the cold, leaned against his car and started to roll a fresh cigarette. Ailsa, on the other hand, spotted me sitting at the kitchen table and sped up.

'*Mum!*' she said, entering the kitchen while still pulling off her shoes. 'Why didn't ye tell me Nevis and Mr Gow were comin' fer tea? I didn't know.' She was still in her school uniform. She pulled her satchel from over her head and dumped it on a stack of old newspapers next to the bin. 'We were at the YM,' she said, throwing her jacket on top of her bag. 'Or at least *I* was. I don't know where Duckman went. He left as soon as we got there and didn't show up again fer two whole hours. That's why I'm late.'

'Where is Colin?' Elspeth asked.

'Outside havin' a fag.'

A plate of food was put in front of me. A limp-looking, half-cooked egg, its white still slimy on top, the burst yolk pouring over a pink piece of meat. I felt a gagging in my throat and chest. On the side were some peas with a blob of butter melting and on the other some straight-cut chips, browned slightly at the corners, not greasy like a takeaway's.

'Oven chips,' Marshall said. He picked one from his plate and waved it at me. 'It's been a while, eh, Nevis?'

Oven chips, I thought and smiled weakly at my father. I picked one of the pieces of potato from the plate and tried to remember the last time I had an oven chip. I couldn't. Marshall had said it as though I should, as though it was something we used to eat a lot of. I put the chip in my mouth and chewed. It was crispier than what I was used to. It had a drier texture. It didn't really taste like anything. I felt it mushy over my tongue and swallowed hard. I wasn't hungry. Or maybe I was too hungry. Regardless, I had a mountain of food in front of me and I couldn't eat any of it.

Ailsa was sitting opposite. I watched her cut away the white from her egg and push what was left of the yolk to the very edge of her plate so her peas and chips couldn't touch it. She scraped the soppy yellow from her meat before cutting it into small bite-size pieces. She did all this while telling her mother about some girl called

Sinclair who was being suspended from school for pushing another girl, called Jordan, down a hill. Apparently the girl Jordan deserved it. 'I have to sit next t' her in science,' she said. 'And she's always gettin' me into trouble fer chattin' and scribblin' notes. But it's *her*.'

It was just like the books, I thought. Girls playing tricks on one another, chatting and swapping notes in class. Bullies pushing people down hills. I imagined the boys as bigger and slightly older Just Williams, bringing in bugs or spiders from outside and trapping them in unsuspecting girls' desks. I suddenly saw Ailsa as a Naughtiest Girl figure mixed with fleeting images of a large and evil headmistress swinging her round the playground by her precious, perfectly straight blonde hair. *The Demon Headmaster*, I thought. *My Teacher is an Alien*. And what about *Boy*? The true story of Roald Dahl when he was at school. The *true* story! He used to have to warm up toilet seats for the older prefects before they sat down to use them.

So when Ailsa asked, 'Why don't *you* go to school, Nevis?' I realised how pleased I was my father had taught me in the van.

'Well, Ailsa, Nevis doesnae really *need* t' go t' school. I'm sure Mr Gow has taught him everythin' he knows. An' Mr Gow is a very clever man. Isn't that right, Mr Gow? You used t' be a teacher.'

'That's right. English. In London.'

'An' only the cleverest teachers can work in *London*, Ailsa.'

'That's not true, mum.'

'Don't be rude. An' eat yer yolk, it's good fer ye.'

'But why *don't* ye go to school, Nevis? Don't ye want to? Now that you live here ye could go t' the same school as me.'

Live here? I thought. *I don't live here.*

I could feel Marshall's eyes hot on my face. 'Come on, Nevis, speak up.'

I shook my head. Closed my eyes.

'Nevis?' His voice had a warning tone.

'No,' I said.

'No what?' said Ailsa. 'Why are ye shakin' your head?'

'No, I don't . . .'

'Don't what?'

My head was spinning. '. . . live here,' I said. The words must've erupted from my mouth louder than I meant them to. Everyone stopped still and stared at me. 'I don't live here. And I don't want to go to school.'

I thought I'd get into trouble for that. Or maybe not for what I said, but for what happened afterwards. I stood up, too quickly, my head spun and I felt myself falling forwards, or backwards, I don't remember, it doesn't matter. I was dizzy anyway. I grabbed onto the table to steady myself and in doing so I knocked the plate and

73

it fell to the floor and smashed a big mess of food and broken crockery. It wasn't intentional. I didn't mean it.

Marshall was silent when he came into the caravan three hours later. I was hiding in the bunkroom, under the duvet. I was waiting for him. I'd rehearsed what I was going to say. Sorry to begin with, but then 'I told you so. I told you I wasn't feeling well.' I heard him unfold the table and make his bed. He didn't say a word. Not a word. Until finally he switched the torch off and through the darkness I heard, 'Just forget about it, Nevis. It's history now. Just forget about it.'

11

Sitting on the floor of the caravan, my back against the wall and my feet flat against the door, I was waiting. That's all I ever did in those first few days. If I wasn't waiting for Marshall, I was waiting for Ailsa to come looking for me or for Elspeth to rattle on the door and ask me if I was ok. One dreadful minute after the next. In those first few days, with Marshall never around, I only ever waited for time to pass – slowly taking me closer to the second when he would come back again. But the morning after the plate-smashing incident there was a knock at the caravan door that I didn't recognise. Then came a sniff. Followed by another knock.

'Ah'm no fuckin' aroon, Nevis,' he said. 'Come oot here.'

I waited. There was no more knocking. When I got to my feet and looked out the window I saw Duckman leaning against the caravan wall, an unlit cigarette hanging from his lips. He didn't look at me. He struck a match and cupped his hands around the end of his cigarette so the flame took to the tobacco. He took a couple of breaths, he spat, he scratched his cheek with his thumb. I watched him. I waited. He sniffed and spat again before looking at me.

'Come oot,' he said. And then, 'It's all right, Nevis, ah don't want t' be yer best friend, ah just want help clearin' these weeds. Ah canna be fucked doin' 'em on ma own.' I looked at the weeds and noticed around the gate he'd already started chopping them down to form a path. I turned back to face Duckman. He had a large pair of shears in his hand and he held them up to me. 'For you,' he said. I looked beyond him to see if Ailsa was hiding anywhere, then scanned the yard and the windows of the farmhouse. 'Who are ye lookin' for?' Duckman had caught me out. 'Yer dad? He's gone intae town.' He waved the shears again. 'Come on, freaky feral child, ah canna be arsed hangin' aboot.' So I opened the door slowly and peered round. Duckman held out the shears. I took hold of them.

'We won't even have t' say a word t' each other,' he said flicking the remainder of his cigarette into the weeds. 'Ah'm no the type fer idle chit chat anyway.' And without waiting for a response he turned his back to me and started haphazardly cutting at the weeds with his own pair of shears.

I watched him for a moment, the muscles in his fore-arms flex as they opened and snipped shut the shears.

He didn't look up at me or say anything. He just silently decapitated the weeds. I felt the weight of the pair of shears in my hands. I opened and closed the sharp blades around the head of a thistle and watched the purple crown fall in among the grass. I noticed how the muscles in my forearms flexed the same way Duckman's did. I took the heads off more weeds and thistles and long grass, enjoying the sound the blades made when they snipped themselves shut, metal sliding against metal. Together we cut the weeds to ankle height, from the caravan door right up to the gate, making a sort of path. I became so immersed in the snip snip of the shears and the cutting down of weeds that I began to smile privately to myself. I didn't notice Duckman stopping, climbing the gate, rolling a cigarette, watching me with that quiet intensity, inhaling, exhaling white plumes of smoke, until at last he spat. The noise interrupted my thoughts. I looked up. Duckman scratched his cheek. Smoked a little more of his cigarette. I waited. He waited. We looked at each other. Finally he spoke.

'Why are you here, Nevis?'

I said nothing.

'You and yer dad,' he continued, 'why offer t' pay rent fer a beaten up old caravan when you could jus' fix up yer van and be on yer way?'

We looked at each other. Duckman frowned.

'Ye know, Nevis, ah think that maybe there's summit

gone wrong wi' you.' He tapped his index finger twice onto his temple. 'Am ah right?' I just looked at him as though stunned by headlights, both my hands still clutching the shears.

Duckman got down from the gate and slowly walked towards me. Did I flinch? Perhaps I moved back or cowered slightly, I don't remember, but something must have surprised Duckman because I saw him raise his eyebrows before burrowing them into a frown. 'There's summit wrong wi' you,' he repeated, more quietly this time, to himself. And then he reached out his hand and took hold of the shears. 'Done,' he said and he turned and started to walk back to the gate, spitting once more into the weeds as though punctuating the event with a full stop.

12

The car park in Kirkcaldy. We were sitting in the front of the van together, I was finishing off the fish supper Marshall had brought back, the greasy warm paper unfolded over my lap. I know exactly what I was doing at that moment, even though it was two years ago. I know because I do it every time I have a fish supper. I tilt the polystyrene tray slightly so all the vinegar runs into the corner and I can hold each remaining chip down in the puddle, soaking it through until it drips. And I know I was doing that at that precise moment because out of the blue Marshall nudged my arm making the vinegar spill onto the paper and over the crotch of my jeans. I dabbed at it quickly with my sleeve. Marshall wanted a pen.

'What is it?' I asked, meaning his new idea. He didn't answer. I passed him a pen from the side pocket of the passenger door and watched as Marshall bent over himself and started to scribble frantically into a notepad.

The car park was behind a nightclub, a run-down

restaurant and a couple of bars. Skips lined the backs of these buildings, bursting rubbish from the top and dribbling dirty-looking liquid from the bottom. It was by the emptier-looking skip I noticed the man. He was old and bent up and mumbling to himself. We were close enough to see his grubby skin, his fat bulbous nose with lumps and painful warts, the dirt in his matted greyish-brown beard. His head was covered with a black beanie. He wore an ill-fitting bomber jacket and joggers, two pairs. I could see the one underneath through the gaping tear in his inside leg. On his feet he wore sandals and socks. They were soaked through from the wet the rain had left behind.

Marshall carried on scribbling, occasionally flicking over to a fresh page in his pad, occasionally stopping. When he stopped he would look out at the homeless man and together we watched him shuffle over to a crate and pull it up to the skip, saw him step up and lean over the edge. We watched as the old man fumbled through the rubbish, found his own meal from the food the restaurant had thrown away. The slops, Marshall called them, the crap customers left behind. I felt the fish supper settle heavy in my stomach.

Later that evening Marshall announced he would be sleeping outside. 'To know what it's like,' he said. And he did sleep outside, I watched him. While the overspill from the nightclub and the bars came round to fight or laugh or linger in dark corners of the car park, Marshall slept. And I watched.

Day twelve, two sets of tallies and two marks complete. I tried to remind Marshall of the car park in Kirkcaldy. 'Do you remember,' I asked, 'the old man eating from the bins?' That morning I had started to wonder if my father's enthusiasm for the farm was a similar case. A new writing project. Marshall was picking at the farm for ideas, picking at the Kerrs for his new characters like he'd done with the old homeless man. That would explain why he wasn't fixing the van or wanting to leave in any hurry. 'Paying rent' was what Duckman had said. So Marshall had offered to pay the Kerrs money to stay with them. Why? Because of a kiss? I didn't understand. Never again, he said. Never again. But that doesn't explain why he didn't just fix the van. If what happened must never happen again, then why couldn't it 'not happen' back in the van?

'The van is broken, Nevis.'

The night before I'd questioned him about it.

'It takes a long time to get things fixed in the middle of nowhere.' He was flicking absentmindedly through a book he'd brought back from the library. 'They need to order in parts from all over the country. Could take weeks.'

'We could call the breakdown service. They come out straight away.'

'Not here they wouldn't.'

'Have you tried?'

Marshall sighed and pressed his fingers into his temples.

'You haven't even tried?' I stared at him in disbelief. 'We've been here more than ten days . . .' I watched him flick even more slowly through the book. I started to feel desperate. What if Marshall never wanted to leave the farm? What if he was settling in? 'Marshall . . . please . . .' I stopped short. So did he. We looked at each other.

It was my tone, I realised later. My tone bothered him. It bothered us both. I can't remember ever pleading with my father. Is that possible? I must have when I was younger. Kids are always pulling at the hands of parents, sobbing because they want ice cream or lollypops or some kind of sweetie. But I don't remember ever doing that. I must have done, surely, but I don't remember. That was why when my please came out, long and begging, 'pleeease', it filled the air around us and stopped us both short. It was Marshall who eventually broke the spell. He said simply, 'Enough now, Nevis,' and turned his eyes back onto his book.

That night I dreamt the moment again. But this time when we stopped and looked at each other, I was looking into the eyes of the old Marshall, the bearded Marshall, not the clean-shaven, cotton-shirt Marshall, but my writer father with long ratty hair and scruffy clothes.

'You've grown your hair again,' I said. I smiled. We laughed. 'A homeless man doesn't shave,' he said. 'A homeless man can't afford razors.' And then I was there, the car park in Kirkcaldy with my father rummaging in bins in search of his story, and me, wandering the tarmac and remembering the night before, alone in the van, guarding Marshall while he slept.

This was why on the twelfth day I woke up thinking it was all a misunderstanding. The farm was just another writing project, I told myself. And at breakfast, when Marshall brought me a bacon butty and a cup of tea, I asked him, 'Do you remember, Marshall, the old man eating from the bins?'

Marshall frowned.

'You must remember,' I said. 'You slept outside that night. By the skips.'

'Not very well,' he said. But I didn't know whether he was referring to the night's sleep or how little he remembered. My question put him on edge. These sorts of questions always did. Marshall didn't like to be asked about the past and memories. 'Once something has happened,' he says, 'no one can ever re-create the event truthfully, accurately, as it *actually* happened. It becomes a fabrication of a truth. It becomes fiction.' Perhaps that's why I've never dared ask him about his life – our life – before the van. He would only tell me to remember it how I wanted to remember it. 'And it would be as

83

much the truth as anything I could tell you,' he would say. But for some reason, on this day, I believed it was important for Marshall to remember. I wanted him so desperately to remember. Anything that might make him pick up his pen again. The sooner he writes this story, I thought, the sooner we can leave.

He didn't stay to talk to me about the car park in Kirkcaldy. Duckman was giving him a lift into town and he had to go. Things to do, he said, he would be back later. I asked if I could go with him.

'No,' he said, 'not today.' And then as he was leaving, turning to close the door behind him, he looked at me. 'Nevis,' he said. And then stopped. Glanced down at his feet, at the laces on his boots. I saw his hand tighten and then relax around the small metal handle of the door. 'Don't stay in the caravan all day, will you, son?' he said. And then left.

LIST 2

The Seats

There were three seats in total, two for me and one for Marshall. I could semi-lie with my legs curled up, head against window while he drove, careful not to kick the gear stick. If you kicked the gear stick it could stall the engine and we could crash. That's what Marshall always said.

The seats were made of a grey material with a faded stripe pattern, dusty-looking. In two places there were splits in the seams where the material met the PVC sides. When I was sitting upright, one of the splits would be directly under my right knee. I used to fiddle with it, pick at the padding when I was bored or hold my finger inside while we were driving along.

I always sat next to the window because Marshall preferred me to. He said the seatbelt was better, the one that went diagonally across my chest. But he didn't mind if I loosened the belt occasionally and put the diagonal bit behind me so I could curl up.

At night I often slept in the front of the van. When my father wasn't driving I could stretch out across all the seats. It wasn't as comfortable as the sofa cushions in the back, but Marshall was often writing late into the night and he didn't always like me lying down next to him. He said he could feel my eyes watching him.

But I didn't mind sleeping in the front of the van so much. I could lie back and look out the window at all the stars, count how many constellations I could see. I had a book on stargazing. I kept it in the glove compartment.

The Stereo

The radio didn't work, but the tape player did and Marshall had a handful of cassettes that we used to listen to now and again. Madonna, Phil Collins, Huey Lewis and the News. Marshall said they weren't his, the previous owner must have forgotten to clear out the glove compartment. He said he didn't like the tapes all that much, preferred driving in silence, but I remember on the odd occasion his finger would tap-tap absentmindedly against the steering wheel or he would forget himself and mouth the words along to the choruses.

There was one other tape that we listened to, more often than the rest. Ivor Cutler – a Scottish comedian and poet. Marshall had bought it for thirty pence in a charity shop. I don't remember anything about this tape other than the strange dreariness of an accordion playing before an old man spoke in a soft, thick, Scottish accent. Marshall would listen to this and smile occasionally. I never understood what was so funny about it. I took my cue instead from the audience on the tape and smiled knowingly when I heard them giggle. Or I slept. There was something about Ivor Cutler's voice that made me want to close my eyes and drift off.

The stereo broke completely a week before my seventh birthday. I know because Marshall was quite cross. He'd bought me a new tape. *Now 13*. Pop music, he said. There were lots of different singers and bands on there and he thought I might like it – although, he added, *he* probably wouldn't. I asked if I could keep the tape anyway, even though I couldn't play it. Marshall looked upset but eventually said he'd got me a book as well, so it wasn't so bad. I don't remember what the book was about. It had a red cover. I'm not even sure if I read it.

The Steering Wheel

When I was really young and Marshall was writing in the back, I used to sit in the driver's seat with my hands firmly on the wheel, turning it this way and that, blowing a brrrm noise through my lips. I couldn't reach the pedals, but I wobbled the gear stick every so often and pretended to beep the horn. Meep meep! – but quietly, under my breath. The horn was in the centre of the steering wheel. Even when the engine wasn't running the horn worked, but I wasn't allowed to press it. It was one of the van rules – or rather, 'no loud noises' was one of the van rules. More specifically, 'no loud noises when Marshall was writing'.

My father always insisted he wasn't in favour of rules. But some rules – he used to say – weren't really rules; they were just common sense. Like making sure we aired the van every day. And keeping the back doors open when we used the gas cooker. And then there were 'courtesy rules'. 'No loud noises', for example. Marshall didn't like being disturbed when he was writing. So no beeping horns or loud brrrrrming. No questions. No talking. It sounds strict when I write it on paper. But the rules only ever applied when Marshall was writing in the van. I could go outside, he said, and be as loud as I liked. Sing, dance, whistle, scream. But in the van everything had to be 'shhh'.

'And there's one other courtesy rule,' he said. 'My writing. You must never read my writing. It's private. Do you understand?'

I nodded.

'Reading my writing would be like reading my thoughts. And thoughts aren't supposed to be read.'

'I promise,' I said.

'Good boy.'

And so the van was aired every day and we always cooked with the back doors open and I learnt how to become very very quiet. And I never read my father's writing.

The Glove Compartment

My space. Marshall used to keep some old rags, an ice-scraper and an out of date road map of Great Britain in there, but I moved these things to the side pocket of the passenger door instead. We never really used any of them anyway. Marshall didn't mind. He said the glove compartment could be my own secret stash and he promised he would never look in it. 'A courtesy rule for me to obey,' he said. And I was pleased. 'I promise never to look in the glove compartment. Cross my heart and hope to die, stick a sausage in my eye.' That's the kind of silly stuff he used to say when I was much younger.

The *Now 13* tape I kept in there, along with my book on stargazing, three pebbles I'd found on Brighton beach, an odd-looking bit of bone Marshall said might be part of a cow's vertebrae, some matches, a pocket book on SAS survival, a bright yellow bouncy ball I found in a public toilets somewhere and a plastic key-ring in the shape of a small frog with big eyes. It's Kermit, Marshall said, from *Sesame Street*. I shrugged and smiled and said I liked the way I could move its arms and legs into different positions and they stayed there.

13

I know exactly what time Marshall left that morning, day twelve, because Elspeth had given us a small square battery-powered clock. We put it on the shelf above the sink with the two mugs – one plain yellow, chipped at the rim, the other white with a picture of Edinburgh Castle on the front – which Elspeth had also given us. We never did get a generator. Instead Duckman had been instructed to bring back from town a twenty-five-metre extension lead, which he rolled out from the tool shed to the caravan. Then Elspeth gave us an electric heater, a desk-light, a toaster and a kettle. Just things that were lying about, she said. Marshall thanked her even though we didn't have any bread for the toaster and the taps in the caravan weren't plumbed in so we had to go to the farmhouse to fill the kettle anyway. Marshall said we should be grateful. I replied that I was, but I was glad it was only temporary. He scowled at me.

It was twenty-seven minutes past ten when he left. He

returned at twelve minutes past five. That meant my father was away for six hours and forty-five minutes.

Six hours and forty-five minutes.

Here's what I did:

I took down the little red clock from the shelf and put it in front of me on the fold-away table. There I sat and listened to it tick and watched the hand counting the seconds. I imagined myself sitting in the car with my father going into town. They'd be at the end of the track by now, turning left, Duckman pressing his foot onto the accelerator, shifting through the gears as he sped up. I wondered what Marshall was thinking. Maybe, 'Slow down.' Or maybe he was going though a list of everything he had to do that day.

What did he have to do that day? Buy some food? Some books? Maybe he was looking for someone who could fix the van. A mechanic. My spirits lifted at the thought. Maybe me pressing him for information had made him think he'd better do something.

My jacket was on the bottom bunk in the narrow bedroom. I went to get it. Pulled it on. Picked up the clock. Ten forty-eight, it said. I put it in my jacket pocket.

I didn't know where I was going. After I clicked the caravan door shut behind me I paused, standing still on the little metal step while I tried to work out what to do. It was Monday, so there wasn't any danger of bumping into Ailsa. That made me feel a whole lot better.

Ailsa was at school. Duckman was taking my father and Elspeth into town. That only left Nigel Kerr and I knew he'd be in the forbidden room staring emptily at the grand piano.

I walked across the field, letting the light wind blow the hair about my face. I climbed the gate and started making my way to the hay barn, a giant stack of hay bales under a corrugated iron roof. This was where I'd managed to escape Ailsa at the weekend by climbing up and into the barn, dropping down in between two bales and pulling some loose hay over the opening above me. Ailsa had climbed into the barn at first. I heard her clambering about, calling my name, telling me how dangerous it was. 'The whole thing can topple if yer not careful, Nevis,' she said. 'It'll crush ye.' And then her voice very close above me, 'If ma uncle finds oot we're in here, he'll go mad on us.' I had sudden visions of her foot stepping onto the loose hay and her whole body crashing through on top of me.

Eventually she left, annoyed. 'I'm tellin', Nevis,' she called back. 'Ye'll be in trouble if you don't come oot.'

I did come out, as soon as she left, and hurried back to hide in the caravan. But that was Saturday. This was Monday and Ailsa was at school. I climbed up into the hay bales and lay down near the very top of the stack where the wind couldn't get at me. I looked up into the rafters and the cobwebs, my hands behind my head.

I sighed, closed my eyes.

Drifted off.

A fat heavy POK sounded itself against the roof above me, followed by another . . . POK . . . and another . . . POK POK. And then downpour. Within seconds the roof rattled with the heavy rain, drumming against the metal sheets only five feet or so above my head. I twisted myself round onto my stomach and looked down from the stack onto the fast forming puddles in the mud. I fished for the clock inside my pocket. Eleven forty-three, it said. I shook it. I felt like I'd been asleep for hours. I tried to remember what I dreamt about. Driving in the van. Marshall had his hand on my leg. He was smiling at me. It'd started to rain. Marshall switched on the wind-screen-wipers. I woke up. It hadn't been a very exciting dream, but I was stiff. I thought about masturbating, decided it was too cold, watched the heavy globs of wet fall thick and fast into the constant ripple of the puddles.

I wondered if Marshall had been caught out in the rain. The old Marshall, I knew, wouldn't care. He'd saunter about at his usual pace or, if the mood took him, stop in his tracks, stretch out his arms wide and raise his face to the sky. 'Open your mouth, boy,' he'd say when I copied him. 'See how many drops you can catch.' But this new Marshall: I imagined him running about town, picking his way past puddles, holding a sodden, limp newspaper above his head; or cowering in a shop doorway or bus shelter, waiting for the weather to pass. I didn't like this new Marshall. Strange and unpredictable. And all because of a kiss? I conjured up an image of a beautiful princess bending low over a lily pad to kiss an ugly toad. KAPOOF! And the toad turns into a prince. Only my father, it seemed, was the other way round.

'It must never happen again, Nevis. Do you understand?' And I'd nodded, said yes, even though I hadn't. I remembered again the time when I was nine and the girl with the green skirt called me gay.

'You prefer fiddling boys. You're a poof. You're a little gay boy,' she said.

'You're ugly,' I told her. So she punched me.

I cried. Of course I did. I remember the blood on my hands and on my t-shirt. I remember the feeling of it warm and sticky on my lips. I remember being afraid. We were in a big town and the van was parked at the other end of the High Street. I ran sobbing all the way, pushing past people with prams and old men with walking sticks and then knocking into a woman who dropped her shopping because of me. I remember her shouting, 'Oi! Kid! You've broken my eggs. Damn you, kid, you've broken my eggs!' But I kept running. I remember hands reaching out for me. Voices calling after me, 'Son, you ok? Where you going to? Where's the fire?'

Or to each other, 'Did you see that young un's face? Blood all over it. He must've had a fall. Or been in a fight.'

The van was parked up in a car park across from a service station. I slowed down when I saw it. I could see Marshall sitting in the front, leaning his pad of paper on the steering wheel. He was writing. I ducked myself down in behind a car and bit onto my lip to stave off the sobbing. I touched my nose. It hurt. It throbbed. The blood had dried and blocked my nostrils. I wanted to pick it out. And I wanted to look at the damage in a mirror. I remember standing and staring at my reflection in the car window. The trees around the edge of the car park cast a shadow over the glass making one half of my face transparent, the other lit by the sun, picking out my pale skin and the almost black of the dried blood under my nose and over my lips. I looked like a boxer, I thought.

It was a while before Marshall noticed anything was wrong. I'd climbed quietly into the back of the van and sat down on the sofa cushions, dabbing at my face with some toilet tissue.

When eventually Marshall did notice he seemed shocked. 'Christ.' He climbed over the seats into the back with me. 'Did you fall?' And I shook my head. He held my face in his hands. I remember that bit particularly, his warm palms and fingers gently cupping my chin and cheeks, his round eyes looking at my nose with concern. 'It's not broken,' he said, 'but it'll swell up and bruise.' He'd ripped a t-shirt for me, dampened it and gently cleaned away the mess. 'A lovely purple colour,' he said. 'Do you want to tell me what happened?'

I told him about the girl.

'Ah,' he said nodding, 'girls don't like being called ugly.'

'I don't like being called gay.'

He shrugged. 'You can't help who you fall in love with,' he said.

That's what he said. Exactly what he said, word for word. I'm absolutely sure of it. I know because I replied. As he kneeled down in front of me and cleaned my face I told him, 'I love *you*, Marshall.' And he smiled, touched my chin with his index finger. 'I love you too, Nevis,' he said and kissed me on the forehead.

And yet now it must never happen again. The more I tell myself that, the more I think about kissing him. The warm of his lips, the bristly hair of his beard full of trapped smells. I wondered what it would be like kissing him now. I wanted to know what shaved skin smelled like. And then I thought about Ailsa with her thin lips, small mouth and little white teeth. The complete opposite, I thought, of my father who had thick lips, fat and dark red, a cavernous mouth full of big teeth. His tongue was slug-like, slow and wet, but soft. I imagined Ailsa's to be thin and sharp like the rest of her. I pictured it moving and flexing and twisting about in her mouth like a snake. I tried to imagine kissing her; her jaw would dislocate and her small mouth would open wide so as she could devour my whole head. I shivered. Ailsa was a snake all right.

And then I thought about kissing Duckman, how his smoky cigarette breath would fill my mouth. And then Elspeth, her lipstick coming off on my face like it comes off on the rim of her mug. And Nigel Kerr. I couldn't imagine kissing Nigel Kerr. He seemed too sad to kiss anyone.

I decided to go back to the caravan. My hands were cold. I cupped them around my mouth and blew into them. Eleven forty-five, the clock said. Hardly any time had passed at all. I put the clock back into my pocket and climbed down to the ground, making sure I didn't rush as I made my way back up the track. I walked slowly through the pouring rain. I felt water seep through the crack in the bottom of my right boot and soak through my sock.

In the short time it took me to walk from the hay barn back up to the yard, I was completely drenched. My jeans rubbed against my legs uncomfortably, my jacket – only showerproof – was heavy across my shoulders and my hair clung to my forehead in clumps. I smiled as I heard the beginnings of thunder rumble across the sky. A flash of lightning forked from the grey clouds in the distance and I counted the seconds. One, two, three, four, five . . . and then came the crack. Only five miles. The wind was picking up. An empty bucket rattled and banged its way across the yard. I shivered as I unhooked the gate, squeezed through and semi-jogged my way back to the caravan.

Five minutes later, naked and wrapped in a duvet, I was thanking Elspeth over and over in my head for the electric heater. 'Thank you, Elspeth, I am truly grateful.' My bare feet pointed towards the hot orange and red bars. I'd folded down the table into Marshall's bed and thrown on the cushions. I leant against the wall, the heater close to my feet, my right hand cupping my balls, and watched the storm through the window above the sink. It was moving further away. I counted the seconds between light and bang. Eleven . . . fifteen . . . nineteen . . . until there was no more lightning, no more thunder and the rain had slowed down to a drizzle.

Twelve thirteen, the clock said.

I missed my books. Waiting around all day wouldn't be so bad, I decided, if I had things to do. Things to read. And what about my clothes? I hated wearing Duckman's cast-off jeans and unwanted tops and now that my clothes were soaked through I had no other choice. I made a mental note to ask Marshall later if we could at least visit the van to pick up a few things. Some books, some clothes. And if not . . .

well . . .

I imagined walking off to find the van by myself and realised I couldn't even remember if it was left at the end of the track, or right.

The rain was on and off for the rest of the day. When Marshall finally came back, at twelve minutes past five, he was shaking a wet umbrella. I must have been wide-eyed staring at it because Marshall said irritably, 'What is it, Nevis? Have you never seen an umbrella before?'

I looked away. 'How was your day?' I asked.

'Wet,' he said. He had bags with him. He started unpacking them into the cupboards above the sink. Some tinned food, some bread, some dried milk. I was pleased. At least I wouldn't have to go to the farmhouse for food any more. Tea, coffee, sugar, a four-pack of dried noodles. The sight of the instant edibles reminded me of the van and put a smile on my face. I asked Marshall if he'd been to the field that day.

'I've been busy,' he said.

I mentioned the clothes.

'What's wrong with what you're wearing?'

'They're not mine,' I said.

'They fit, don't they?'

So I asked for the books.

'There's too many to cart back,' he said.

'Two or three, that's all.' I was starting to feel desperate. 'Maybe the one about the kings and queens of Britain and the science encyclopaedia . . .'

'You've read those ten times already.'

'So I'll read them again. It's non-fiction. You're supposed to read them over and over.'

Marshall fell silent. I watched him screw the empty bags up into balls and stuff them into a drawer. 'It's good,' he said finally, 'that you have such an interest in history and science.' He coughed to clear his throat. 'Would you like a cup of coffee?'

I mumbled for tea and watched him open a bottle of water and pour it into the kettle.

'I met someone today,' Marshall said. 'A man, and I'd like you to meet him too. His name's Hamish Galbraith. He's very interested in you.'

'In me?'

'Yes, I spoke to him about you. About how clever you are. Mr Galbraith is a teacher.'

Marshall put the kettle on the floor and plugged it into the free socket next to the heater. 'Nevis, has this been on all day?' He pointed at the hot bars by my feet. 'Christ, you'll be costing the Kerrs a fortune.' He pulled out the plug and the red died to dark instantly. I listened to it click as it cooled. 'You mustn't waste electricity, Nevis, it's not free you know. It costs a lot of money.'

'Does it?'

'Yes and don't be smart. Just put some more clothes on if you're cold.'

That annoyed me. 'I don't *have* any more clothes,' I said. 'They're at the van.'

Marshall sighed and closed his eyes. 'No more about the van, Nevis. Please. I want to talk about Mr Galbraith. I think you'll like him. He'll be able to teach you more about history and science and geography and maths and lots of other things besides. You won't have to just read books any more.'

'I *like* reading books,' I said.

'He's also fluent in French and German.'

'Good for him.'

'Nevis!'

'What?'

The kettle clicked off. Marshall shook his head and went to get the mugs from the shelf. I crossed my arms and stared at my knees, already cold without the heater on. This was shit, I thought. Everything was shit. Why couldn't we talk about the van?

'I've made an appointment for you to meet Mr Galbraith next Monday.'

I sighed.

'Did you hear me, Nevis?'

I didn't look at him.

'You keep asking me to take you into town, well next Monday you can go.'

'I *do* want to go into town – with you. But not to meet some teacher. Anyway, *you're* a teacher, aren't you? Why don't you just teach me stuff? You always used to in the van.'

'Stop mentioning the van, Nevis.'

'What do you *mean* stop mentioning it?' Now I really was annoyed. 'We can't live here forever. We need to get it fixed.'

It was then, without warning, Marshall raised his hand and brought it down with a bang on the kitchen unit. 'Enough!' He stood staring down at me, his hand gripping the edge of the unit. 'Enough, Nevis. There'll be no more talk of the van, do you understand?' He shook his head, looked away, let his hand fall from the unit to his side. 'And don't cower from me like that,' he said. 'I'd never hit you.'

I'd pushed myself into the very corner of the caravan and was holding my knees, tucked tight to my chest. He looked at me closely. His eyes moved from my bare feet, up the pale blue of the borrowed jeans and plain red of the t-shirt, and then stopped on my face. 'I think . . .' he said quietly. 'I think maybe it's time we went back to normality.' His eyes seemed sad when he said it. 'Do you understand what I mean, Nevis?'

'No,' I said.

'I mean . . .' and he trailed off. 'I mean I'm sorry.'

I frowned.

'For being a bad father.'

'Who said that?'

'But things can change, Nevis. That's what we're going to do. Change.'

'But what if I don't want to?'

'Wait here.'

'What?' I suddenly felt panicked. 'Why? Where are you going?'

'Wait here,' he repeated. 'Don't follow me.'

The caravan door banged shut. I shouted after him, 'What do you mean *wait*! I've been waiting all day!' But I didn't open the door. I didn't follow my father. I just watched through the window as he strode full of purpose across the field, through the gate and then disappeared into the yard. 'Where are you going?' I leant my elbows onto the unit, gripped my hair tight with my fingers. 'Where are you going? Come back, Marshall . . . please.'

14

One of the most bitter nights. It dropped well below zero. I couldn't sleep. Marshall still hadn't returned. I guessed he was at the van. Where else would he go? I knew Duckman had taken him somewhere. I'd seen them in the yard talking and then they both got in the blue Sierra and drove off together. I paced the caravan back and forth, blowing into my fists for warmth. I imagined him at the van. What was he doing there? I sat myself down. What was all this about being a bad father? Going back to normality? The van *was* my normality. I felt panicked.

Eventually the cold made me move into the bunkroom and pull the heater into the doorway. I didn't care how much it cost the Kerrs, at least it would keep me from freezing. I climbed into bed, the small room lit with an orangey-yellow glow. Fully clothed and tightly wound in the duvet, my hands up underneath my jumper and t-shirt, I hugged my stomach. I waited.

I don't remember falling asleep, but I remember

waking up, so I must have done. Either that or the cold must have knocked me out – made me lose consciousness. When memories of the evening finally caught up with me, I almost fell out the bunk, a tangled mess, in my rush to check on my father. He was there, sleeping, his arms hugging the pillow underneath his face. I sighed. Leaned back against the wall. Closed my eyes with relief. When I opened them again I looked down at my father and smiled. He must have crept about like a cat so as not to wake me.

The heater had been switched off. I switched it back on and pulled on my boots, not bothering to do up the laces. I'd make tea, I thought. The sound of the boiling kettle would wake Marshall up and then I could ask him where he'd been. I clicked on the kettle.

My eyes fell onto a black-labelled bottle on the kitchen unit, a third full with a brown liquid. Alcohol. I picked it up, pulled off the cap and sniffed. It was whisky. I recognised the smell. My father used to drink it most nights when I was younger. But then he stopped. Almost overnight. I remember the morning he poured the whisky away. 'Things are going to change,' he said when he caught me watching him. And he tried to smile, but his smile only made him look sadder.

I know very little about the prehistory of my father – his life before the van. He was a teacher. He lived in London. My mother left him. That's about it. And I don't remember much about those first few years living in the van with Marshall either. Most of my memories start after the age of seven. Apart from brief instances, snapshots, or just 'things' from the earlier years – like the silver hipflask my father would swig from. And I remember my father red-faced and laughing. And I remember him being sick once, leaning against the side of the van, holding himself up. And I remember our conversations.

'You remind me of her. Your face. You look like her.'

'No.'

'You do. You have her chin. You have her eyes.'

I placed the bottle back on the kitchen unit and turned to look at my father, sleep-breathing and dribbling on his pillow. I didn't want him to start drinking again. When my father got drunk he'd stop writing and start talking about her – my mother. And I hated it.

I approached carefully so as not to wake him and bent low over his face to sniff. Whisky. Mixed with vomit. And smoke. Had my father been smoking?

And then his eyes shot open.

My head banged against the wall. It happened before I could see or feel it happen. His hand was around my neck.

'What the hell are you doing?'

'Jesus . . .'

'What the *fuck* are you doing?'

'Nothing,' I said.

I tried to focus on his face, taut, tight-lipped, staring into me. He pulled me away from the wall, forced me down onto the cushions, his fist on my chest pinning me still. I felt the sob bubble up and out my mouth before I could stop it.

'Were you trying to kiss me?' he said. 'Were you trying to kiss me, Nevis?'

'No.'

'Don't lie to me!'

I was shaking, holding my father's wrist and arm weakly with my hands. 'Don't *lie* to me, Nevis!' He shook me hard.

'I'm not . . .'

'Then what were you doing?'

'Smelling . . .'

'Smelling me? For *fuck* sake!'

'Smelling you . . .' I cried, '. . . for whisky!'

And then it was over. Marshall pulled away. He stood up and started pacing the caravan up and down, hands on hips, then hand running through his hair. I held my head where it had hit the wall and hid my face close into the pillow. I cried.

'Jesus Christ,' he said just as the water came to boil. The kettle clicked off. Steam poured from the lid. 'Jesus Christ.'

15

I hate Marshall, I hate the farm, I hate the Kerrs, that's what I spent the rest of the morning thinking after the incident in the caravan. I hated everything. The only thing I liked was the dull bruised throb of pain the lump on the back of my head created whenever I pressed or prodded it.

Marshall had gone to the farmhouse to wash. I was sitting on the grass, leaning against the wire fence that ran along the track towards the hay barn. I'd positioned myself perfectly so when Marshall crossed the yard on his way back to the caravan he'd see me sitting there alone, picking at the grass and flicking it onto the track. He'd feel sorry for me. Come across. Talk to me. Say nice things, like everything will be ok and I shouldn't worry and he hadn't meant to hurt me. That was what I wanted.

The back door of the farmhouse opened and closed and the dogs got to their feet wagging their tails. I picked and flicked my grass, not looking up at first, but when nothing happened and nobody approached, I glanced across the yard and saw Duckman climbing through the window of the tool shed. I sighed and leaned my head back against the fence.

The sky was a clear blue with wisps of white. Cirrus; cirrostratus; cirrocumulus. The highest clouds made entirely of ice crystals.

In the summertime Marshall and I would sit together with the back doors of the van wide open. Marshall could never write when it was hot. His skin itched with sweat, he said, he couldn't concentrate. So we often sat together, side by side with our legs dangling over the edge of the van, his ending with his feet in a bowl of cold water. We'd sit and watch the world go by, that's what he called it. We looked at the sky and he taught me the words for the clouds. Cumulonimbus; altostratus; nimbostratus; cumulus. Beautiful words that rolled off the tongue. Words to be chanted, Marshall said.

I didn't hate him. I could never hate my father. I just wanted him back.

Footsteps. I looked across to where they were coming from. Duckman had climbed back out of the tool shed carrying a bucket and was now walking straight towards me. I didn't move. I stared at my boots and willed him to pass.

'What a lovely fuckin' day, eh, Nevis? Do ye mind if ah join ye?' He flipped the bucket upside down onto the track and sat. 'It's all right,' he said, 'I know better than t' wait for a response.' He took the half-smoked brown roll-up cigarette from behind his ear and fished in his pocket for a lighter. 'D' ye mind if ah smoke?' He lit his cigarette and inhaled deeply. 'Ahh that's better. Ma lungs jus' don't feel right unless ah'm fillin' 'em full o' cancer.' He spat and took another drag on his cigarette.

I heard the back door of the farmhouse open and close and the dogs start beating their tails against the ground. I craned my neck around Duckman to see who it was. Marshall. He was walking across the yard back to the caravan. He saw Duckman sitting down the track, smoking on his upturned bucket and then he saw me. He nodded. Semi-smiled. And then carried on his way. Damn you, Duckman, I thought. Fucking Duckman. I hated him.

He turned to glance over his shoulder to see what I was looking at and then sighed a long weary sigh. I glared at him. He was shaking his head, staring at his yellow fingers and fag burning down to its filter tip. 'God help me,' he said. 'Ah must be a fuckin' fool. Why ah give a shiny shite is beyond me.' He flicked his ash. 'It's a bit weird though, no? You and 'im. Dinnae go thinkin' ah've no noticed. It's like yer obsessed.'

I turned my face away, glared at the muddy track instead, pretending I wasn't listening, but I was.

'Ah've seen the way ye look at 'im, Nevis. It's weird. Big bug-eyed in awe of 'im. And what's with callin' 'im Marshall? He's yer father, no? D'ye catch me callin' ma dad by 'is first name?' He shook his head, scratched his cheek. 'Ah dinnae get ye, Nevis. I dinnae get you or yer father.'

What's there to get, I thought. I love him. I wondered if Duckman had ever loved anything in his life. Maybe only his dead mother, I thought. And now she's gone, love's gone. I could suddenly see Duckman for what he really was. An empty, bitter, smoking shell. Jealous because at least I *could* wait for Marshall to come back when he'd gone away.

'Listen,' he said, 'ah'm gonnae be honest wi' ye, Nevis. Ah don't like ye. Ye piss me right off with yer no talkin' and yer weedy wimpin' aboot the farm tryin' t' avoid everyone. In my opinion, you need someone t' take ye aside and beat the livin' shit intae ye. An' believe me, by Christ, ah've thought aboot it.' Duckman paused, took a drag on his cigarette and held it in his mouth before blowing out the smoke in one long jet of white. 'Yer a wee shite, Nevis. Ah knew it as soon as ah saw ye. A spoilt wee shite who doesnae have t' open his own gob 'cause his father speaks up fer 'im. Am ah right or am ah right?' He hawked up the phlegm from the back of his throat and spat it at the ground. 'Ah'm fuckin' right,' he said.

The thick greenie-yellow spit lay inches from my boot.

'Ah'm surprised yev no tried t' run off yet. Ye can ye know. Ah'm no stoppin' ye. Go on back t' yer caravan an' hide if that's what ye want. Go back t' yer father. Or *here's* an idea, Nevis, ye can stay an' chat wi' me. Would ye like that? For a fuckin' change would ye like a wee chat?' He let a silent space fill the air between us, long enough for an answer – which I didn't give him – and then he laughed quite suddenly, aggressively. 'Christ,' he said. 'Ah long fer the day ah can tell *you* t' shut the fuck up, Nevis.' He shook his head.

I watched him tread his dead cigarette into the mud and pull out his tobacco tin for another. I could leave, I thought. I could stand up and walk off and not have to sit through Duckman blowing smoke at me. I could go and see Marshall in the caravan. But then what? We'd argue . . . or not speak. Just stare at each other.

'You look depressed,' said Duckman. 'Maybe ye should kill yerself.'

I stared out towards the road.

Duckman sighed and shook his head.

'Ah must be a fool,' he said again. And then, 'Ah've got somethin' of yours.' My ears pricked. 'Or at least, ah think it's yours.' He shifted slightly on his upturned bucket, squeezed his hand into his jeans pocket and pulled out something green. Held it out to me. My key-ring.

'Where'd you get that?' I grabbed it from his outstretched hand.

'Where'd ye fuckin' think?' he said. 'And no need t' snatch.'

I stared at the frog and felt an unexpected grin start to warm and spread across my face.

'Ah used t' collect key-rings,' Duckman explained. 'Don't any more mind. But ah saw it in yer glove compartment an' it was kinda automatic, ye know?'

'When were you at the van?' I asked.

'First day ye got here,' he said. 'Ah went back later that night fer a wee rummage.' He shrugged. 'Sorry. Couldnae resist.'

I moved the frog's legs and arms up and down, rubbed some grime away from the white of its eyes.

'Christ,' Duckman said with a relieved sigh. 'And ah thought I'd be in the shite. Look at ye grinnin'. Careful yer face doesnae crack, Nevis, it's no use t' the exercise.' He spat. 'Ah still think yer an eejit mind and fair weird t' say the least. Dinnae go gettin' the wrong idea jus' 'cause I owned up t' nickin' yer poxy key-ring.'

'It was a present,' I said. 'From Marshall.'

'Aye, of course it was,' he replied. 'Who else?'

I shook my head in disbelief. The frog looked unreal in my hand, a memory out of context.

'You have to take me there. Please, Duckman, will you take me there?'

Duckman snorted and then shot me a confused uncomfortable smile. 'Ok,' he said. 'But ah dinnae see the point. Yev got all that's left in yer hand.'

16

Fire, it seems, can twist metal, bend it, dent it, beat it out of shape. There must have been an explosion. The bonnet bent back and broken, blackened doors popped from their locks. The passenger side hung heavily from one hinge. Slide door blown free from the side, lay flat on the grass, littered with sharp shattered glass. The tyres had melted leaving only their rings of steel wire wrapped around the small, ugly metal wheels.

Marshall must have watched this burn for hours. Drunk his whisky. Walked back to the farm, alone.

There was very little left of the interior except the skeleton of the seats and the red and yellow wires that twisted out from where the radio used to be. The dashboard had part collapsed, part remained, still framing where the round dials of the speedometer and fuel gauge had been. The glove compartment had completely disappeared.

And nothing left of possessions. The books, the sofa cushions, our clothes and bedding. *His stories*. Nothing left. I climbed into the back of the van on hands and knees and felt around. Not frantically, but with a stolid determination to find something. What I found was a battered pot and frying pan and three hooks. Rifts of grey ash rose up around me. I found the clasp of the food chest, a drawing pin, a broken bulldog clip. I carried on searching. I was blackened from head to toe before my hand closed around something thin and solid. A fork. I lifted it from the mess. One of the prongs had bent and stuck out slightly at a jaunty angle. Eleven years, I thought. This is what's left of eleven years. And I wondered then what the smoke of eleven years looked like.

Duckman beeped his horn. Three times and then waited. Twice more. Then waited. I heard the sound of his engine start up and drive off.

I lay down. Pressed my cheek into the now cold metal of the floor and watched as the soft grey ash settled or shifted or was lifted by the slight wind that blew through the open van, spiralled up and out of the back doors.

17

It's all in the wrong order. I know it is. I'm missing bits out, changing things round. I'm not being honest. Just like what Marshall's always said; you can't recreate an event truthfully, as it actually happened. 'It's history now, Nevis, forget about it,' he says. But I mustn't forget. I'll not allow myself to forget anymore. If it means writing and re-writing lists for the rest of my life, keeping records, diaries, bottling my memories, then I will. History *is* important. Why can't he see that? Everything past has brought me here. Everything past has created me. Memories are like milestones. They show you where you've been. I can almost hear Marshall cluck his tongue in a kind of tut tut tut of disapproval. I know what he'd say: 'Memories are like milestones, eh? With such a poetic tongue in your head, Nevis, you should be a writer yourself.' Whenever I used to say something foolish, my father always seemed to suggest I became a writer like him.

I should have started from the very beginning. My

conception. Not that I know anything about it apart from that it definitely happened. My father had sex with my mother and made me.

I know about sex. I've known ever since Marshall bought me my science encyclopaedia. Reproduction ensures that the human species does not become extinct, that's what it says. The man inserts his penis into his partner's vagina and releases millions of sperm. If sexual intercourse happens within twenty-four hours of ovulation, a sperm may penetrate the egg. This is called fertilisation. And that's how babies are made. There were diagrams. Not of the actual sexual act, but of the male and female 'reproductive systems'. But I know all about sexual intercourse. The night my father slept by the skips. The car park in Kirkcaldy. I've been missing things out.

A girl in the doorway behind the nightclub, leaning drunk, one arm against the wall, holding herself up for a boy who fiercely kissed and bit her neck, holding her breasts, groping her sides. He lifted her skirt and lifted the girl against the wall, her legs wrapped around his waist. I can still see her face; the pallid, pasty skin and drunk watery eyes that tried to stay open, her head limp, and her hands hung over the shoulders of the boy who moved inside her. I watched. Not knowing what to do, not knowing what sex was, on the edge of my seat staring at this boy and girl and my father only a few feet away, slumped against the side of a skip, eyes closed, mouth open, fast asleep. And I was scared. The boy looked angry. His voice was hard. The girl's legs kept slipping from around his waist. 'Hold still,' he kept saying. 'Hold yersel' up fer fuck sake.'

Some memories you can't forget, no matter how hard you try. They haunt you. I used to dream I was the boy pinning her against the wall. But in the dream I lost my balance. The girl's right hand fell from my shoulder and her arm dropped heavily to her side. The shift in weight made me stagger. We fell. And when I looked at the girl to make sure she was all right, her eyes were set open, bloodshot and staring right through me. Dead.

I was thirteen then. It was later that year I was given my science encyclopaedia and put two and two together. That's how you make babies, I thought. The man inserts his penis into his partner's vagina. I remembered the girl in the park. How she'd pressed my fingers against her bits and there was nothing there. Just a fold. And I struggled to pull my hand away.

'What's wrong with you? Don't you like it?'

'No.'

'Well most boys do.'

A girl's insides – her uterus – look like the head of a ram. Or at least it did in my book. A boy's insides – I'm not sure what they look like. Complicated. Sperm duct, testis, urethra. I know these words. I can spell them. Give me a diagram and I could label it. Epididymis. That's my favourite. Although I don't really know how to pronounce it . . . or what it actually does. But what I do know is that if I accidentally hit my balls it hurts. Jesus Christ, it hurts. It doesn't say anything in my science encyclopaedia about that. But what it does say is that two hundred and fifty million sperm are made each day in a man's testes. Two hundred and fifty million! I've decided that's why men have to masturbate. You can't keep producing that much sperm and not get rid of it somehow.

Masturbate: arouse oneself sexually or cause another person to be aroused by manual stimulation. That's what it says in the dictionary. I didn't even know there was a word for it. All the dictionary games we used to play together; all the times I just sat on my own and leafed through the pages reading random words, I never read that one. But that's how I discovered it in the end, just randomly flicking through, picking out words and reading their meaning. Masturbate. It didn't say how to do it, but I knew what it meant. I'd been doing it for years. Just not with other people.

'It must never happen again, Nevis.'

Why not? Where in the dictionary does it say it's so wrong?

'Do you understand, Nevis?'

No. But if I could turn back time and change everything, I would. Right back to the moment I closed the dictionary and it made that dull thump of thick pages closing against pages. It was at that moment I saw Marshall asleep, not bothering with blankets. He'd get cold, I thought. It's October.

Or did I think that? Is that really the truth?

Arouse oneself sexually, it said, or cause another person to be aroused by manual stimulation.

18

I don't remember Duckman returning. I don't remember being lifted and put into the car and driven back to the farm. When I woke up I was alone in a bed. And I mean a proper bed, with a thick quilt and big pillows. A double bed. I felt myself sinking into the soft mattress. The curtains were drawn across the window, thin and flimsy. The bright morning sun shone straight through the pinkish material, giving the room a soft bubblegum glow. When I remember waking up that morning, in that room, in a bed – a proper bed – for the first time, I remember it like waking up in a bubble. Warm and safe. And then it popped, just like a bubble would pop. I smelt the ash and dead smoke in my hair, tasted it in my mouth, on my tongue. I gasped. A sudden intake of breath like I'd been underwater for a long time and only just made it back up to the surface.

They visited me. They came in, one at a time, sat down on a wooden chair next to my bed and talked. Marshall was first. He didn't knock but opened the door slightly, peeked in and saw me there, staring up at the ceiling with my mouth open. He coughed, pushed the door a bit further. 'Nevis?' I kept my eyes on the ceiling. 'Nevis?' and he coughed again. 'It's me. Your father.' Perhaps he thought I'd hit my head. Perhaps he thought I was delusional, that I couldn't recognise his voice. 'Do you want to talk to me?' he said. I closed my mouth. He came in. Sat down. Coughed. Why was he coughing so much? Maybe it was the smoke, it had infected him too. I thought maybe I should cough. Maybe my lungs were filled and choked with smoke and that's how I could taste it. I could smell it, clogging my nose, sticking to the walls of my nostrils. I didn't cough. I didn't sneeze. I didn't move. I just lay there staring up at the ceiling.

What followed was my reprogramming. That's what I've called it since. I lay there like a redundant robot, all broken and out of place, and my father sat over me like a mad scientist, twisting words into small intricate tools, rewiring my system.

How can we distinguish memory from simply imagining? he said. We experience an event and then days later we try to remember what happened. We conjure up an image in our head, we conjure up a feeling, but who's to say that our image is clear and complete? Who's to say we haven't added bits or exaggerated our emotion? And after thinking about it for such a long time, boiling over the event, trying to recreate the moment in our memory, it becomes distorted. And then it's the distorted image we remember and think of as fact. We have new feelings tied to the incorrect image, feelings that perhaps weren't there at the time of the event. So we remember it wrongly. The event becomes fiction, an untruth. Worsened still if we try to speak about it. I've told you before, Nevis, about the incompetence of words. There are not enough in the world to describe a past event perfectly. Or even if there were, what is a word except our experience of what it means? And what is experience except memory? Do you understand what I'm trying to say, Nevis? *Now* is the only truth. It is safer to live in the present, easier to change your future. This is us now . . . this is how things are going to be . . . are you listening, Nevis?

And he told me about how he'd found a job at a local pub called the Crofter's Inn. He would start the next day, he said. And he told me about how he's going to pay rent to live in the caravan, but that the Kerrs have kindly invited me to move into the farmhouse with them. It's warmer in the house, he said, and he told me about central heating and about how cold it gets in the Highlands through the winter, as though this was something I didn't already know.

He spoke about Mr Galbraith, the teacher who was

still very interested in me and was looking forward to our first meeting. Marshall had postponed it until the following week on account of me being ill. Apparently I was ill. I don't remember being sick or feeling sick. I didn't have a fever. But that's how Marshall described it. When you're feeling better again, he said, you can meet with Mr Galbraith. Education is important. You need outside help. I've taught you everything I know now.

He told me about how much I love science. You love science, he said. You could learn so much. You could go to university if you do well in school. And you will do well, I know you will. You're smart, Nevis. Really smart.

Repetition: like telling me the same thing over and over again would make me believe it. My reprogramming. Me staring blank-faced up at the ceiling listening to his words wash over me, through me. Maybe my emptiness gave him the impression I was hypnotised.

... and you're getting on so well with Ailsa and Duckman, he said. I can see that we're going to be happy here.

That's when I let my head fall sideways onto the pillow to look at him. And there he was, sitting forward on his chair, hands clasped in front of him. He stopped talking. We looked at each other.

I know about robots. I know the word 'robot' was invented by a playwright called Capek. He wrote a play

125

about an army of robots that became so clever they took over the whole world. Capek was from Czechoslovakia. I was thinking about this when my father and I stared at each other. 'Did you know,' I said, 'the word "robot" comes from the Czech word *robota*?' Marshall looked blank. 'It means "slavery",' I added and then turned my attention back onto the ceiling.

The Rot

Two bodies breathing, sleeping, sweating among unwashed clothes, on top of filthy torn sofa cushions pulled from a skip, never rid of that slight smell of rubbish. I could press my face deep into the padding, breathe in and smell it, the fousty, wet, garbage. Rotten. The back of the van smelt of damp and dust and skin even though we aired it every day. We opened the windows and doors and pulled out the sofa cushions if it wasn't raining.

We'd notice the smell more if we spent time away, come back and it would hit us. A proper punch, Marshall said. Could stun a dead man. We tried aerosol air fresheners once. Marshall bought a pack of three, but the sweet, strong smell of a fake summer breeze made us gag, turned our stomachs. We used one spray instead as a flame-thrower. Marshall held a match to the nozzle and sprayed so a jet of fire flew out. We did it at night in the pitch black. Our own fireworks display. Marshall scorched his fingers, but didn't care.

For a time we used incense sticks instead. Almond. Cedar. Coconut. But even they made me queasy. Marshall said they helped him write so wouldn't stop buying them. I'd go for a walk or sit outside while the heady scents crept out through the open windows. Soon the smell of skin and sweat and bodies deep in the sofa cushions were mixed with a faint flowery hint. Sandalwood. Jasmine. Patchouli. And then one day, Marshall just stopped burning them. It happens like that sometimes. You do something for months, maybe even years and then one day you just stop. Like me and stories. Fiction, I mean. From now on I'm not going to read anything that isn't true.

The Windows

The smell was so bad if we closed the windows at night. Some days we'd wake up and the van walls would be dripping with the wet from our breath and the windows would be steamed up. I would write in them: good morning, hi, hello, good day or draw a round face with a big smile. Marshall used to write and draw things too. I think therefore I am, he wrote once. Then he added, I can say 'I think', therefore I am. Once he drew a picture of the van and when he finished I added a picture of us holding hands just next to it. Very good, he said. Marshall called the windows our morning etch-a-sketch. I had a real etch-a-sketch once. I stood on it and the plastic cracked. The windows were better in that respect.

The Slide Door

We very rarely used the side door of the van, not as a door anyway – too much like hard work climbing over all the books and heaped clothes we piled around it when we could just jump in through the back or front doors instead without any bother. So the slide door was purely for ventilation. In the summer the van would get hot and stuffy. We'd open all the doors and windows and let the air blow through. I loved the sound the door made when it was pulled back, the whirring of those little plastic wheels on metal and when we slammed it shut again, whooooBOOM.

The Exhaust Pipe

The one part of the van I despised. I hated the exhaust pipe. It reminded me of cities and traffic jams and sickness. The smell of exhaust fumes makes my heart beat faster and my chest tighten like at the beginning of a panic attack. I don't know why. It's a city smell and I hate the city, perhaps it's as simple as that. But I remember times being ill – lying on the sofa cushions in the back, my eyes glued to the rusty metal roof, a sick bucket nearby and I could feel every vibration of the van's engine and I could sense the exhaust pipe pumping out its horrible black smoke. Whenever I was ill and Marshall was driving, the exhaust pipe became fixed in my mind and I couldn't think of anything else until we stopped moving again.

19

Perhaps I really was ill. I couldn't eat. I couldn't read. I couldn't move. Or rather, I could move, but I didn't want to. I'd just lie there in that big double bed, looking up at the ceiling. I'd drift so much in and out of sleep I never felt awake, I was always dreaming or in between dreams. I was told later that I was like this for five whole days. Even when I got up to go to the toilet or have a bath, escorted by my father, I was empty. That's how Ailsa described it. My eyes were empty like I couldn't see what was right in front of me.

Five days.

I remember one time I woke up to the sight of a girl in the corner of the room where there was a dressing table. The girl was singing to herself, not words, just la's and hmm's. She was tying her hair back in a ribbon, admiring herself in the mirror. She picked up colourful glass bottles from the table that clinked when she put them back down again, she dabbed perfume onto her wrists and neck. I could smell it, sweet and flowery in the air. The girl dabbed more onto a handkerchief, turned round and looked at me. You're awake? she said. I replied 'no'. Well your eyes are open, she said. So I closed them. It might have been Ailsa. But when I thought about it closely I pictured the girl having a green skirt, like the girl from the park. And when I woke up again later she was still sitting there, although this time the girl had grown up and it was a woman sweeping her hair back and tying it with a ribbon. I didn't recognise the woman at first, but then I thought – Catherine Kerr. Duckman's mother. It was Catherine Kerr, so I really must have been dreaming. I watched her clink the bottles and dab her wrists and neck and handkerchief with perfume. She turned around. You're awake? she said. No, I replied and closed my eyes. When I woke again the heady flowery scent was right by my nose. The handkerchief folded on my pillow.

Another time I woke up lying out in the heather, looking up into sun shining through the tops of trees. I could smell the soil and the moss and the woodland. I heard the birds and the distant river. I must have been lying there for quite some time because spiders had woven their webs around me. It was warm. It was summer. I closed my eyes. I opened them. I was still in the woods, but this time behind some trees looking over at myself lying in the heather, spread out like a star. It was a younger me. I remembered this moment from years

131

before. It actually happened. I closed my eyes again. I wanted to get back into my head. I wanted to be lying down not standing up. This was me five years ago. Me when everything was ok. I opened my eyes. I saw the younger me get to his feet, brush down his clothes. He looked happy. He started walking through the trees, touching each trunk as he passed. 'Nobody around, nobody in sight,' I said. And then I heard him. 'Nobody around, nobody in sight,' he said. I closed my eyes. I opened them. Why couldn't I get back into my body? I followed him. I started blinking furiously. I wanted to get back into his head – my head. Why couldn't I get back into my head? He started to run. This part didn't happen in real life. I hadn't run through the trees like this. I shouted, 'Wait!' He ran faster. 'Wait for me!' I was chasing him at full pelt. I was starting to catch up. I could hear his breathing. He glanced over his shoulder at me as I was gaining on him and I saw his face, terrified. He sped up. 'Wait!' I shouted. And then his voice – my voice – panic stricken, screaming through the trees, 'Why are you following me? Leave me alone!' I stopped. 'Leave me alone!' he was crying. This hadn't happened in real life. This wasn't the memory. I watched myself run ahead, lifting his feet high to clear the twisted roots of the heather. I watched myself disappear. I closed my eyes. It hadn't happened like that. There had been no running, no fear, no crying. That wasn't how it went.

They woke me up quite regularly in those five days to tell me I was having a bad dream. 'I know,' I said to them once. 'So why won't you let me sleep?' In the evenings Marshall would shake my shoulders, gently so as not to frighten me. 'It's seven o'clock,' he'd say. 'It's time for your bath.' I'd make myself move. Not because I wanted to, but because I knew Marshall would lift me like an invalid if I didn't. So I pulled back the covers, slowly swung my legs round and out of the bed and stood up. The first time this happened Marshall took hold of my arm as though I needed steadying. I remember that moment, seeing him clasping my elbow, the greenish veins branching across the back of his hand. I stopped and stared at his nails, clean and clipped short, and at the small black hairs on the bottom of his fingers just above the knuckles. His hands were pale, well scrubbed. I could smell some sort of perfume on him, an unfamiliar musky scent. Marshall saw me staring and let go of my arm. 'Follow me, Nevis,' he said. So I did.

The room with the double bed was on the top floor of the farmhouse at the bottom of a dark corridor with patterned wallpaper, greyish in colour, with a faded red flowery crown print all over. Fleur-de-lis. Where one strip met another it had started to peel away from the wall and around the light switch, where it was cut badly, it had been clearly picked. There was a large painting in the corridor with a thick gold frame. Two deer running in the woodlands, painted in dark colours, old looking. Dusty. The corridor smelled thick with ill-kept age, the carpet threadbare green. There was a foldable table. It looked out of place in that narrow corridor, like it was left there because there was nowhere else to put it. On the table there were photographs in silver or gold or wooden polished frames. Every time I went past I would look at them and try to take in something new about each one.

Five in total. Three of a woman who I know was Catherine Kerr. Catherine Kerr sitting on a bench, legs crossed, hands neatly folded in her lap. She was holding her head back and smiling at the person taking the picture. A proper smile, not a photo smile. You can tell it was real because she had a shine in her eye, like she'd just been laughing.

Another Catherine Kerr, this time holding a baby in her arms. She was looking down into the baby's face. Duckman, I thought. The baby was tiny, eyes tight shut, wrapped in a shawl so only his pale pinkish newborn face poked out.

The third Catherine Kerr was younger, black and white, not looking at the camera. She stared into the distance. She didn't smile. She was posing, a thoughtful longing pose. She was beautiful, I thought. She was dead. Maybe death is what makes someone beautiful.

It had been this Catherine Kerr that I woke up to in my dream, tying her hair back and perfuming her wrists. The beautiful dead Catherine Kerr.

There was another black and white photograph, a picture of a wedding: a man and a woman standing close together in the door of a church. The man was straight-faced and solemn in his suit and flowered pocket, the woman smiled brightly in her white dress, holding on tight to her bouquet. Around their feet on the stone steps were the remains of scattered confetti. It wasn't Catherine and Nigel Kerr. The woman in the photograph was short and dark haired with a round face. Catherine Kerr was tall and blonde with big bright eyes. And the photograph was too old. I thought maybe it was Nigel Kerr's parents. The small round face of the woman reminded me of his small round balding head.

And then there was my favourite photograph, the oldest of the five, in sepia, a man – in his seventies perhaps – wearing a tweed jacket and cap, in a field leaning on his walking stick. I liked the man's smile. His lips were puckered like he didn't have any teeth, but one side lifted into a happy lopsided grin. In the distance I could see the farmhouse. It looked the same, but older in the brown and reddish tones. Ironic. It was older now of course. I worked out that the field the man was standing in was the field directly in front of the farm-house – the one with the long lines of hay bales. It pleased me that I'd stood where that happy man had stood all those years ago. It pleased me that these old photographs of people no longer alive still lived and were on display for others to see. History, I thought. The past. Not everyone is so afraid of memories.

Marshall would lead me to the bathroom and hold the door open for me. 'Lock the door, Nevis,' he'd say, 'we don't want people walking in on you while you're having a bath.' I'd lock the door. I'd take off my clothes. I'd step right into the bath without testing whether the water was too hot. It was never too hot.

So I lay there. I didn't move. I didn't scrub at myself. I lay there and looked at the ceiling as though I was still lying in the big double bed. Five days, five baths. Half an hour and then Marshall would knock on the door. 'You can get out now, Nevis.' After that first bath I got out, dried myself with the clean towel folded and warming over the radiator. I put on the fresh underwear and socks left for me on the toilet seat. I unlocked the door.

'You haven't washed your hair,' Marshall said. 'You need to wash your hair, it's filthy.' When I didn't move he took hold of my wrist. He pulled me back inside the bathroom, made me kneel down on the floor and bend over the tub. I let him turn on the taps and wet my hair, I let him squeeze an orange peach-smelling gel into his hand and start scrubbing at my skull. He wasn't gentle with me. His fingers felt impatient and firm. 'If you don't start washing your hair I'm going to cut it all off,' he said. 'You need to look after it. You need to be clean.' My reprogramming. I watched the water and bubbles form a puddle around the plughole.

There were times when I woke up and Ailsa was lying on the bottom of my bed. She'd be singing to herself or reading things out loud from a magazine. When I saw her I would close my eyes again straight away and pretend I hadn't. But one time she was there at the bottom of my bed, not singing or reading, but just watching me. 'Nevis,' she said. 'I saw ye open yer eyes. You're awake. Don't pretend.' So I opened my eyes and looked at her.

'Are ye feelin' better, Nevis?'

I moved my eyes to the ceiling.

'D' ye want somethin' t' eat? Mum made ye a piece in case ye woke up. It's jus' next t' ye.' After she said it I could smell the ham and butter and bread on the bedside table. I felt sick. 'Ye don't look very well,' she said. I closed my eyes. 'D' ye want some water, Nevis?' I felt her move from the bottom of the bed to the empty space beside me. I felt her body close. 'I want t' help, Nevis. I want t' look after ye. Why won't ye let me?' She leaned across my body and reached for something next to me. 'I've got some water,' she said. 'Open yer mouth.' I turned my face away. 'Why won't ye let me help you, Nevis? It's not fair. I want t' help ye get better.'

There was a knock at the door. Marshall came in. 'Hello, you two,' he said and smiled. And then to me, 'It's seven o'clock, Nevis. Time for your bath.'

After the hair-washing incident I learnt to wet my hair properly before leaving the bathroom. I'd pinch my nose and slide down the back of the bath until my head was fully underwater. I'd count the seconds and listen to the hollow clunks rattling through the pipes of the old farmhouse. I'd listen to my heart pumping blood around my body. I liked these underwater bath noises and made my own, drumming my fingers against the enamel, or blowing small bubbles of air out from my mouth.

Half an hour would pass. Marshall would knock. I would climb out of the bath, dry myself with the clean towel and then dress. 'Good boy,' Marshall said when he saw my wet hair.

One time I woke up and Ailsa was lying right beside me, her arm over my body in a sort of slumped hug. I could smell her skin, soft and girl-like, sweet like peaches and coconuts. She was asleep. I wanted to move her arm, but didn't. Worse would be to wake her up and start her talking. So I left her there. Marshall knocked quietly and poked his head round the door. He saw me, eyes open, with Ailsa asleep beside me, her arm hugging my body and he smiled. 'You're getting on so well,' he said. 'I'm so pleased, Nevis,' and then closed the door. I was distraught. I flung Ailsa's arm from me, which made her body twist awkwardly and she woke with a yelp.

'Get out,' I said to her.

She started to sob and hold her arm.

'Get out!' She could hear it in my voice. She moved off the bed and left the room, still holding her arm, still crying softly to herself. 'And don't bother coming back. I don't want you here.'

I'm sure this wasn't a dream. I remember it vividly. Yet nobody told me off. And Ailsa kept coming back.

20

I woke up. Eventually I had to, although my waking up was unexpected and happened when I was already awake. Seven o'clock. Time for my bath. Marshall led the way. 'Remember to lock the door, Nevis. You don't want . . .'

'I know,' I said. Marshall nodded. I went into the bathroom. I locked the door. I undressed. And then there I was. I don't know how I hadn't noticed myself before, staring out from the full-length mirror on the wall right next to the toilet. It was misted from all the hot water, but I recognised myself instantly. Nevis Gow. I stared at the blurred figure in front of me. I lifted my arm and watched my image lift his arm. I took my finger and wrote into the glass without thinking – *today is the day for song and dance.*

I'd written that once. One morning in the van when the windows were all misted up. Marshall had seemed particularly pleased. Yes, he said when he saw it. Yes, it is! And he started laughing and beating the van walls and hopping from foot to foot over the sofa cushions. I couldn't stop laughing. We sang all morning: 'Ging Gang Goolie', 'Ten Green Bottles', 'Kookaburra Sits in the Old Gum Tree' and all the other silly songs we knew. Marshall finished off by bursting into 'Oh Flower of Scotland' and when we settled down to drive after breakfast he turned to me and said, 'That's where we're going now, boy. Back to Scotland for the summer. How'd you like that, eh?' I loved it.

I don't know when I wrote it in the window again, but I did, on a morning when Marshall was quiet and thoughtful and I was bored: 'today is the day for song and dance', I wrote. When Marshall saw it he took his hand and wiped it straight through the words. 'A good writer never writes the same thing twice,' he said. The condensation dribbled where Marshall's hand had been and through the window I could see the picnic bench we'd eaten at the night before and the empty, dusty car park and the trees all around. It was raining. Marshall took a deep breath and I looked at him. 'You can't relive a memory, boy,' he said. He was staring at the wet on his palm. 'It just wouldn't be the same. Do you understand?' I didn't answer.

Years later and it was my turn to take my hand and wipe it through the words on the glass. I saw my face: long and narrow with long narrow nose, thin lips, pointed chin, dark brown eyes, thick black eyebrows, pock-marked cheeks. Three spots: one on my jawline, two on my forehead. I noticed the soft dark hair on the corners of my upper lip. Facial hair, I thought, and I wondered how long it would take to grow out like Marshall's old beard.

I grabbed the towel warming over the radiator and rubbed the glass clear. Nevis Gow: the whole of me, from head to toe. Tall, thin, gangly, bony-looking. I could see my ribs. I counted them. I lifted my arm and inspected the thin strip of armpit hair, remembering the thickness and length of Marshall's. And around my penis short dark curly hair was growing. I touched it. I lifted my cock, held it in my hand. I pulled back my foreskin, touched the raw red of the tip.

There was a knock at the door.

'Nevis?'

Half an hour already.

'I want more time,' I called.

'What?'

'I want more time.'

There was silence at the other side of the door and then, 'Ok, son,' and I heard Marshall move down the hallway. I turned my attention back to the mirror.

One morning last year while standing by the fat trunk of an old tree, taking a piss, I saw some ants, lots of them, scuttling about all over the roots and leaves and broken bark. I watched them as the pee streamed down the trunk and hit them like a miniature tidal wave, their little black bodies swamped by the oncoming rush. Fuck me, I thought, I'm *alive*. And suddenly I was aware of my hands, my fingers, my dick sticking over the top of my boxers. And I saw my brown leather boots, as if for the first time, loose-fitting and scuffed; black, knotted laces, pulled tight. It was as though I'd never felt them on my feet before. And then my jeans, with gaping holes in the knees, I could feel the damp air against my skin and the wet that had soaked in from the thick bracken and heather. My body was warm. I was wearing my father's blue woollen jumper and underneath that my own thin sweater. I wondered what I looked like. If someone had passed me then, what would they've seen?

Boy pissing in the woods. Scraggly-looking boy: unwashed, grubby-skinned boy with a thick greasy mop of black hair wearing hand-me-down clothes and boots too big for him.

But I was *alive*.

That's what I remembered when I stood and stared at myself in the mirror: that day, pissing in the woods and the ants getting washed away. I woke up.

21

'Do ye mind if ah smoke?' Duckman hauled the window up as he asked, not waiting for a reply, and then took the cigarette from behind his ear. 'Ah'm no supposed t' smoke in the house,' he said. 'But they've all gone intae town.'

I started to sit up. Duckman lit his cigarette and watched me. 'Gotta headache?' he asked. I was rubbing my head. 'You've been drugged,' he said.

'What do you mean?'

'They've been crushin' the tablets an' puttin' them in yer water.'

'I haven't drunk any water.'

'Aye, ye have.'

I looked at the bedside table. There was a pint glass, half filled with water, a stripy green and white straw sticking over the brim. The water looked clear, not cloudy.

'Are you lying?' I asked Duckman.

'No,' he said. 'Why would ah lie?'

'I don't know.'

'Sleepin' tablets,' he said. 'Nothin' bad. It won't kill ye.'

'But why?'

Duckman shrugged. I looked back at the water.

'Yer father said it was 'cause o' the nightmares. Elspeth said you'd rest better if ye took some o' her sleepin' pills.'

'I feel like shit.'

'Ye look like shit.'

I held my head.

'I'm lyin',' he said.

'What?'

'Aboot the sleepin' pills. They haven't drugged ye.'

I frowned. 'Why did you say it then?'

'Thought it would be funny,' he smiled.

'For fuck sake, Duckman.'

'That's the spirit.'

And despite myself I smiled.

Duckman flicked the cigarette out the window and walked to the bottom of the bed. He sat down. 'So what d' ye want?'

I frowned again.

'Look,' he said, 'ah said ah'd keep an eye on ye. So what d' ye want? Some food? Some painkillers for yer bangin' headache? D' ye want some fresh water?' He nodded towards the pint glass. 'Ah'm no gonnae pitter-patter aroon' tryin' t' guess, Nevis; placin' ye offerins on yer bedside table like yer some god or other. Ye'll jus' have t' tell me.'

'You'll get me anything?' I asked.

'Aye,' he said. 'Well, within reason.'

'I need some paper,' I said. 'And a pen.'

22

I want to remember everything.

The dents, the scratches, the brown flaking rust, the petrol cap that wouldn't come off without a slight wiggle of the key. The black wheels without their wheel trims. The grime and dust thrown up from the road, the mud that spattered the sides. The bird-shit on the roof, the windscreen, the bonnet. The spiders that wove their webs around the wing-mirrors. The weathered GB bumper sticker, peeling slightly. The sticky residue left underneath. The sound of the slide door being pulled back, sticking half way. The sound of it slamming shut. The broken brake light, cracked after reversing into a bin in a supermarket car park. The blackened exhaust, for a time tied with string to the undercarriage after taking a speed bump too fast. The blue and white and curled letters of the Ford badge. The registration plate BA51 CPD. The breakdowns. The AA men in their brightly coloured overcoats and the vehicles with flashing orange lights. Their curiosity when they looked over the van, when they saw inside, when they realised we lived there. The smell. You could see the smell wash over their faces and clog up their noses. If only I had a camera. If only I knew how important a camera would have been. I ache for the photographs I could have taken, to have them now, wave them high and say look, Marshall, look, here's the fucking evidence. It did happen. We did exist. It was real.

I won't forget.

23

I was no longer sure how many days had passed since arriving at the farm. It was impossible to say without my tallies. I guessed at twenty. Marshall knocked on my door in the morning, poked his head round the corner and said, 'Are you awake, Nevis? Can I come in?' He came in. It was early. Marshall had already showered and shaved. I could see his hair was still damp. I could smell the steamy bathroom and the shower gel and aftershave as he sat down on the bottom of my bed. This pleased me. And then I became angry because it pleased me. Angry because I'd forgotten I was supposed to be angry. I'd been writing my lists late into the night. In the beginning my writing had felt desperate – trying to scrape everything I could remember about the van together, to put it all on paper, immortalise it. My lists started as bullet points. I wrote pages and pages.

- Sofa cushions
- Blankets

- Water container
- Food chest
- The smell . . . the rot . . . sweat, skin and bodies

And then I stopped. It wasn't how I wanted to remember the van. A list of black dots. So I started again with headings and subheadings. Sentences this time. Paragraphs. Punctuation. I lost myself in the details of the memories. It felt good. I remembered Marshall and the way he used to bend over his paper, scribbling frantically. The way he'd scratch behind his ear with his pen when he paused for a moment. The way he frowned in concentration. Licked his lips. Touched his beard. The way his eyes glistened when he came out of his writing reverie and smiled. I started to feel, when I was writing those lists, that I was only just beginning to understand it all. His obsession. I fell asleep. Happy. Tired. And woke in a peaceful forgetfulness a few moments before my father knocked. And then I remembered.

'How are you feeling today, Nevis?'

I looked at him.

'You seem better.'

I looked away. I wondered if I was supposed to say 'thank you' to this. That was what naturally filled my mouth – 'thank you' – but I refused to voice it. I decided I didn't want to thank Marshall for anything. Not just yet. I wanted to make him suffer. Marshall touched the blanket where my foot was and I pinched my lips together. I meant them to say, why are you touching me? You have no right to touch me. I hate you. And I must have said that successfully because when he saw my face he lifted his hand back onto his lap immediately. And that upset me. And then I was annoyed I was upset because I was upset for all the wrong reasons. *I hate you,* I said in my head towards Marshall. *Shut up,* I said in reply to myself. *No, you don't.*

Marshall nodded. I don't know why he nodded, but he did. He looked across at the dressing table in the corner of the room with all the pretty glass bottles of perfume. I watched him look for the right words and wondered if he'd find them in amongst all that coloured glass. The sort of words hiding there, I thought, might not be appropriate. Euphonious. Efflorescence. Ineluctable. I imagined these words squeezing themselves inside and behind the pretty bottles with hand-pumps and tassels.

'Are you hungry?' he said.

I was disappointed. Perhaps he wasn't looking at the dressing table at all, his head was just pointed in that direction.

'No,' I said. It was my first word of the day. As soon as it was out I wished I could take it back. I'd been enjoying my silence. I felt as though it gave me some sort of control over things. I was right because when

Marshall heard my 'no' he smiled as though he'd won a point. It was only a quick smile though. I pinched my lips again just to let him know he could lose his ground at any moment. And then I thought, *this is a stupid game*. I unpinched my lips. I sighed.

'You really haven't eaten much these last few days,' he said.

I hadn't eaten 'much' he said. That would suggest that I'd eaten *something*. I tried to remember eating. Duckman had brought me a packet of dry-roasted nuts the night before along with a pad of paper and three pens. The empty nut packet was on the floor. I could see it crumpled on the carpet. The pad and pens were underneath my pillow. I tried for a moment to concentrate on my stomach. Was I hungry? I felt empty, but not hungry. Perhaps through lack of eating my body had started to feed on my insides and I was slowly becoming hollow. It triggered a memory. A poem. Something about a fat boy called Horace who loved eating so much he started to eat himself. His arms, his legs, his heart, his spleen . . . everything until he was nothing more than a stomach on a plate. And then other memories came flooding back. There was another poem about a boy who woke up and all the clothes in his wardrobe were starting a revolution, angry because they hadn't been treated well. And another poem about a toilet kangaroo. And another about a boy with a magical eraser who started rubbing out buildings and buses and people. What was the poetry book called? *The Vampire's New Socks*? Something about a vampire anyway. And socks. I wanted to reach under my pillow and pull out the pen and paper. I wanted to start writing it all down.

'Nevis?'

I used to read under the blankets. I remember that now. With the hand-torch Marshall got me for Christmas one year. What year? I have such a good memory for presents, but I forgot all about that little red torch. It broke. No, I lost it. Something happened to it anyway because I stopped reading under the blankets. Or maybe I just got older and lost interest in the tent-like atmosphere of under-cover reading. Although, I don't remember doing it that often in the first place. So maybe I got the torch the same time as I got the poetry book and actually, I only remember the torch because I loved the book so much . . . and I only read under the blanket because I wanted to use my two presents together, at the same time. That's it, I thought! That's it! And then I wondered how much of that memory was actually true and how much of it was just . . .

'Speculation,' I said out loud.

'What?' My father was staring at me. He looked confused, a little worried. 'Did you hear me, Nevis?' he said, 'I just asked you a question.'

I frowned. He asked me if I was hungry, I thought.

I'm sure I told him I wasn't. 'I'm not hungry,' I said again.

'I didn't ask you if you were hungry.'

'You didn't?'

'No . . . well, yes, I did,' he sighed irritably. 'But that was before. Were you not listening to me?'

The word 'no' popped into my mouth but I didn't let it out. I let it bounce against the walls and roof of my mouth before settling quietly on my tongue, dissolving. I waited for Marshall to continue.

He eventually did. 'Angry, I asked you if you were angry. And then you said . . .' He paused. '. . . speculation.'

How apt, I thought.

'Are you smiling?' he asked.

I thought I'd covered it up. It wasn't really a smile anyway; it was more of a smirk. I turned to face him and glared. With all my will power I gave him the filthiest, angriest look I could muster. It seemed to work. To top it off I said, 'And what have I got to smile about?' *Yes!* He hung his head in shame. He sat for a moment, quite still, hanging his head like that with his hands resting one on each knee. And then he nodded and rose to his feet. He moved slowly, quietly to the door, opened it and looked at me. I didn't want him to go.

He went.

LIST 4

The Lights

If Marshall left the key in the ignition and turned it only half way round, the van wouldn't start but the lights would come on. In the evenings we often sat on blankets outside together in front of the van, another blanket over our knees. I used to always wipe the squashed flies from the lights with the sleeve of my jumper so that if I wanted to read a book, the dead flies wouldn't leave dirty black spots on my page. When I was younger Marshall would tell me ghost stories and try to scare me by pointing into the shadows that escaped the semi-circle of light. 'What's that? Can you hear something?' And we'd listen, ears straining for unusual sounds in amongst the whispers and noises of the night. But as I grew older the ghost stories petered out and eventually stopped. Instead we just cooked and ate together in front of the lights, or I would read and he would write. Sometimes I would sit out the front alone and look into the shadows. Once I kept the lights on for so long it drained the battery and Marshall couldn't start the van the next morning. He was angry. 'The engine's getting old now,' he said. 'We can't use the lights like that any more.' And that was that.

The Sun Visor

There was a small rectangular mirror on the back of the passenger sun visor. I remember in the days when Marshall would shave, he'd unclip that mirror and take it into the back of the van with him where he'd prop it on some books. With a cup of water, some soap, a towel and a disposable razor, he'd shave. I remember this well. He would do it every two, maybe three, days and I'd sit and watch him, curled up in the corner. I liked the way he lathered the soap in his hands and then rubbed it over the bristly hairs, thickening the soap more, turning it white. And the careful strokes and movements with the razor, turning his face side to side or bearing his neck when he shaved underneath his chin. He'd cut himself often and have to tear tiny bits of tissue from the toilet paper and stick them to the blood. I always wanted to try shaving for myself, so one day when my father was writing, I unclipped the mirror, poured myself a cup of water, took his soap, his towel and his razor and walked off to find somewhere private. How old was I? Eight? Maybe nine. We were pulled in by the side of a country road, thick hedgerows on each side fencing in farmland. Potato fields. England. It was summer. I remember walking along the road, trying not to spill my water. I climbed over a gate into one of the fields and sat behind the hedgerow. I balanced the mirror in the thicket and stared at the small square of my reflection.

I took the soap, lathered it, rubbed it on my face – it didn't thicken as much as when Marshall did it. I took the razor and dunked it into the cup of water – and then remembering Marshall's movements I bore my neck at the mirror and dragged the razor upwards towards my chin. The razor removed the soap and I dunked it in the water again, waggled it about to clean it, just like Marshall used to do. I continued shaving until all the soap was removed from my face and I was beaming into the mirror. No blood. I wondered how my father could be so bad at shaving. It wasn't until later I realised you were supposed to take the little plastic head off the front of the blade. Although it was a good thing I didn't, the way I dug that razor head into my throat and pulled upwards. However, I did draw blood that day, even if it wasn't from shaving.

The mirror I put into my back pocket. I returned everything else to the right place, but the mirror I forgot about. Later that evening, we were outside cooking. I sat awkwardly and it snapped under my weight and its broken corner stuck into my behind. Marshall heard my yelp and saw me pull out the broken mirror. He chuckled. 'That's when vanity comes back and bites you on the arse,' he said. 'Why are you carrying a mirror about in your pocket anyway?' My face burned red. I returned the mirror, even though it was broken, back into the visor. The long diagonal crack from one corner to the next meant that whenever I caught a glimpse of myself my face was distorted. Marshall used the rear-view mirror to shave for a little while after that and then gave up and just let his beard grow.

24

'What day is it?'

'Sunday.'

I nodded.

'Why?' Duckman asked. 'Ye wannae go t' church? Repent?'

Repent. I'd never heard that word being used before. Not out loud. *Repent.* I repeated it over in my head and then, remembering the pen in my pocket, wrote it on my hand. 'No,' I said.

We were sitting in the wood behind the caravan field – me on a large rock, which wasn't particularly comfortable, and Duckman on the dirt, leaning against the trunk of a tree.

'What kind of trees are these?' I asked.

'Rowan,' he said.

I studied the straight clean boles and grey bark of the trunks. They looked as though they'd been knife-scarred repeatedly with horizontal scores all the way up. Thirty maybe forty feet tall. They swayed and creaked in the breeze. Crows cawed from the topmost branches. I continued digging in the ground with my twig. I must have been digging for quite some time before I realised Duckman was leaning forward, his elbows on his crossed legs, looking at me intently.

'Nevis . . .' he said, when eventually I looked up and made eye contact with him. He didn't say anything following this. He just let my name drift into the air and linger. We looked at each other. I saw the apple in Duckman's throat slide up and then down again as he swallowed. It was him who broke the eye contact. He turned his face away and stared down at the ground and the gnarled roots of the tree.

I thought about asking him if he was ok, but I didn't. Instead I looked down at my hand holding the twig. I started scratching at the earth in a new place. My name must have still been in the air because without thinking I carved an 'N'. And then for some reason, not wanting to be seen carving my initials, I scored a diagonal line through it – linking the beginning of the 'N' with the end.

'An hourglass,' Duckman said looking at it. And I suppose from his perspective it did look like an hourglass. He sighed and leant back against his tree. Closed his eyes.

Something was missing, I thought. And then I realised Duckman was neither smoking a cigarette nor rolling one. He was just sitting quietly.

'Have ye never wondered, Nevis, why there's no live-stock here? Why we aren't all oot pickin' tatties? Have ye never thought it's odd?'

I eyed Duckman carefully and thought for a moment. I remembered how Marshall had warned me not to mention Catherine Kerr. Still an open wound, he'd said. So I shrugged. 'We're sellin' the farm,' he said then.

I stared at him blankly.

'Did ye know we were sellin' the farm?'

I shook my head. I knew they'd sold the livestock. After Catherine Kerr died they auctioned it all off. I hadn't considered the farm would be up for sale. And that would mean . . .

'We'll all have t' leave,' Duckman said.

'Leave,' I repeated.

'Aye,' Duckman said. 'Ah thought ye'd be pleased.' He looked at me. His look said, I *know* you're pleased but if you show it right now I'll have to hurt you. I lowered my eyes to the muddy ground and continued digging into the hourglass. *Leave*. The word kept returning to me. I tried to hide my smile. 'But what are ye gonnae do, Nevis? Where are ye gonnae go?' Duckman sounded angry. 'The van's gone. Or have ye forgotten that?'

I stopped smiling.

'Ye think yer father's gonnae buy another one? Ye think life's jus' gonnae switch back t' what it was?'

I glared at him. 'And why not?' I asked.

161

'Because life doesn't work like that, does it? Things change.'

'They can change back.'

'Not if yer not in charge.' Duckman stared at me. 'Are ye in charge, Nevis?'

He knew I wasn't. We both fell silent. I could feel the blood in my face, my cheeks hot. The twig I was using to dig into the hourglass snapped.

'D'ye hate him?'

The word 'who' started to automatically form from somewhere, but I stopped myself. I hate answering questions with questions that I already know the answer to.

'Ye should hate him,' he said, not waiting for a reply anyway. 'Ah would. After what he's done.'

I thought about this for a moment. Or at least I tried to. Actually, my brain had begun to go numb. I was just staring down at my broken twig, looking at all the little scars and potholes in the dirt. Do I hate him? The question was picking out my head just like I'd been picking out the dirt. And it left nothing.

'Will you tell me what happened, Duckman?'

'When?'

I looked at him. My look said, 'you know what I'm talking about, so why ask?'

Duckman sighed. He put out his cigarette and instantly started rolling another one. 'Ah was in the tool shed,' he said. 'Smokin'.' I watched his hands spread out the tobacco on the brown paper. 'I heard yer dad shoutin'. I didnae hear what he was sayin', but there was a bang. Like he'd hit summit.' He ripped a square off his Rizla packet and rolled it between thumb and fore-finger. 'Ah left the tool shed an' went roon' t' the corner.' He looked at me then. 'It wasn't like ah was spyin',' he said. 'It was jus' . . .'

'Go on.'

'Yer father came oot. Ah tried t' get back intae the tool shed, but he came stompin' over an' saw me climbin' through the window. He told me t' gi' him a lift. He said, "Colin, ah need a lift." At first ah jus' stared at 'im fer a minute, pissed off 'cause he called me Colin. An' then pissed off 'cause he expected me jus' t' drop everythin' an' gi' him a lift some place. Maybe he could see ah was pissed off 'cause he changed his tune. Offered me a twenty.'

'Twenty quid?'

'Aye.'

'And you took it?'

'Course ah did.'

I shook my head. 'Go on,' I said.

Duckman looked at me for a moment then licked his tongue across the rolled cigarette and finished folding. He didn't light it. He put it behind his ear instead. 'Ye sure?' he asked.

'Go on,' I repeated.

'We got intae the car. Ah mind ah looked across at the caravan an' I saw you at the window. You were grippin' yer hair in yer hands an' rockin' like a crazy person. But ah didnae say nought t' yer father. He felt crazy himself. A cold kinda crazy. He gave me the twenty an' said he needed t' go t' his van. So ah took him.'

Duckman stopped.

'There's more,' I said.

'Ah didnae know what he was doin',' Duckman looked at me. 'But even if ah did, Nevis, ah wouldnae been able t' stop him.'

'I know.'

Duckman nodded. 'When we got there he tol' me t' go back t' the farm. Before that ah'd jus' thought he wanted t' pick up some stuff, ye know? Clothes and shit. Books. But when he tol' me t' go back withoot 'im, ah knew summit was up. So ah hung aroon'. Ah drove doon the road a wee way an' then walked back t' the van. He was inside. There was no light, but ah could hear him pullin' shite aboot an' the van was rockin'. Then it stopped fer a bit. I reckon yer father was sittin' in there in amongst all that stuff wi' his bottle o' whisky, 'cause that's what he was swiggin' when he came oot ten minutes later.' And then he added, 'Along wi' the smoke.'

'How did he set fire to it?'

'Ah dunno,' he said. 'Wi' a match?'

'No, but *how*? What did he burn first?'

'Nevis, ah wasnae in there wi' him. Ah don't know.'

I was gripping my hair.

'Are ye goin' mental?'

It made me grip my hair harder. I felt like tearing it out. I could smell the smoke. I could see the fire and Marshall feeding the flames, sitting back, drinking his whisky and watching it all.

'There was an explosion,' Duckman said. 'Ah don't know how . . . ah mean . . . ah didnae think diesel exploded. No like petrol.'

'We had gas,' I said.

'Boom,' he said.

It was his stories, I told myself. That's what he set fire to first. I consoled myself with this thought. Perhaps it was the stories he wanted to get rid of and then the fire got out of hand. It took to the books; then the clothes caught alight, then the cushions. The plastic water container would have melted. The wooden food chest would've gone up. And then the gas. Boom. Wild fire. Black smoke billowing out and up.

'Ah could smell it fer miles doon the road,' he said.

'You didn't stay.'

'Not after the explosion. Didnae want yer father t' see me. He came over t' sit on the bank an' watch it all. Ah left.' Duckman took the roll-up from behind his ear and held it between his lips. 'So that's all ah know,' he said and sparked up.

25

We sat on the roof of his Ford Sierra. Duckman had wound down the passenger window so he could prop his feet on the glass. He was leaning on his knees with his elbows, looking between his legs at the ground and spitting. I think he was trying to spit on top of his first spit. Some kind of game.

I had my feet on the roof, my legs tucked close to my body, my arms wrapped around my knees. I could hear Elspeth laugh from the kitchen and imagined my father sitting at the table, smiling and nodding at her. There was always something sad about the way he smiled these days. He wasn't happy. The farm wasn't good for us. I sighed.

'What's up wi' you?'

'Nothing,' I said.

It was 8 o'clock and already dark. Duckman was sitting in just the right position so that whenever the back door light switched off he'd wave an arm and it would come back on again. Whenever he waved an arm the dogs would raise their heads and look at him. Occasionally Murdo would bark under his breath or wag his tail.

There was a knock from the kitchen window. Elspeth had wiped a circle into the steamed glass and was peering through it, smiling. 'Come on, boys. Dinner's ready!'

Duckman pulled a face. 'Ah hate her.' He spat once more, viciously, at the ground. There was another knock at the window, 'Boyees.' Duckman looked at me. 'At least,' he said, 'when we have t' leave ah'll be gettin' shot o' them, her and Ailsa. He jumped down from the roof and started to make his way to the house. *When we have to leave . . .* I mouthed the words silently after him. I tried to smile but Duckman's voice filled my head, 'Are you in charge, Nevis?'

I slid down the side of the car and jogged after Duckman. He was kicking his boots off under the bench.

'Do you know when, Duckman?'

'When what?'

'When we have to leave by? I mean . . .' I realised a little too late my question might upset him. His eyes darkened.

'Dinnae you worry yer wee head aboot it, Nevis. You'll be rid of us soon enough. By the end o' the month I reckon. The Estate has already agreed to buy. Probably got the next tenants lined up as we very speak.'

I'd upset him. Duckman did not sit down at the table

when we entered the room. He walked straight through the kitchen and out again. Elspeth went after him but stopped at the doorway. 'Colin! *Colin!*' and from somewhere near the top of the stairs I could hear Duckman reply, '*Don't* call me *Colin.*' And while Elspeth continued to tut and sigh and mumble her irritation under her breath, I for the first time just quietly went to the table and sat down next to my father without being asked. He looked at me. I stretched the corner of my mouth up into a kind of smile. Marshall raised his eyebrows.

'. . . that boy jus' doesnae appreciate anythin' I've done fer this family. That's the trouble, ye see. I move here t' help, uproot Ailsa oot o' school, away from her friends . . . away from her father, although in fairness that wasnae such a bad thing, fat lazy lay-aboot that he is.' I looked at Elspeth then. She was dishing up food, oven glove over one hand, tipping chips onto plates with a spatula. I studied her tight leggings and baggy black flower print t-shirt, sequins sewn into the petals. It hung straight down from her breasts, mostly covering the bulge of her belly. Her blonde hair was tied up into a loose bun, showing off the small gold hoops of her earrings. I noticed the colour of her neck was much paler than the colour of her face and that her blood red toenails, poking out from the sandals on her feet, were chipped. I don't think I'd ever properly looked at Elspeth before. I knew her more by smell – the sweet perfume she squirted behind her ears and on her neck and wrists, covering up the cooking fat and sweat.

Such an odd body shape, I thought: big belly, big breasts, but thin legs, emphasised by her clothes, baggy t-shirts over tight leggings. Corpulent, Marshall would say, bulky in the body – although he didn't. Marshall never spoke to me about his opinions on the Kerrs other than to say how *good* they've been to us and how *grateful* we should be. If we didn't have to be so grateful then Marshall and I would have had fun describing her together.

We used to do that whenever we were hanging around somewhere busy. We called it the pure poetry game. Pick a person to look at and then think quickly, come up with words or phrases, lots of adjectives, one after the other that describes them. There weren't really any rules. Repetition and rhyming were good, alliteration excellent and exaggeration came quite naturally without trying, so that in the end the person you described sounded more like a comic book or cartoon character.

'Corpulent.'

'Big belly and breasts.'

'But not all fat.'

'Skinny-thin legs in leggings.'

'Squeezed like a sausage in its skin.'

'Big lips.'

'Red lips.'

'Powdered nose.'

'. . . and painted toes.'

'Cheap perfume and manicured claws.'

'A shop in town files away the flaws.'

'Not in the least a farmer's wife.'

'Yet she cooks and cleans.'

'The farm's her life.'

'Pure poetry.'

That's how the game always ended. When one of us came up with a good final line, the other said – or sometimes we both said in unison – *pure poetry*. And then we thought up a title. Cosmetic Countryside. Not all of the games worked. We both had to be in a good mood for a start. But even then some poems flopped. We'd go off at a tangent and list words that were synonyms or simply rhymed with each other and actually had nothing to do with the person we were describing. Sometimes we made up words, firing gibberish that made little sense.

'. . . he was a snoot, the moot.'

'Filling his boots.'

'A coot . . .'

'That loots . . .'

'Copious shoots . . .'

'Mongolian fruits.'

'Pure poetry.'

I smiled and glanced at Marshall next to me. I

wondered what *he* was thinking. He nodded politely at Elspeth and spoke when he thought it was necessary. Carefully selected words. My father wasn't wasteful in conversation; only, it seemed, in silly word games with his son. His hand nearest to me rested on the table over his fork. I rested my hand close to his over my knife and willed him to touch me. *Touch me,* I closed my eyes, *touch me and I know everything will be ok. In a couple of weeks we'll be gone from here. We can start afresh, just the two of us.* And he did. He touched me. He ran his finger over the back of my hand close to my thumb. My eyes shot open.

'Repent,' he said and looked at me.

'What?'

My father touched the black ink on my hand, the word written in dark block capitals. 'Are you waving the white flag, Nevis?'

And then a memory of my father's arm reaching out through the driver's seat window, his hand holding onto a small stretch of toilet tissue and me sitting with my legs crossed and arms folded, my back against the front wheel of the van. I was in a mood. 'I surrender,' he'd said. 'I'm waving the white flag. I surrender. Mercy.' It hadn't been a real argument. He'd just snapped. I think I must've been making some kind of noise or maybe I kept asking questions while he was writing.

Repent, I thought. Surrender. My father thought I was

giving in, that I was feeling sorry. Perhaps he thought he'd won me round.

'Nevis,' he said, 'tomorrow I'm going to take you into town to meet Mr Galbraith.'

I nodded. Had he won? Or was I just letting him think that he'd won? Is it possible to wave the white flag as part of a surprise attack? Marshall smiled. And so did I. Or at least I tried to.

26

The day of Galbraith. It was a Monday. The meeting was set for nine o'clock. But before that I was taken into town in the Land Rover: Nigel Kerr driving, Elspeth in the passenger seat, me sitting behind with Ailsa on one side, my father on the other; the two dogs in the back snuffling and sniffing around my ears – before all that – this is what happened.

It was early, the sky only just breaking into the beginning stages of inky blue. I wasn't asleep. I was sitting up in bed with my notepad on my lap and pen in hand. This is what I'd written:

He is the mad puppeteer and I am his puppet.

The door opened.

'Duck—'

He held his finger to his lips. 'Get dressed,' he whispered and he picked my trousers from the floor and threw them at me. 'Have ye got shoes up here?' I shook my head. Duckman left and then came back a short while later with a pair of Wellington boots. 'Hurry,' he said.

'Where are we going?'

'Ah want t' show ye summit,' he said. I pulled on the boots. They felt strangely cold and airy. I'd never worn wellies before. They were too big. I tucked my jeans into them like Duckman. 'Ye ready?' he asked. I nodded.

We sneaked down the corridor, past the painting of the deer and the table with the photographs, past the bathroom, careful at the top of the stairs with Ailsa's room just opposite, the door slightly ajar. I could hear her light breathing. I thought at first Duckman was taking me to his room – further along the hallway, past the room where Elspeth slept and then up another narrower flight of stairs. I'd never been in Duckman's attic bedroom, but I'd seen him up there once or twice before when I was still sleeping in the caravan. He'd sit on his windowsill at night, one foot in his room, one on the edge of the sill and I'd watch the glow of his cigarette move to and from his lips, brighten as he inhaled, soften as he exhaled.

But we didn't go to his room. We went down the stairs. It was dark, but there was a light on in the hallway to the kitchen. I kept my hand out, brushing the wall as I stepped quietly behind Duckman and felt the velvety raised pattern of the wallpaper underneath my fingertips. At the bottom we stopped. Duckman held up his hand so I wouldn't move. I listened. Through the oval mirror on the dresser in front of us I could see Duckman's face concentrating. I could hear nothing but the ticking of the polished brass clock on the dresser top. It said ten past six. Round to the right of the stairs was the narrow hallway to the kitchen. I leant over the banister and peered towards the closed door. The kitchen light was on.

'He's in there,' Duckman whispered.

'Who?'

Duckman moved left where the hallway opened out into the small square reception area, cramped by old-looking furniture and two-to-a-wall gilded or carved wooden framed paintings, similar to the running deer upstairs. The door to the music room was shut. For a split second I thought that Duckman was taking me there – into the forbidden room – but he moved quickly and silently over to the front door where the two windows on each side were letting in the yellowish-red of a fiery sunrise. Even Duckman, who was trying to undo the catch as quietly as possible, stopped to look at the light creeping above the hills and across the fields.

'Red sky in the mornin',' he said.

'Shepherd's warning,' I finished.

Duckman looked at me.

'What?' I asked.

He pulled the door open and nodded for me to go through.

'Duckma—'

'Fer fuck sake, Nevis. Jus' go.'

We went outside, closing the door with the faintest click behind us. It was cold even though the sun rising was the colour of burning hot coals. The sky was a red gradient, in one part the clouds were high, wispy mares' tails; in another they were like thin veins. Around the sun there was a salmon-pink halo. A single crow's caw from the woods broke the morning silence.

We edged down the side of the house like burglars. When Duckman came to the window that looked into the kitchen he ducked low, crouch-crawled underneath it. So did I, although I wanted desperately to look in. Just a glance to see who it was we were hiding from. I was starting to suspect it was Marshall. We went round the corner of the house. I was told to wait. Duckman straightened up and walked directly to the dogs before Murdo could start barking. He patted them, calmed them down and then beckoned me to follow.

We went behind the kennels, climbed over the wire fence and into the woods where we hid close to a tree. Murdo stood bolt upright and stared after us, wagging his tail. He tried pulling on his chain. He started to whine. I glanced at Duckman who didn't seem bothered. He watched the farmhouse unblinkingly. I started to shiver.

'Du—'

He held up his hand. Just as he did so Murdo started to bark, but not at us. The back door opened and Nigel Kerr stepped out.

He was wearing a checkered cap and a long waxed jacket, his jeans – like ours – tucked into muddied rubber boots. He stopped for a moment by Murdo and let him lick his hand. He was carrying something over his other arm, something long and V-shaped. I couldn't tell what it was. Something metal. I saw the trigger. A gun. One of those long guns that I'd seen pictures of cowboys use. I nudged Duckman.

'He's got a gun,' I whispered.

'Ah can see.'

'I thought guns were illegal.'

'What?'

'Guns . . .'

'Shut up, Nevis. He's a farmer. All farmers have guns. And it's called a shotgun.'

Nigel Kerr had started walking across the yard and we could no longer see him from our viewpoint behind the kennels.

'. . . a double-barrelled shotgun. And it's not illegal,' Duckman carried on. 'Ye just need a licence. Christ, Nevis, ye really did live in the back of a van fer eleven years, didn't ye?'

I frowned.

'Come on,' Duckman said.

We moved through the trees trying to tread softly. Duckman told me to keep quiet. Behind the tool shed we could see the caravan field and Nigel Kerr moving through the long grass and weeds. My father would be asleep, I thought. I imagined him lying on the fold-down table in the caravan – sprawled on his back, his head on the pillow and mouth slightly open – and I had a sudden urge to break away from Duckman and go to him. I wouldn't wake him. I just wanted to look through the window and see him lying there asleep. And then I felt something so strong in my chest, an even bigger urge well up, as I imagined kissing him. I was lying next to him, our bodies close to each other, his lips near my neck and I could feel his breath. I had my arms around him. We were hugging. And then the words boomed through my brain as though they'd just managed to break down a locked door. *I love you. I love you.* It never hit me so hard as when I was sneaking through the woods with Duckman that morning and I realised I really *was* going to wave the white flag, I really would be his puppet if it meant having him close again.

'*Nevis!*' Duckman was a good few metres ahead. He'd noticed I wasn't behind him anymore. I started moving again, glancing one last time at the caravan, but now with every step the words *I love you, I love you,* drummed into my head. I wasn't angry. I didn't hate him. I just wanted him back. I would have to win him back. *Two weeks,* I thought, *there's two weeks left until the end of the month.* In my pocket I felt the little plastic limbs of the frog key-ring stick into my leg. I placed my hand over it as we walked.

Duckman stopped, crouched, waved at me to do the same. He pointed. Ahead of us in a small clearing Nigel Kerr sat with his back against a tree. I recognised the clearing. I recognised the tree. It was where Duckman and I had sat only the day before. And Nigel Kerr sat just as Duckman had, with his head back and his eyes closed. I looked at the boulder opposite where I'd been. The little potholes and marks where I'd dug into the ground were still there.

The gun lay across Nigel Kerr's legs. It was not broken anymore. It was perfectly straight and pointing towards us. I nudged Duckman who scowled at me. I could feel my heart start to get nervous, beating harder.

'The gun,' I whispered.

'He never does it,' Duckman whispered back and just as he did I saw Nigel Kerr lift the gun and put the metal in his mouth, his arm stretched to the trigger. I grabbed Duckman's shoulder so hard we both stumbled back-wards.

'*Fucking idiot . . .*' He was still speaking in whispers. '*Get off me, fer fuck sake.*'

And then the shot rang out. Duckman's eyes widened as the crows scattered from the treetops, flew into the air and cawed. He pushed me roughly on my chest to get him back into his crouching position and then straight away ducked behind the tree. I tried to read what had happened on his face. Duckman held his finger over his lips. Then from the clearing came the quiet sobbing. I got slowly back up. Nigel Kerr was still leaning against his tree, head in one piece, but he was crumpled, broken; his shoulders shook as he sobbed and saliva dribbled from his mouth and onto his lap where he still held the gun. My wrist was grabbed and pulled. Duckman was moving back through the woods the way we came, less quietly but still avoiding the broken branches or sticks that crunched underfoot. When we got back round to the other side of the caravan field, to the place where I'd stopped earlier and thought of my father, Duckman turned round sharply, and with a tight clenched fist, punched me in the stomach. I doubled over, fell to my knees. I held one hand over the place I'd been hit and with the other I gripped onto the ground. Duckman was pacing back and forward.

'Ye *fucking* idiot.'

I managed some big breaths.

'Ah *told* ye he never does it. Ah fuckin' *told* ye.'

With my hand still over my gut I managed to move back towards a tree and slump against it. My head was spinning, not because I was dizzy, but because I couldn't make sense of it all.

'Why did you hit me?'

'Why did ye grab me?'

'Because your dad was going to shoot himself.'

'Ah *told* ye he never does it!' Duckman was still pacing and running his fingers through his hair. 'Ah fuckin told ye, Nevis.' And then, as though he only just remembered, he grabbed his tobacco tin from his shirt pocket and sat himself down to roll a cigarette.

The sun had risen now behind a thick veil of cloud, the red sky had darkened to a grey. It was cold. It was going to rain. I shivered, pulled the sleeves of my jumper over my hands and wrapped my arms around my legs. I breathed onto my knees.

'It's been goin' on fer months,' Duckman said after a while. 'At first it was only once a week. He'd come oot here at dawn wi' his gun. But now it's almost every day. Ah used t' jus' sit at ma bedroom window an' watch him walk across the field t' the woods an' then wait fer him t' come back again. He'd always come back. But then ah heard the shot one day an ah thought he did it.'

'But he didn't.'

'Well obviously not, Nevis.' Duckman threw his cigarette away. His voice softened, 'He never does it.'

'But he might.'

Duckman shrugged.

'And you'll see it.'

'Maybe ah want t' see it.' He looked me straight in

the eye when he said it, so hard I had to turn away. 'Ah wanted t' show ye 'cause ah thought ye'd understand.'

'Understand what?'

'Escape,' he said. 'He's jus' tryin' t' escape. We all are, everyone on this farm. And that includes your father.'

'How?' The thought was ridiculous. Marshall didn't want to escape. I'd have been right there next to him, my hand in his, if he had. 'You're wrong,' I told Duckman. 'I bet Marshall's even sad the farm has been sold.'

'I'm no talkin' aboot the farm, Nevis. Are you completely blind? Your father set fire to everythin' he owned. Ah've never seen a man run so fast from his life before. An' ah watch ma dad stick a gun in his mouth most mornins.'

I felt a drop of rain on my cheek.

'Nevis,' Duckman said, so I looked at him. 'Ah'm leavin'. Ah'm gettin' oot. Ah was gonnae ask if ye wanted t' come wi' me.'

27

The day of Galbraith. It was a Monday. I was taken into town in the Land Rover: Nigel Kerr driving, Elspeth in the passenger seat, me sitting behind with Ailsa on one side, my father on the other; the two dogs in the back, Murdo trying to stick his nose out the open window, Red sitting quietly with his chin down on the backrest of my seat, breathing close to my ear.

Elspeth was talking. 'An' there's the Mayfair, Nevis. An' there's the newsagent's. An' see that ol' man donderin' doon the road? The one wi' the tartan tammie on? That's Douglas.' I watched Nigel Kerr as he drove, not saying a word. I wondered what he was thinking and if he still had the taste of gun in his mouth. I looked at his bald head and the greyish-brown of the remaining hair above his ears and around the back. I looked into the rear view mirror and studied the horizontal frown lines in his forehead, the creases around his watery eyes, staring ahead, unfocused and distant. Perhaps he was wishing he'd pulled the trigger, I thought. Perhaps he was telling himself there was always tomorrow. Or maybe he was thinking of her, his dead wife.

This was the closest I'd ever been to the farmer. If I leaned forward I could reach out and touch him on the shoulder. He was right there, watching the road, changing gears, feet pushing pedals, as though this was just another day, another trip into town, the most normal thing in the world. And yet only a few hours before I'd seen him come near to killing himself. I could still feel Duckman's fist in my stomach where he'd punched me. 'Idiot!' he'd said. 'Ah *told* ye he never does it.' But what if he had? And we'd witnessed it? Or what if I'd shouted out at the shock of seeing him lift that gun into his mouth? What if I'd startled him and his finger slipped and BANG! Dead. That *could* have happened. That *could* have happened.

I felt sick. It wasn't helping that Ailsa had spent the entire journey into town trying to hold my hand. I could see out the corner of my eye her edging her fingers towards mine. Every now and then her pinky would stretch out and brush my skin or she'd try to burrow the tips of her fingers discreetly under my palm. No amount of scowling or warning elbow nudges deterred her. Eventually I took both my hands and clasped them firmly between my legs. My father took this as a sort of sign of nerves and whispered, 'It'll be all right, son,' in my ear.

'I feel sick,' I told him.

'There's nothing to worry about,' he said.

My father was clueless. I wanted to turn and pinch him hard on the leg. 'Wake up, for fuck sake, wake up! You think you can read my mind? You think I'm just nervous about meeting some crumby old teacher? Why don't you ask me what's wrong? And I'll tell you I've just seen Nigel Kerr almost blow his head off. And Ailsa, *fucking* Ailsa, I can't *stand* her. She won't leave me alone. Ask me what's wrong and let me tell you I'm miserable. We shouldn't be with these people. Damn you, Marshall, we were better off on our own.'

Ailsa started waving frantically out the window at three girls with satchels hanging over their shoulders. The girls smiled and waved back. 'My friends,' Ailsa said. 'Can you drop me off here please, Nigel?' So Nigel Kerr pulled in and Ailsa jumped out squealing and slamming the door behind her that set Murdo to barking.

'Wheesht, Murdo, wheesht.' Elspeth flapped her arms at the dog making it bark even more. '*Wheesht, Murdo!* For pity's sake.' My father stretched his arm behind me to try to push the dog down. '*Wheesht, Murdo. Sit!* Nigel, can't ye do somethin' about this dog o' yours?' I saw Nigel Kerr's eyes focus for the briefest moment, flit to the rear-view mirror to look at the dog.

'Murdo. Sit,' he said. And the dog sat down and licked his jaws.

'Chaos,' Elspeth sighed. 'Thank you, Nigel.' My father removed his arm from behind me and I sat back up. Nigel Kerr I noticed was still looking in the rear-view mirror, but not at Murdo. He was looking straight at me. My heart dropped. *He knows,* I thought. *He knows we were in the woods this morning.* And then I felt the wet tongue of Red lick my ear.

'Just push him down, Nevis,' said Elspeth and as I pushed him away the Land Rover started moving again and Nigel Kerr's eyes were firmly set back on the road.

Marshall began talking about Mr Galbraith and how much he thought I was going to enjoy lessons with him. 'Science, Geography, History . . . you're going to learn so much.' He'd already told me all this at breakfast. The meeting was going to take place in Mr Galbraith's house. At first this had worried me, but as I looked out the window at the groups of boys and girls wearing their grey uniforms underneath jackets and carrying bags, all of them filing up the road in the same direction towards the school, I felt relieved. I didn't want to be in amongst them.

We drove past a large playing field where boys and girls were kicking a ball about or sitting cross-legged on the grass, others swarmed towards the ugly grey block of granite caged in by a chicken-wire fence. 'That's the school,' said Elspeth. 'That's where ye'll be goin' soon,

Nevis. You'll be in that field playin' football like the rest o' them. Won't that be good?' I turned to look at Marshall. *Say something!* But he wouldn't meet my eye. Surely that's not what he wanted?

'It looks like a prison,' I said under my breath.

'But it's far from it.' Elspeth had heard and was quick on the uptake. 'Ye'll get yerself a good education in school an' that'll give ye freedom to do whatever ye want in life.'

'She's right,' my father added. I stared at him. Shocked. 'Close your mouth, Nevis. There's no need to gawp at me like that. Elspeth's right.' I closed my mouth. *She's right?* But then that contradicts everything he'd ever said to me before about schools. My instant reaction was to turn on him and remind him of the times we'd parked outside or near a school in the van, or even just drove past, and he'd say, 'Bet you're glad you're not in there, boy. Out here you're free to wear what you like, read what you like and learn what you like. In there there's nothing but limitations. They call it curriculum.' How could he forget all that? He said it so much. Yet I always liked parking near schools. In fact, if I saw a sign I'd suggest we'd turn and drive by because I knew that after his talk on the 'institutionalisation of the mind', 'freedom versus curriculum' or 'schools stunting brain growth', he'd buy me a new book. Whether it was later that day or a couple of days later, he'd always buy me a new book and say, 'Freedom's all very well, but it's not clever to be stupid.'

Mr Galbraith lived in a small white bungalow in a cul-de-sac surrounded by other identical small white bungalows. The only thing slightly different about them were the gardens: each had a drive, whether it was tarmac or gravel, and most of them had a square of grass, but some were scattered with children's toys, others with a border of flowers and plants. One had a very rickety-looking swing. We pulled up onto the pavement alongside a bungalow where the garden had a water feature as its centrepiece. A pile of neatly arranged rocks with the tip of a copper pipe just visible and poking out the top, water bubbling and trickling down into a very small puddle-like pond. On top of the rocks sat a smiling, rosy-cheeked gnome, red cap and blue tunic, fishing rod in hand, line dangling in the water.

The front door opened and an old man appeared in the doorway. He was wearing grey trousers and a grey cardigan with a white shirt underneath. My first thought was, *is that him? Is that Galbraith?* Followed shortly by, *why do old people always wear grey?* It's like colour drains out of their skin and hair so they let it drain out of their clothes as well. And Galbraith had certainly lost the colour of his hair. It was bone white and so was his beard, neatly trimmed around the sides, longer at the chin, cut into a point. He wore half-moon spectacles.

'Come on, Nevis,' Marshall said. He got out of the car and I followed.

'Do ye want us to wait, Marshall?' Elspeth asked. I turned and looked at her. Since when had she started to call him by his first name? In the beginning it had been Mr Gow this, Mr Gow that. But now it was Marshall? Such familiarity scared me. And the way she said his name . . . it sounded so comfortable on her tongue.

My father said yes.

'You're not staying with me?' I asked.

'I've already spoken to Mr Galbraith, Nevis. Now it's your turn.' I followed my father silently over the drive, looking back only once to give Elspeth a final glare.

At the door Marshall shook hands with the old man who smiled at him but looked at me. He was tall, taller even than Marshall by at least three inches. I had an urge to hide behind my father like I did years ago when I hid behind his back and poked my face round to spy at people.

'So you're the boy?' he said when Marshall had finished his piece. I didn't answer. I just looked from his face to my father's who was glowering at me in that 'say something' way I'd grown to recognise. But before

I could even open my mouth Mr Galbraith had turned to Marshall and said, 'I can take it from here, Mr Gow. Thank you.' And my father smiled and nodded. With one last glower he turned and walked back down the drive.

'We'll pick you up in one hour, Nevis,' he said and as he slammed the door Murdo started barking in the back and Elspeth started flapping her arms again. I watched them drive away.

'So . . .'

I turned to the old man.

'Shall we go inside?'

Every room in the Kerrs' farmhouse had a slightly different smell – the corridor at the back door was dirt and rubber boots and waxed jackets, the kitchen was warmth and food, the hallway was dusty and old with the furniture and clutter. But throughout the whole of the farmhouse I could smell the intermingling of the people inside it. Especially in the bathroom: Elspeth's sweet perfume, Ailsa's peach bubble bath, the bottle of blue shower gel I could smell on Duckman and my father alike. The aftershave. The deodorant.

In the bungalow there wasn't a clash of smells other than that of furniture polish and books. Mr Galbraith lived alone.

In the hallway there was a family photograph on

the wall: a younger Mr Galbraith stood with his hand on the shoulder of a woman sitting in front of him. I knew it was Galbraith because he still had the neatly trimmed beard and glasses. The woman had a happy round face and bobbed curly brown hair. Two boys sat on either side of her. They were all smiling, shiny-eyed at the camera.

'My wife and two sons,' Mr Galbraith said. He was standing at the end of the hallway watching me. He smiled. 'The study's this way,' he said and then gestured to the open door he was standing beside.

The smell of furniture polish and books was stronger in the study – and also something else I didn't recognise at first; I found out later it was the soft leather of the armchairs facing the electric fire, which was on and glowing when I walked in, yellow and orange flames flickering over plastic coals. Every wall except one was lined floor to ceiling with shelves and filled with books; even above the door there were books. The shelves stopped only on each side of the fireplace – over which there was a large framed print – and the one wall without any shelves had instead a big bay window that looked out onto the garden and the little fishing gnome. Underneath the window was a desk made of dark wood; on it there was a pile of books, a pen-pot, a lamp and a small clock, ticking. The study wasn't dirty but there were books everywhere and where there are books, there is always dust. The morning sun shone through the window and I could see the little flecks and hairs swirl and dance.

'Your father has told me a lot about you, Nevis.'

I turned to face Mr Galbraith who was still standing at the doorway.

'Would you like a cup of tea?' he offered. 'A glass of water? Or milk? I'm afraid I don't have any juice.'

'What did my father say?' I asked.

He smiled. 'Has your father told you anything about me?'

'You're a teacher,' I said. 'And you're interested in me.'

'The latter is true. But the former should be changed to past tense. I *was* a teacher. I'm retired now. Take a seat, Nevis.'

I sat down in one of the deep armchairs. Mr Galbraith sat himself down next to me; we were angled partly towards the fireplace and partly towards each other, but I kept my eyes on the orange and yellow and did not look at the old man.

'Your father told me you've never been to school. Is that true?'

'Yes,' I said.

'You were taught at home.'

'The van.'

'By your father.'

'Yes.'

'And from books.'

I didn't reply. They didn't seem much like questions anyway.

'Do you know why you're here, Nevis?'

That was a definite question, but Mr Galbraith didn't wait for an answer.

'Your father wants me to teach you to get you up to speed, so to speak, with the national curriculum.'

I cringed from the words.

'He wants you to go to school.'

'I don't want to go to school,' I said.

'No. I can't imagine you do.'

My eyes moved onto the old man sitting across from me. It was his turn to be staring into the fire, his eyes – blue – reflecting the flickering light. They looked almost glassy, breakable, like blue ice. I imagined his eyes melting as he watched the fire, dribbling down his face and into his beard. He turned towards me and smiled. I switched my own look onto my knees.

'Could you do me a favour please, Nevis? There's a pad of paper on my desk. Could you get it for me? And a pen please. I'm not lazy but I may as well make good use of your youth.' I was already on my feet and at the desk. 'Oh and Nevis, whatever you do – and this is important – *don't* read the note.' I plucked a pen from the pot and picked up the paper. I saw my name. *Nevis Gow. 15.* The handwriting was neat and easy to read.

Never been to school. Lived in a van. How long? Can read and write. Interest in science. Apparently v. bright. Why was Galbraith writing notes about me? Maybe that's what teachers did. So why did it matter whether I saw it or not? I handed the pen and paper to the old man and sat down. My father must've told him all that. *Interest in science.* Why did he always have to insist I was so interested in science? I liked facts. The truth. That was all.

'Did you read my note?'

'No,' I said. The lie was out of my mouth before I could stop it and I felt my cheeks redden. Mr Galbraith smiled and nodded and wrote something more on the paper. I watched him, wishing I could read his writing by the movement of his pen alone. Perhaps the old man sensed my curiosity because he asked, 'Do you mind if I keep notes of our conversations? It will help me build my lesson plans later.' I looked away. Mr Galbraith carried on writing and then stopped, put his pen down. 'I need some water,' he said. 'Would you like anything?'

I shook my head.

Mr Galbraith pushed himself up onto his feet, placed the notepad and pen down on the coffee table between us and walked out the door. There was movement in the next room, the sound of a tap turning on and water hitting a metal sink. I quickly grabbed the pad from the table. 'Oh and Nevis,' the old man's voice was raised so as I could hear him clearly, 'please don't read my notes. They're private.' I hurriedly read the note.

Hey diddle diddle, the cat and the fiddle, the cow jumped over the moon,
The little dog laughed to see such fun and the dish ran away with the spoon.

The man was crazy. I placed the pad back on the table and the pen at the same angle as before. Mr Galbraith came back with two glasses of water. 'Just in case you change your mind,' he said and placed the water on the table. He looked at the paper. 'You didn't read it, did you?' he asked. 'My notes?'

'No,' I said. I was starting to feel uncomfortable.

'Promise?'

I looked away. 'I promise,' I said. Mr Galbraith picked the pad up and turned over the page. He sat back down in his armchair.

'Do you have any questions?' he asked.

'No,' I said.

'Well I do. Lots. Do you mind if I go ahead and ask them?'

'I guess not.'

'What's the capital of Scotland?' he asked.

I frowned. *Was he serious?* 'Edinburgh,' I said.

'And what's the capital of England?'

'London.'

'Russia?'

'Moscow.'

'Japan?'

'Tokyo.' I smiled. This was just like the games Marshall and I used to play when we were driving along. I was good at capitals. I started hoping Galbraith would ask me what the capital of Venezuela was or the Philippines or Turkmenistan.

'Who is the current prime minister?'

I smiled even more. 'John Major,' I said.

Another game we used to play – Who Am I? One person had to think of someone famous, dead or alive, and the other would have to guess who it was only by asking yes or no questions. I used to hate this game. When Marshall was driving along and suddenly said, 'Who am I?' I would always groan. 'Come on, boy, you'll know this one. And if you don't, then you'll learn someone new. So who am I?'

'You're not a politician, are you?' I often asked. 'Because if you're a politician I'm not playing.'

'But you know plenty of politicians.'

'John Major,' I said. 'That's all I know.'

'And who's John Major?'

'The prime minister.'

'And what does the prime minister do?'

'Run the country.'

'Good. But no, I'm not John Major. But yes, I am a politician.'

'I'm not playing then.'

Even so I managed to learn about Winston Churchill, Abraham Lincoln, Margaret Thatcher, Bill Clinton, the list goes on. The game Who Am I? should really have been called History Lesson. I preferred guessing kings and queens, but only if they were British. When they weren't British:

'Are you a king?'

'Yes.'

'British?'

'No.'

'I'm not playing.'

Marshall would laugh. 'I'll give you a clue,' he said once. 'I'm Spanish.'

After which I tried to explain to my father, not for the first time, that the game really wasn't any fun unless I would be able to eventually guess the answer.

'Juan Carlos the First,' he said. 'The King of Spain since 1975. Did you know he was a descendant of Queen Victoria?' He would always follow up the name with a fact. 'I believe it was through his grandmother.' Even if the fact was completely useless.

Mr Galbraith continued with his questions. They seemed to be endless. And every time I answered, he made a mark on his page.

'What's Newton's first law of motion?'

I thought back to my science encyclopaedia where I remembered learning the words 'momentum' and 'inertia'. 'If something is still it won't move until a force hits it.'

'What's Charles Darwin most famous for?'

'His theory on evolution.'

'What planet is closest to the sun?'

'Mercury.'

'Who was the first man on the moon?'

'Neil Armstrong.'

'What's your favourite colour?'

I stopped.

'What's wrong?' Mr Galbraith looked up at me from his list of questions. 'Do you not have a favourite colour, Nevis?'

'No,' I said.

'But do you know how colours are formed? For example, why the grass is green?'

'Yes,' I said. 'The absorption and reflection of white light.' I wondered if that was enough or whether he wanted me to explain in more detail. '. . . frequencies,' I added. Mr Galbraith made a mark on his page.

'What music do you like?' he asked.

I didn't like these new questions. 'I don't listen to music,' I said. I thought back to the van and the tapes in the side pocket. 'Our radio broke.'

'I see.' He made a mark on his page. 'And what's your favourite television programme?'

'We never had a telly.'

'Film then. What's your favourite film?'

I looked away.

'Have you never been to the cinema, Nevis?'

'No.'

'The theatre?'

I thought back to a puppet theatre on a beach. Marshall had sat me down among a swarm of other kids sitting cross-legged, staring unblinkingly at the horrible big-nosed puppets that squealed in high-pitched voices and hit each other round the head with bats. I hated the noise. I hated the other kids around me falling about laughing and shouting at the little stripy theatre. Or no, I didn't hate them, I was scared. When Marshall bent down to my ear and whispered he was going to get some ice cream I got straight to my feet, jammed my hand in his and said I was going too. 'Don't leave me,' I said.

'No,' I told Mr Galbraith.

He nodded and put the pen and notepad back onto the coffee table. He leaned forward, his elbows on his knees and his hands clasped in front of him. 'Nevis, why don't you want to go to school?'

I kept my eyes lowered to the carpet.

'You like learning new things and that's what school's

all about.' There was a knock at the door. 'That'll be your father,' Mr Galbraith said. 'But just one more thing before you go. Next time we meet we'll have a proper lesson. You'll be here for three hours. One of those hours is yours. You can decide what you want to study. It can be anything. Comic books if you like. Music, film, art . . . you choose.' I looked up at the old man and he smiled. 'Any ideas?' he said.

'Could you tell Marshall I'm nowhere near the national curriculum?' I asked. 'I don't want to go to school.'

Mr Galbraith stopped smiling.

'I already intended to advise him against it, Nevis.' There was another knock at the door. Mr Galbraith sighed and pushed himself up from his chair. 'Come on,' he said. I got to my feet and as I did so I looked at the table with the two glasses of untouched water and the notepad of questions – except there weren't any questions written on it, just a page full of squiggles. Mr Galbraith must've seen me look at the pad because he said then, 'Pretty, isn't it? Just like confetti.' He placed his hand on my shoulder and led me out the door. 'I want you to think about that hour of yours, Nevis. You don't have to give me an answer today. Unless you have an idea already?'

I shook my head.

'Something scientific maybe? Your father tells me you love science.'

'I *hate* science,' I said.

'Oh.' Mr Galbraith coughed awkwardly. 'Is that so? Well something else then. Anything.' He handed me a card with a number on it. 'My telephone number. Call me once you've thought of something. Think of it as your first homework assignment.' He unhooked the latch of the front door and opened it to my father who was standing on the step, waiting.

'Everything ok?' he asked.

'Yes, yes, everything's fine.' Mr Galbraith tapped my shoulder.

'Good.' Marshall looked at me. 'Go wait in the car, Nevis,' he said. 'Please.' So I went.

As I walked across the driveway towards the Land Rover I looked at the little fishing gnome sitting alone on his rocks, smiling to himself, his line in the water and then my eyes caught sight of some unusual colour in the flowerbeds behind him. More gnomes, poking their heads round plants and flowers, hiding behind boulders and shrubs. At the gate I noticed that one gnome had been completely buried right up to his neck, his head sticking out of the soil, little rosy cheeks and big grin smiling up at the sky. I looked back at Mr Galbraith who was talking to my father. He was nodding and holding the point of his white beard in his hand and I wondered just how crazy he was.

The petrol cap

The key to the petrol cap was stiff, a little rusty. You had to wiggle it in, but not all the way. If it went all the way it wouldn't open. You had to wiggle it in and then pull it back a notch, after which, with a little twist of the key, the petrol cap would come off as easy as you like.

I never went into service stations with my father. Once he said to me, 'Nevis, boy, will you run in and pay while I fill up.' And I said, no but we could do it the other way round. So that became my job. I would always fill up the van while Marshall went in to pay. I always managed to get it dead on ten, fifteen or twenty if that's what Marshall wanted. Or I'd just let it run until the trigger automatically switched off. I remember the first time I did that and I thought there was something wrong with the nozzle, so I kept pressing it over and over again until at last the diesel came splurting from the tank and all over the forecourt, my trousers and shoes. We put sand on it. They always kept buckets of sand at service stations. And I remember then Marshall telling me that diesel wasn't as bad as petrol. Petrol was highly flammable, get it near a naked flame and WHOOSH, up in smoke, he said. But throw a match into diesel and it'll go out.

The windscreen wipers

How I first learned about God. Marshall and I had come back to the van after visiting a park. I remember that afternoon well. I'd been pretending to be a spy; hiding under the slide or behind the seesaw, skirting around my father to make sure he didn't see me. Marshall wasn't playing at all. He was writing. I remember losing interest in spying on him because he wasn't paying me any attention and instead I started spying on birds instead. Sneaking up on them very quietly, trying not to be heard. The challenge was to get as close as you could before they flew away. I got bored with that too after a while and spent the rest of the afternoon poking a molehill with a stick and then making my own molehills in the loose bark that lay around the play-castle. When finally my father had a lull in his writing and suggested we go back to the van I remember kicking all the molehills flat again. None of this is relevant to windscreen wipers or God, but it's a memory so it's important and has to be included.

At the van there was a flyer stuck under the windscreen wiper. Marshall pulled it out, scanned it quickly then screwed it up and threw it on the dashboard. I must've been young because when I unscrewed it and looked at it for myself there were some big words I couldn't read. 'Redemption,' Marshall said when I pointed to one. 'Enlightenment. Fulfilment.' Amongst other things, the flyer said that Jesus Christ, son of God, died for us on the cross. I asked my father what it meant. Jesus, he said, was a very clever guy who lived a long time ago and preached lots of good things to people about loving their neighbour and being kind to one another. But all the rulers and emperors and priests at the time were scared of Jesus. They heard the people were starting to think of him as the son of God, their saviour. So the government killed him because they were worried Jesus would become too powerful.

'Nailed his hands and feet to a big wooden cross and left him there to die. That kind of punishment is called "crucifixion",' he said. And then, 'Not a very nice story, is it?' I shook my head.

The next day Marshall went for a walk and came back with a new book for me, a children's bible. I read about Adam and Eve, Cain and Abel, Noah and his great Ark. I learnt about the life of Jesus and his twelve disciples.

'They liked killing people back then,' I said when I finished. 'Even God kept killing people and he made a law against it.' Marshall taught me the word 'hypocrisy'.

'An eye for an eye, a tooth for a tooth,' he said. 'That's

according to God in the Old Testament. Yet in the New he tells us to forgive and forget. Love our neighbour as though he were our own brother.' Marshall tutted and shook his head. 'Couldn't make up his mind really, could he?'

'Is it true?' I asked. 'The stories?'

'Maybe; maybe not,' he replied. 'I wouldn't know. I wasn't there.'

28

For the rest of the day after my first meeting with
Galbraith I hid myself in my room, the chair jammed
under the doorknob so Ailsa couldn't get in. I lay on
the bed, thinking about Galbraith's list of non-existent
questions. If he really hadn't wanted me to read his
notes, I thought, why did he ask me to get them in the
first place? And why did he write so clearly in black ink?
Perhaps he knew I'd read them so he wrote them in code.
Hey diddle diddle. Or perhaps he really was just mad.

I placed the bedside lamp on the carpet so it shone
like a torch under the bed and I crawled under. My
notepads and pens were stored in the far corner so
Marshall wouldn't find them. I lay flat on my stomach,
propping myself up with one arm as I wrote.

The truth.

*My name is Nevis Gow. I am fifteen years old. I
have lived in a van with my father for eleven years.
His name is Marshall Gow. He is a writer.*

I stopped and crossed out the last sentence ~~He is a writer~~ and then rested my head on my hands. I could smell and taste dust from the carpet and the corners of the room. I could smell the paper from the notepad. I looked into the bright light of the light bulb, shining, and when I closed my eyes little circular spots drifted behind my eyelids, yellow and green and red. He *was* a writer, I thought, *used to be*. Now I'm the writer.

29

Very early the next morning, I was standing by the window, watching the rain and waiting for Nigel Kerr to cross the yard with his gun. I'd not seen Duckman since the morning before, and at dinnertime Elspeth had asked me if I knew where he'd disappeared to. I'd shrugged. Ailsa said, 'I bet you *do* know, but you're not saying.' And Marshall had looked at me. 'I don't know,' I told him, so he continued eating his dinner.

The next morning and still the yard seemed empty without Duckman's rusty blue Sierra. He'd told me he was going, but hadn't said where or when.

'What about you?' he asked. 'Are ye comin'?'

I told him I couldn't.

'Why not?'

'I just can't.'

'Ye can,' he said. 'If ye want.'

I shook my head. I couldn't leave Marshall.

While I stood waiting for Nigel Kerr to make an appearance, I watched the caravan and thought of my father. The heavy rain was falling on the slightly sunken caravan roof, creating a small puddle and trickling over the edge, dribbling over the little square window into the weeds. There was a movement from inside, I saw a shadow get up and go to the sink. My father was awake. His face appeared at the window, looking out at the rain. He pressed his nose against the scratched pane and I pressed my nose against mine. *Look at me*, I thought. His lips started moving and his warm breath steamed the window. He stepped back. I could no longer see him. I waited another five minutes, but Nigel Kerr did not leave the house with his gun and Marshall did not reappear at the window. I returned to my lists.

The truth.

My name is Nevis Gow. I am fifteen years old. I have lived in a van with my father for eleven years. His name is Marshall Gow. And I love him.

30

I sat with Marshall at the table for breakfast, looking at him while he drank his coffee and read a newspaper. He held his mug close to his lips and took small and careful sips. Underneath the table his legs were crossed. I noticed that occasionally he bounced his foot up and down. Odd. I'd never seen Marshall Gow sip his coffee so carefully in this way. And I'd never seen him cross his legs. And to read a newspaper? Marshall didn't read newspapers apart from quick glances in shops.

Elspeth hummed while she fried up some bacon. If I closed my eyes and ears the smell alone could send me drifting back to days in the van. Bacon days. When Marshall brought back a pack of bacon from town and we'd have to eat it within a day or two. We'd cut it into slices and mix it in with pasta or mashed potatoes, or fry up a bacon omelette, or just have a bacon butty with ketchup. I loved the smell of my clothes on a bacon day. Bacon grease clung like no other. It made me feel rich. Not in the money sense. I've never been aware of money and the value of things. But a bacon day made me feel like I had a lot. I felt content and full and happy.

I ate my bacon butty in silence. When I finished I got up from the table and Marshall said, 'Nevis, Mr Galbraith mentioned something about a homework assignment.' He looked at me. 'Have you done it yet?'

'No,' I said.

'Well perhaps you should. Your next lesson is on Thursday at five o'clock.'

I wondered how to respond to that and in the end plumped for 'Ok.' I started towards the door.

'Nevis?'

I turned.

'Aren't you forgetting something?'

'What?'

'Your plate,' he said. 'Take it to the sink.'

I frowned, returned to the table, picked up the ketchup-smeared plate and took it to the sink. 'Do you want it in the sink?' I asked. 'Or on the side?'

'Don't be cheeky, Nevis.'

Cheeky? I placed the plate on the side. How was that cheeky? He was the one who wanted it by the sink.

'Thank you, Nevis,' Elspeth said and beamed at me.

'Thank you, Nevis,' said my father. I left the kitchen. Confused.

*　　*　　*

By early afternoon the sky had cleared to a cool blue. I was sitting with the window open, perched on the sill, notepad on lap. I was remembering the way I used to lie down on the roof of the van, looking up at the sky and making pictures with clouds; and I was writing the memory into my list when I heard the sound of a car bumping and splashing through puddles up the track. It was Duckman. He swung into the yard, switched off the engine and got out the car, smoking. Straight away he looked up at my window.

'What are *you* lookin' at?' he said.

I was pleased to see him.

'Come on, I've got beer. We're goin' t' the river.' He got back into the car, started the engine and waited a few seconds before poking his head out the door and over the roof again. 'Are ye fuckin' comin' or what?'

In the back of his car Duckman had four bottles of beer and a large blue tarpaulin. He grinned at me as I got in, slammed the car into reverse to turn round and then sped off down the track. He didn't care about the uneven bumps, he laughed when the undercarriage scraped against the ground. He turned his music up. It didn't have any words just unusual sounds and a big bass beat. I felt quite unsteady when he finally stopped and parked up by the river.

He spread out the tarpaulin on the bank like a picnic blanket and lay down. I sat beside him on the blue plastic. Duckman opened two bottles of beer with his keys and handed one to me.

'So,' he said, 'are ye no gonnae ask me where ah've been?'

'Where've you been?'

'Inverness. Dossin' wi' mates.'

'I didn't think you'd come back.'

'Did ye miss me?' He poked me in the side with the neck of his bottle and grinned before taking a swig.

'I thought you said you were going.'

'Ah am,' he said. 'Jus' wanted t' make sure ye hadnae changed yer mind like.'

I shook my head. Duckman spat and scratched his cheek. We sat in silence for a while watching two ducks paddle up and down stream. They kept coming to the bank where we were sitting, watching us with their beady black eyes.

I looked at the bottle of beer in my hand. I'd never tasted beer before. I'd tried whisky with Marshall when I was much younger, but didn't like it. Marshall had laughed at my disgusted face when I swallowed my first mouthful. 'That'll soon put hairs on your chest, boy,' he'd said.

I remember when Marshall decided to stop drinking. The police pulling us over, blue lights flashing and asking Marshall to step out of the van. 'Do you know how fast you were going, sir?' When Marshall got back in he waited for the policemen to return to their car and then he blew on my face. 'Can you smell the whisky?' he said. I nodded. 'Then that was close, boy. Too damn close.'

I thought about my lists and made a mental note to write up the memory of the speeding ticket when I got back to the farmhouse. Under the heading 'Speedometer'. I placed the bottle to my lips and took a small swig. The liquid trickled into my mouth, bitter-tasting. I grimaced as I swallowed. How could people drink this for enjoyment? And then I remembered the hipflask and my father silent and red-faced when he drank too much. 'You look like her, you know,' he used to say. 'You have her chin. You have her eyes.' I hated him telling me that.

'I look like you,' I'd reply. 'I have your nose.'

'You have her eyes.'

'Her eyes were blue.'

'They were brown. I remember.'

But when Marshall stopped drinking so did these memories. 'It's in the past now. Forget about it,' he'd tell himself. And I felt pleased. I remember the morning he poured away the alcohol, staring down into the ditch and the whisky soaking into the ground. I walked over to him. Stood beside him. Held his hand. 'I won't leave you,' I said. And he tried to smile at me. 'Things are going to change now, boy. You'll see,' he said.

I watched Duckman cock back his head and down the rest of the beer. People didn't drink for enjoyment, I thought. Duckman wasn't enjoying that beer, he was thinking about his mother. I could tell. He was drinking because he remembered her, like when Marshall used to remember my mother. Memories can have such a hold over people. I turned to Duckman and held the bottle of beer out to him.

'Don't ye want it?'

I shook my head and watched as Duckman drew back his arm and hurled his empty bottle into the river, almost hitting the two ducks paddling near the bank. They quacked and flapped and fluttered further down stream. He turned and took the bottle from my hand.

'Did ye no like it?'

'No,' I said.

He took a swig.

'Why do they call you Duckman?' I asked.

He shrugged. 'Killed a duck once.' He looked at me, then back at the river. 'Two years ago. Got suspended fer it.'

'Suspended from what?'

'From school, ye eejit. Most kids have t' go, ye know.' He spat. 'Count yersel' lucky ye no had t'. Ah hated school.'

'Why don't you go anymore?'

'Ah left when ah was sixteen. T' work on the farm.'

He looked at me again. 'Ask me how ah killed the duck,' he said.

'How did you kill the duck?' I asked.

'Ah drowned it. The fuckin' irony, eh? In the duck pond. The rest o' the class were all boppin' aboot in their kayaks, happy as ye like, practising their front an' back paddle, an' ah grab a duck, its wings flappin' crazy, tryin' t' fly away, an' hold it underwater till it stops. The girls were screamin' when they realised what ah was doin'.' I pictured Duckman knee deep in a pond holding the fighting duck underwater. 'Have ye ever felt life just seep away from between yer fingers, Nevis?'

'No,' I said.

'Well, yev had it easy.'

We sat in silence. Duckman took out his tobacco to roll a cigarette.

'Road kill,' I said then.

'Wha' aboot it?'

'We've hit things on the road before.' I thought back to the time Marshall and I had come across a swarm of frogs hopping over the embankment of the road, bouncing across to the other side. He didn't stop. He slowed down, but it was too late. He drove straight over the frogs and we felt them squish underneath the wheels. 'Badgers. Foxes. Frogs. And a stag,' I added.

'Ye hit a stag?'

'Almost.' We'd been driving at night. The stag's eyes

caught the full beam of the headlights. Marshall slammed on the brakes, stopped just in time. Right in front of us, looking in with wide eyes, was the huge head and antlers of the stag; we could see its nostrils flaring and its frightened breath bellow out in white plumes in the cold air. Then the stag turned its massive head and fled into the shadows. Marshall pulled over. He was shaken up, but excited. 'Wasn't he beautiful?' he said. 'What a magnificent beast.'

'Good thing ye didnae hit it,' Duckman said. 'It woulda made a right mess o' the van.' He flicked the tip of his cigarette. 'Tell me summit else,' he said. 'Another memory.'

I tried to think.

'Anythin',' Duckman said.

But the only memories that came to mind were the ones I didn't want to share. Private memories – like Marshall by the bunker. Or the kisses when he slept. 'I can't think of any,' I told Duckman. It wasn't really a lie.

'Try,' he said. 'Jus' take me through a day in the life of Nevis Gow.'

'I don't know how,' I said.

'What do ye mean ye don't know how?'

'I mean . . .'

But Duckman interrupted me. 'Start with the sentence, "I wake up . . ."'

'I wake up . . .' I said.

'And then?'

I thought for a moment. I closed my eyes. I opened them. 'I wake up,' I said, 'and see if Marshall is writing. Or if he's still asleep. Or if we're moving.'

'Keep going,' Duckman said.

'I can't.'

'Why not?'

'Because everything depends on everything else,' I said. 'If I wake up and we're moving, I'm going to have a different day than if I wake up and Marshall is writing. And if I wake up and we're in the country, I'm going to have a different day than if I wake up and we're in a city.'

'Ah like that,' Duckman said. 'No routine. No ties. Ah like that.'

I nodded. 'We were happy,' I said. 'We were free.'

Duckman was leaning back onto his elbows, beer in hand, looking across the water. He seemed to be squinting, even though the sun wasn't bright. 'Do you remember a time before the van?' he asked finally.

'Yes,' I said and told him about the plastic tub full of little metal cars and how I used to play on a mat printed with roads and houses and traffic lights and shops.

'Ah know the kinda mat ye mean,' he said. 'Ah had one o' those too.'

'Did you?' This surprised me.

'Aye. Loads o' people have 'em.'

For some reason I smiled. 'Do you still have it?'

'No.'

We both stared out at the river and from somewhere we heard a salmon jump and plop in the water. 'So what's your first memory?' I asked.

'Ma shoes,' he said. 'Ma new school shoes.' He looked at his boots when he said this. 'Ah just have a memory of lookin' at ma feet while ma mum drove me t' school fer the first time. Ah remember they felt stiff, the leather was hard. Ah didnae like 'em.' He took a swig of his beer. 'It's no very interestin',' he said.

'I think it's interesting,' I said and lay back onto the tarpaulin. I put my hands behind my head and stared up at the sky. I knew Duckman was watching me so I continued with this thoughtful relaxed pose. I was enjoying the attention.

Duckman turned onto his back and lay down beside me. I felt good, I realised then. For perhaps the first time since arriving at the farm I actually felt calm and content. Perhaps because I remembered days when I would lie like that and look up at the sky with Marshall. Or perhaps because I was soothed by the silence, which wasn't really silence, but filled with the river and the birds and the salmon and the breeze. And the ducks. And the occasional fly fisherman's rod. I fancied even being able to hear the ants and spiders scuttling about in the grass, the worms in the soil, moles digging, rabbits burrowing . . . and then deeper, deeper – if I stretched my ears far enough – the bubbling and boiling of the earth's core. I thought of Marshall – With such romantic imagery in your head, boy, you should be a writer yourself. I closed my eyes and enjoyed the noise-filled silence.

Beside me I felt Duckman move. I wondered if he'd turned onto his side to look at me with my eyes closed, the way I used to look at Marshall when he slept. I heard him whisper my name. 'Nevis?' And then felt him gently nudge my arm. Maybe he thought I'd drifted off. I remained still and completely silent. 'Nevis?' And then the slightest touch on my thigh. He held his fingertips over me, so close, only just touching, that at first I wasn't sure if he was really touching me or not. But then he moved his hand. Softly. Slowly. To the inside of my leg.

I opened my eyes.

The hand was removed.

I turned my head to look at Duckman who was now sitting up, rolling a cigarette. It was on the tip of my tongue to ask him – did you just touch me? But I didn't. Duckman carried on slowly breaking up the tobacco with his fingers, lining it up on the little brown paper. I watched him for a moment. Then looked up at the sky. He definitely touched me, I thought. I don't need confirmation. I sat up and crouched forward to hide my erection. Duckman didn't look at me; and I didn't turn to look at him. I wondered then if he was waiting for some sort of acknowledgement. Maybe I was supposed to say something. It's ok – I tried out in my head, it doesn't matter. I thought about Marshall. Maybe I should tell Duckman that I loved Marshall. I closed my eyes and willed my erection away. I could get up and go into the woods – I thought. Say I was going for a piss. Or I could wait it out. I opened my eyes. Duckman was looking straight at me.

'Wanna puff?' he asked. I looked at the rollie he held out pinched between thumb and forefinger, thought for a moment, then shook my head. Duckman grinned. 'Good boy,' he said. 'Daddy would be proud.' And he put the cigarette to his lips and cupped the lighter flame with his hand. I could smell the tobacco begin to burn.

'Duckman,' I had to ask, 'did you just touch me?'

'What?'

'A minute ago. When I was lying down.'

'Did ah touch ye?'

'Yes.'

'Why the fuck would ah touch ye?'

'So you didn't?'

'No.'

'You didn't touch me?'

'Where?'

'On the leg.'

'No.'

'Are you sure?'

'Aye, ah'm fuckin' sure. Jesus Christ, Nevis, ye were asleep.' He was staring at me wide-eyed in disbelief. 'Generally speaking ah tend not t' molest ma friends when they're asleep.'

I looked at Duckman carefully. 'I was asleep?' I asked.

'No fer long like. Less than five minutes. Ye jus' drifted off.' Duckman shook his head. 'Nevis, are you ok?'

'Why?'

'Because ah'm starting to think there's a high possibility that yer completely fucked up in the head.' He seemed almost concerned. He looked down at his burning cigarette, then placed it to his lips. Inhaled. He looked back up at me. 'Ye know, Nevis, ah've been thinkin' long an' hard aboot yer situation.' Threads of smoke twisted from his mouth as he spoke. He pocketed his lighter. Exhaled fully. 'Ah mean, eleven years is a long time. It's almost sick, don't ye think? Ye hear aboot kiddies bein' locked up in basements by demented parents – it's no so far off it really, is it?'

I was confused. I felt like I'd missed out on some essential part of a previous conversation.

'Did he fiddle wi' ye, Nevis? Is that it?'

I frowned. Even when I watched Duckman's lips move it didn't make any sense.

'Yer father, Nevis. Did he fiddle wi' ye?'

He was talking about sex, I realised then. He was talking about masturbation.

'Ah mean, it jus' doesnae make sense. Why else would he keep ye all to himsel' like that? For *eleven* years.' Duckman was shaking his head. 'It's dirty,' he said. 'It's sick.' And he took another long drag on his cigarette. 'Ye know it's wrong, right? Ye know it's against the law, don't you?' Duckman looked at me. 'It's called incest, Nevis. You can't splash aboot in yer own gene pool. You know that, right?'

'I know,' I said. I lied. I had no real idea what he was talking about anyway.

Duckman scratched his cheek and spat at the grass. 'Good,' he said and the intensity seemed to ease between us. Duckman flicked his cigarette into the river and lay back onto the tarpaulin. I also lay back. Tried to relax.

'So I was asleep?' I asked again.

'Aye, Nevis. At least, ah thought ye were. Ye didnae move anyway. You seemed asleep t' me. That's why I started rollin' ma fag.'

I put my arms behind my head and looked up at the mackerel sky, rippling tufts of cloud. There was a tinge of pink where the sun had started to set and I remembered the morning before, sneaking out with Duckman at the red sunrise.

Duckman must have heard my thoughts. 'Red sky at night,' he said, 'shepherd's delight.'

'Red sky in the morning,' I continued.

'Shepherd's hat's on fire,' Duckman finished. And I laughed a sort of short bubbling laugh. It made me close my eyes very briefly. And when I opened them again my laughter had turned into a smile and a warm kind of buzz was running through my body. No, not a buzz. A buzz makes you think of vibration or electricity or excitement. This was more of an oozing warm presence. It was as though when I'd closed my mouth it had stopped the laugh from escaping, so it went inside instead and was creeping through my body, making my insides happy, tingly, warm. It felt good after the uncomfortable intensity moments before. I looked at Duckman. He was not smiling.

'My mum used t' say it,' he said.

I looked away, back up at the sky. I wondered what to say next. I could feel it in the air. Whatever it was. The tension returning and it made that warm oozing feeling go away.

'Ye should ask me what she died of,' he said.

So I did. 'What did she die of?'

'Cancer.'

I didn't tell him I knew this already.

'Ye should ask me what kind o' cancer,' he said.

'What kind of cancer?' I asked.

'Ovarian,' he replied.

There was silence. There was the river. There was the

pink mackerel sky. There was another salmon jumping and plopping as it made its way upstream. There was a light cool breeze. I could feel the tension. It was coming from Duckman, I was sure of it.

'What else should I ask?' I asked and I imagined my words and breath breaking up all that intensity. It felt good. I wanted to keep speaking. I wanted more words to fill the air and break down whatever it was leaking out from Duckman. 'What else?'

'She was beautiful,' he said.

'Was she beautiful?'

'No, ah'm tellin' ye she was beautiful. It's no meant fer a question.'

'I know she was beautiful,' I said, trying to make up for my mistake. 'I've seen her in pictures. In the corridor upstairs.'

'So why did ye ask?'

I shrugged.

'Are ye thick?'

'No.'

'Ah hate you,' he said.

'Do you?'

'No. But ah wish ah did. Ah feel as though ah want to.'

'You want to hate everybody,' I said.

'How would you know?'

'I can tell. I can feel it.' That's what it was, I thought.

That's what was filling the air. And then I shrugged, not because I doubted myself, but because I thought perhaps it would have been more appropriate to doubt myself. For Duckman's sake.

He was getting to his feet. 'Are ye no gonnae ask me where ah'm goin'?' he said.

'Where are you going?'

'Do ye wannae come wi' me?'

'Depends,' I said.

'On what?'

'On where you're taking me.'

'Does it though?' he asked and started walking. 'Stay here if ye like.'

I watched his back for a moment moving away from me down the path towards the car. *Fuck*. I rolled onto my knees and reluctantly stood up. 'Wait.' He turned. 'Wait for me,' I said.

'Bring the tarpaulin,' he replied.

31

Small metal pots with round holes in the lid, plastic flowers – coloured cloth petals – sticking from the top. Nearly every grave had one although some had no flowers. Some only had the dented metal pot, tipped over, lopsided, trying hard to be silver. Neat rows of knee-high polished marble, black or grey mottled stone or ivory white. Occasionally a grave with more extravagance: a carved stone angel or cross; or a grave with real flowers, planted or left tied in their bunch, wrapped in pretty paper. We walked in between them all, Duckman leading the way. We didn't speak.

I read the names in gold lettering as we passed. I read the dates, born and died. I remembered Marshall. 'Epitaph,' he said. 'Is it a) an animal that lives in the body of another animal, especially as a parasite; b) a form of lyric poem written in couplets, in which a long line is followed by a shorter one; or c) a phrase or form of words written in memory of a person who has died, especially as an inscription on a tombstone.'

Call My Bluff: Marshall would open the dictionary at random. Scan the page for a good word and then choose three definitions, one of which would be the right one.

'Polymath: is it . . .

'a) A spiritless coward.
'b) An expression of more than two algebraic terms.
'c) A person of much or varied learning.

'Now guess . . .'

That's how I learnt such words as exanimate, gingivitis, hotchpotch and whiffle. 'Limpid' means clear, transparent or easily comprehended. 'Immure' means to shut oneself away. 'Castrate' upset me. 'Castrato' upset me more – *why would someone do that to a child?* As did 'scatology'. I remember Marshall laughing. 'You know, boy, some animals *eat* their shit, not just play with it.' And yes, when I shat later that day I had a proper look at the solid brown lump that hit the bottom of the bagged bucket with a 'foomp'. *Sick,* I thought. And then realised there were probably people who had morbid fascinations with that too. Puke. And piss. And other bodily fluids. What's worse, I thought, there are words to describe those people. And then I wondered that perhaps if the words didn't exist, the people wouldn't exist either. Or at least, I wouldn't be aware of them. They wouldn't exist to me.

I read some epitaphs while Duckman led me in between the graves. *Asleep in Jesus. Not my will, but thine be done. Gone but not forgotten.* And then a small grave, a tiny white block of stone with an angel resting on top, playing a harp. *God's garden has need for little flowers,* it said. The angel had a tear running down her cheek.

Duckman had stopped in front of a polished black marble tombstone, identical to many of the others surrounding it. *In loving memory,* it said. *Catherine Kerr (3 April 1955 – 1 September 1993).* But she wasn't the only name on there. Underneath hers another was inscribed: *Mary Abigail Kerr (15 March 1992).*

'Ask me,' he said.

'Who is it?'

'Ma sister.' Duckman didn't look at me. 'Ma mum was diagnosed with ovarian cancer two years ago. She was pregnant. Doctors had t' cut Abby oot a month premature so they could start chemotherapy. Abby died. Respiratory distress syndrome.' The words sounded strange coming from Duckman. They seemed too serious, too clinical. Rehearsed. I imagined them rolling on a continuous loop inside Duckman's head. I imagined him closing his eyes at night trying to sleep, counting the syllables instead of sheep. Respiratory distress syndrome. Chemotherapy.

'Nobody said,' I told him.

'Nobody does.' He looked at me. 'It's easier t' forget,

don't ye think? T' pretend it didn't happen. If it's no spoken aboot, it's no there. But it did happen. She was there.' He looked back at the names on the gravestone, 'She did exist.' And then feeling as though maybe he'd taken off one too many layers of skin, he grinned at me and nodded towards the grave. 'Room fer one more, ah reckon. What do you say, Nevis?'

'What do you . . .' and I watched him take two fingers and cock them to his head.

'Bang,' he said.

'But he never does it.'

'Maybe he will.'

I looked at the bottom of the tombstone at the inscription. *Earth has no sorrow that heaven cannot heal*.

'What are you going to do?' I asked him and with that he hacked his saliva to the back of his throat and spat. The yellow phlegm flew through the air, hit the stone and dribbled over Catherine Kerr's name. He turned on me with his index finger pointing and poked me in the chest. 'Your life,' he said, 'has been nothin' but freedom. An' ah want a piece o' that.' He recoiled his hand when he saw me flinch. He stepped back, quietly pulling his jumper sleeve over his hand and wiped away the spit on the gravestone. 'Come on,' he said and with eyes lowered to the ground he started to walk again, leading me back towards the gate and the car park.

32

I looked at the telephone, a grubby white, its curly cable tangled and drooping over the edge of the kitchen cabinet. In my hand I held the small card Galbraith had given me, I flipped it over and looked at the numbers scrawled in black ink on the back. Underneath it said, *Mr Galbraith. Homework assignment.* I looked back at the phone. I knew what to do. Sort of. I'd seen people in telephone boxes before. They pick up the receiver and hold it to their ear, they press in a number, they wait and then they start speaking, presumably when the person on the other end picks up. And I knew how a telephone worked – sound waves creating electrical currents and then back into sound waves. I lifted the receiver a couple of inches and heard the buzzing instantly, a continuous humming noise. I held it at arm's length. Maybe it was broken? I slowly moved my ear towards the receiver until I was bending low over the unit. Three high whistling notes sounded, going up in scale, and then a voice, a woman's voice. She said,

'Please replace the handset and try again.' I slammed the phone down and stared at it. I hadn't even dialled a number. I picked up again and listened to the humming, waited for the three notes to come – and they did, followed by the woman telling me to hang up and try again. So maybe that was supposed to happen, I had to dial a number before the three notes sounded. There was a time limit. The number pad was underneath the receiver. I placed the card on a pile of papers on the cabinet, face-up so I could read it, and picked up the phone for a third time. I pressed in the numbers. I waited. There was a ringing, a brrrrp brrrrp. It was connecting me, I thought. I was doing it right. And then it stopped.

'Hello?' It was Mr Galbraith. His voice sounded cracked, as though he'd just woken up from a deep sleep. He cleared his throat. 'Hello?' he said again.

'My homework assignment.'

There was a pause. 'Nevis?'

'Yes.'

'What time is it?'

It was amazing, I thought. He sounded as clear as when we were in the same room together. 'Mr Galbraith, my homework assignment.'

'Dear God, it's three thirty in the morning.'

'I've chosen my topic.'

'Right . . . oh right.'

'Memory,' I said.

'Memory?'

'Yes,' and then I thought for a moment. 'Please,' I added for politeness. And then hung up the phone.

33

He used words such as 'encoding', 'storage' and 'retrieval'. 'Neuron networks' and 'synapse molecules'. You're a clever boy, he said. Stop me if you don't understand. 'Cortex', 'lobes', 'limbic system'. He told me about the sensory information store: how information flows from everything we see, hear, smell, touch and taste into our brain. A lot of this sensory information is ignored, he said. If it wasn't, our brain would become overwhelmed and shut down. He told me about short- and long-term memory. He showed me labelled diagrams. 'Hippocampus.' I liked that word. From the diagram I could tell it was a large lump near the bottom of our brain. 'This is where we consolidate new memories,' he said. He talked for forty-five minutes, showing me colourful diagrams and teaching me words until at last he stopped and smiled. 'Any questions?' I looked at my hands, spread my fingers wide and then closed them again.

'Can you teach me how not to forget?' I asked.

Mr Galbraith sighed and sat back down in his leather armchair. 'Well,' he said, 'do you remember what I told you about long-term memory?'

'I mean the past,' I added. Mr Galbraith raised his eyebrows. 'I want to remember the past *exactly* how it happened.'

At the end of the lesson Mr Galbraith led me to the door with his hands on my shoulders, just like he had at the end of our first meeting.

'Your next homework assignment,' he said as I opened the door, 'is another question, although perhaps you already know the answer to this one. What do you want to be when you grow up?'

I looked at him blankly.

'Think about it,' he said. 'And call me with your ideas. Although, maybe not at three thirty in the morning, eh? Social etiquette. You shouldn't call after nine at night and never before nine in the morning. Remember the nines,' he winked at me.

I hovered at the bottom of the step for a moment, glanced over my shoulder. Marshall was standing by the open door of the Land Rover. Nigel Kerr at the wheel, engine still running, Elspeth's round face peering out at me from the passenger window. Smiling. Waving. My father beckoned me towards him. I turned back to Mr Galbraith who had stopped smiling.

'Nevis?'

I stared at the white socks on the old man's feet.

'What's wrong?' Mr Galbraith asked.

I kept my head down, my eyes on the step. 'I read your notes on Monday,' I said. My confession was met with a long uncomfortable silence. I couldn't bring myself to look up into Galbraith's face. I imagined it working through emotions – shock, disappointment, anger. 'You told me not to. But I did,' I said softly – and then to myself I thought, I should apologise. But I didn't. I remained quiet and staring at the old man's feet on his welcome mat.

'Nevis.' Galbraith's voice was calm when eventually he spoke. 'Nevis, if only you'd stop staring at my feet and look at my face, you'd see I was smiling.' And indeed he was. When I looked up he was smiling warmly down at me. 'Hey diddle diddle,' he said and chuckled. 'You must have thought I was a madman.' He didn't sound angry in the slightest.

'I'm not in trouble?'

'Not at all. Why would you be? Such a curious young boy, I expected you to read them.'

'You did?'

'Yes.'

'I wanted to tell the truth,' I said.

'Ahh,' he nodded and wagged his finger in the air. 'The truth. The truth is important to you, isn't it, Nevis?'

I glanced back at my father again who was standing with his hands on his hips. He was frowning. He wanted to know what I was saying, I could tell. Or maybe he just wanted me to hurry. I lowered my voice.

'I write lists,' I said.

'Lists?' Galbraith lowered his voice too, so we were both speaking close to whispers.

'About me. The past. So I won't forget.'

'I see.'

'That's what I want to do,' I said.

'What do you mean?'

'My homework assignment,' I answered. 'You asked me what I wanted . . .'

'You want to write?'

I nodded. 'And not forget.'

I told him not to tell Marshall and he promised. 'Maybe you could bring your lists to our next meeting?' he said. I had to go. Marshall had moved from the Land Rover to the front gate and was calling my name. 'Nevis, I'm late for work.' So I nodded a goodbye to Mr Galbraith and moved off down the drive.

'How did it go?' Marshall asked when we were both sitting in the Land Rover. I could smell Elspeth's over-powering sweet perfume, her hair products and make-up mixed with a base scent of farm and mud. I could pick out each smell individually and label it. Information drawn into the sensory store, I thought, paid attention to and passed into short-term memory where it's labelled from data stored in long-term. I've experienced these smells before. I remember them. But what I'll forget is that I smelled them here and now. I'll forget this moment like I've forgotten so many moments.

'Nevis?' My father was wearing black trousers and a freshly pressed black shirt I'd never seen before with *Crofter's Inn* sewn onto its breast pocket.

'A new shirt,' I said.

'I asked you a question.' My father looked stern, his forehead furrowed. I studied his eyes, large pupils. I could see dark flecks in the brown of his iris and thin red threads in the whites of his eyes. 'When someone asks you a question, Nevis, you should respond.' I thought about this and remembered the hours sitting in silence in the van while my father was bent over his papers writing, or bent over the steering wheel driving. The times I broke the silence with a question and my father would not even turn his head. An eye for an eye, I thought. Forgive and forget. Love thy neighbour. Hypocrisy. My life in the van was the Old Testament, my life on the farm the New.

'It was fine,' I said and I watched the muscles in my father's face and shoulders relax.

'What did you do?'

'Tests,' I told him. In the first hour Galbraith had sat me at his desk overlooking the garden and the gnomes. He handed me five sheets of paper with printed questions and spaces for answers. 'Answer as many as you can,' he said. 'If you get stuck move onto the next question. Do you understand, Nevis?' I nodded. The questions had been divided into groups and each group had a heading: Maths, Science, Geography, History, Modern Studies . . . Ten questions to each group, I could only ever answer the first three or four.

'Did you pass?' asked Marshall.

'I don't know,' I said.

'Well how many did you get right?'

'I don't know.'

'Didn't you ask?'

I was starting to dislike the new rule of having to answer every question. 'No,' I said.

Elspeth had started humming. I noticed she was wearing more make-up than usual. Her lips were painted a reddish-brown, her cheeks brushed with powder and her eyes darkened. Her hair was scooped up into an elaborate style on her head and held together with pins, not the usual tight bun. It flicked out in different directions. She was wearing a silver necklace and placed her hand over it while she hummed. I noticed her nails were not chipped, but painted perfectly a reddish-brown the same as her lipstick. A silver bracelet, similar in style to her necklace, slipped down her arm a little. Her top was glittery, low cut. I could see her cleavage. On her lap she held a black handbag with sequins.

We were in the town square. Nigel Kerr indicated and pulled up onto the pavement near a tall stone obelisk with large unpolished copper plates on its base. From where I sat I could see a list of names on one side of the copper and on the other an image of a soldier running with a rifle. Question: what date did World War II begin and when did it end? I could answer that one. 1st September 1939 to 2nd September 1945. Question: why had a Cold War developed by 1949? I wrote 'because of World War II'. Question: why was Israel able to defeat the Arab states in the Six-Day War of 1967? History wasn't my strong point, I decided.

Ailsa appeared from behind the obelisk, waving to a group of girls clustered around a bench. She stepped up into the Land Rover.

'Hi, Nevis,' she said. 'Hi, Marshall. Hi, Mum. Hi, Uncle Nigel. Hi, everyone.' She pulled the door shut. 'You look nice, Mum,' she said. Elspeth smiled and reached back to squeeze Ailsa's knee while Ailsa leaned over to me and whispered, 'She must be on the pull.' The squeeze turned into a slap.

'I heard that young lady,' Elspeth said. We drove on. Elspeth told us that there was a plate of food each waiting for us in the oven. 'There's one fer you too,

Nigel,' she said. 'So ye dinnae feel left oot.' Ailsa once again tried to sneak her fingers against mine. I jammed my hands in between my legs. 'And there's one fer Colin too, although I havnae seen him since Tuesday.'

'Oh!' piped up Ailsa. 'Sally Jordan said she saw him in Inverness.'

'What's he doin' there?'

'Dunno,' she said. 'Havin' a fag probably,' and she giggled into her hand.

'Ailsa, be sensible, please. Who's he stayin' with?'

'Who cares?'

'Ailsa!'

She shrugged. And then said, 'Sorry, Uncle Nigel.'

We'd pulled in again, this time at the bottom of the High Street outside an open door with a black sign above it, *Crofter's Inn*. It had the same curly writing as on Marshall's breast pocket. Both Elspeth and Marshall moved to get out. When I clicked open my seatbelt to follow my father he turned to me. 'You're going back with Nigel and Ailsa,' he said. I just looked at him. 'Your dinner's in the oven.'

'Can't I come with you?'

'No, Nevis,' and he closed the door. I stared after him. As Nigel Kerr began to drive I saw my father reach behind Elspeth and press his hand into the small of her back as though guiding her through the door of the pub.

I felt sick.

'Nevis?' Ailsa was whispering into my ear. I felt her palm and papery skin rest over my hand. 'Nevis?' I did not tell her to leave me alone. Instead I picked her hand up in mine and watched a warm smile snake across her vicious thin lips. 'Nevis, I just wanted to say . . .' and I squeezed her fingers so tightly together she let out a yell and whipped her hand free from mine to shake into the air. 'Bully!' she said with such distaste, the words spat from her mouth like venom. I shuffled across to where my father had just sat and tried to ignore the intensity of Ailsa's glare and her vigorous massaging of fingers. Leave me alone, I thought. That's all I wanted. Why couldn't she leave me alone? And why couldn't her nasty fat mother leave Marshall alone? It was quite simple. We didn't need them. We didn't want them. Soon we'll have moved away from the farm, on to the next town – and then, I thought, *then* I'll only be too happy to hear Marshall's words, 'It's in the past now, Nevis. Forget about it.' I tried to console myself.

And yet throughout the entire ride back my head was filled with the vision of my father's arm reaching around Elspeth, guiding her through the doorway of the pub.

34

I could only just pick out the black silhouette of the caravan in the dark. I wondered if Marshall had finished work. I wasn't sure what time it was or how long I'd been asleep, but it was dark. Perhaps it wasn't so late. Night arrives earlier in the winter – and it felt like winter now. From behind the single sheet of glass I could feel the hard frost creeping out and settling its white crystals on the ground.

I imagined curling up close beside Marshall like we used to in the van, his arms wrapped around me. We had blankets – so many blankets – hats, gloves and our sleeping bags. I'm sure they must have been good quality because I never felt cold. But of course, it *was* cold. It was freezing. We'd wake in the morning with the hair and snot in our nostrils frozen together. There'd be ice on the inside of the windows. The sofa cushions were stiff where the condensation and damp had frosted up. We would sigh and see our breath blow white into the air. But it wasn't often we stayed in Scotland after autumn ended. We'd make our way south, like migrating birds, seeking warmer climates. But winter is cold wherever you are in Britain. And so be it, wherever we travelled we would still sleep close together, arms wrapped around each other, for body warmth.

I was hungry. I didn't realise this until I turned away from the cold window and moved back into the middle of the bedroom. I hadn't eaten Elspeth's food. After the incident in the car, witnessing my father hold Elspeth in that way and then Ailsa pestering me, I wasn't in the mood to eat. 'Feed it to the dogs,' was what I told Ailsa to do when she got my plate out from the oven and offered it to me. Yes, she offered it to me, even after our argument. What's more, she asked if I wanted it to be heated. She'd already explained while getting out of the Land Rover that she'd decided to forgive me. Usually, she said, when a boy did something nasty like that it was because they fancied her. Boys were always pinching her at school and chasing her about the field at break time. 'They're babyish like that,' she said. 'Girls mature faster than boys. I left that kind o' rubbish behind in primary school.' She said it pointedly, staring at me with lips pinched. 'Perhaps ye should consider growin' up a bit, Nevis. Actin' yer age an' not yer shoe size.' We were in the kitchen by this point; Nigel Kerr was still outside chaining the dogs to their kennels. Ailsa had fished two plates of food out from the oven. Burger and chips.

'Shall I heat one up for ye, Nevis? Would ye like some beans? Will ye sit wi' me like a civilised human being and eat dinner?' She was trying to act like Elspeth. Her facial expressions and body movements were in adult emulation and not her usual churlish thirteen-year-old self. I did not answer her question outright, but did so in my own manner. I started to walk off down the hallway.

'Nevis!'

'Feed it to the dogs,' I said and left her in the kitchen alone.

But now I was hungry. I picked up my pen and paper, moved the chair blocking the door and crept off down the hallway, making sure I was on tiptoes outside Ailsa's bedroom door.

My dinner was still in the oven. I picked the cold burger from the plate and took a bite, feeling pleased that Ailsa hadn't actually fed it to the dogs. I looked down at the empty sheet of lined paper on the table in front of me. Sat down. Waggled my pen in between thumb and forefinger and took another bite from my burger. Once upon a time – I wrote. Now there's a classic beginning. I should have started my lists and records like that, like the beginning of a fairytale. Once upon a time there was a young boy who lived in a van with his mad writer father.

. . . And the mad father would write day in and day out, chewing on the end of his pencil for inspiration, twisting his long beard around forefinger as though twisting out words, squeezing every last drop from himself. For the greatest stories, the father always said to his son, came from inside a man, they had to be sweated out.

'Who am I?'

'If you're a politician I'm not playing.'

'I'm not a politician.'

'A monarch?'

'No.'

'A singer?'

'No.'

'A writer?'

'Of sorts.'

'I'm not going to get it, am I? You might as well tell me.'

'I'm a Russian structuralist scholar,' he had said with a broad smile. 'Vladimir Propp.' And he taught me about the man who analysed folk and fairytales and came up with thirty-one building blocks that gave the narratives their structure.

I am the hero of this fairytale, I thought. Elspeth and Ailsa the villains. Duckman the aid. And the reward at the end of it all? What the hero struggles and strives for throughout?

* * *

. . . The young boy admired his father with a passion, loved him beyond words, was loyal to the point of obsession. When his father spoke the boy listened with growing ears; when he slept he watched over him like a guard dog, unblinking saucers for eyes. The boy was young, but he knew and understood with every inch of his self that he loved and would forever love this man, his father. And he had made a vow – when old enough to understand the betrayal of a woman his father had once loved, the boy's mother – he had spoken a secret onto his lips, whispering one night while his father slept. 'I shall never stray from your side. I shall never leave you like she.' Later, when the boy was older still, he sealed this vow with a kiss.

Interdiction: You must never do that again, boy. Do you hear me? Do you understand?

. . . And the fire boomed about the van. The flames licked at its tyres and smoke billowed out and up and up into the sky. For many nights the boy's dreams were filled with that smoke and echoes of his father's warning. But when the black clouds cleared, the boy looked about him and saw that there was nothing left but the vow, his love. 'I shall never leave you,' he whispered. And from then his dreams were filled with the kiss, every night in his sleep they pressed lips.

*   *   *

'What are ye writin', Nevis?'

I jumped. It was Ailsa leaning against the open door of the kitchen, arms crossed and staring in at me. I covered my paper instinctively with one hand and tried to slow my heart. I had been so completely immersed in my writing I hadn't heard her sneak up on me.

'You look strange,' she said. 'When ye were writin' you looked . . .' she paused dramatically, '. . . possessed.'

I could get up, I thought. I could push past her and go upstairs. Lock myself in the bathroom. Barricade myself in the bedroom. Oh, you're one of the villains all right, I thought glancing across at Ailsa who was still leaning with arms folded in the doorway. I'm trapped here. I can't get out. Even if I escaped this room I'd have to go and lock myself in another. And what good would that do? She'd be there on the other side of the door, taunting me.

'Are you ok, Nevis?' She had stopped leaning now and unfolded her arms, her thin face almost concerned. 'Ye look as though ye might be sick.' She moved quickly then, into the kitchen, across to the sink, and poured out a glass of water. She sat down at the table opposite and pushed the offering across to me.

I *was* thirsty, I thought. I felt light-headed. I noticed when I went to pick up the glass that my hands were shaking.

'Your hands are shaking,' Ailsa said. 'Oh, and speaking of hands, mine is fine. Thanks for asking.'

I drank the water, the whole glass, starting with small gulps and then draining the rest with one swig. Ailsa raised her eyebrows.

'You want some more?'

I shook my head and turned my face away to close my eyes.

'Nevis,' she said. She started to reach across to my hand still covering the notepad and then thought better of it. I shot her a look – a very obvious 'if-you-touch-me-you-will-regret-it' look.

'I don't like being disturbed when I'm writing,' I told her and heard my father's echo.

'Sorry,' she replied softly. And for a split second, with her head lowered and her hands tucked together on top of the table, I felt like returning the apology. But I didn't.

There was something strange about Ailsa I noticed then, something that didn't seem to fit my picture of her. I remembered how when we'd first met she'd interrogated me about the van, in particular about personal hygiene. I remember her shrill voice stating with near disgust that she could never live without a bath. 'I have to wash and straighten my hair every day you know,' she'd said. And I remembered the day she accosted me by the hay bales in the front field, how she'd inspected her nails and tutted at the filth underneath them. I remembered how her eyelashes had stuck together with black mascara. 'Look at me, Nevis, why don't you look at me?'

And now here, sitting before me was the girl who took such pride in her appearance, yet her hair fell in kinks, unbrushed, not straightened, her face was free from make-up and her nails, which I could see had been bitten, had grime underneath them and her fingers were grubby where she'd been playing outside.

'I wish we could be friends,' she added, even more quietly than before.

This could be the 'trickery' in my fairytale, I thought. Ailsa was disguising herself, speaking softly while she cast her spell. Things are not always as they seem. I thought of Elspeth and the way she'd been dressed so differently. Her sweet perfume and pretty jewellery, her top cut low. She was trying to trap my father. She was trying to steal him away from me. And in my head the image of his arm around her, his hand pressing gently into the small of her back.

I quickly drew my notepad close to my chest and stood up. Ailsa looked at me.

'Nevis . . .'

'You can't fool me,' I said to her. And then left.

35

I must've fallen asleep. I woke on the double bed early, in the midst of the sunrise, and was annoyed. After leaving Ailsa the night before I'd meant to stay awake. I wanted to see my father when he returned from work. I wanted to warn him. But I must have fallen asleep, pen still in hand.

My dreams had been filled with my fairytale. Duckman, the farmhand, had appeared and given me a magical charm, the frog key-ring. He explained how he'd saved it from the van and how at first it had burned him with the 'wrath' of my father's fire. 'But now it holds only the fire's strength,' the farmhand had said. 'I think it will bring you great luck.' And I dreamt the frog key-ring had glowed in my palm.

Now I sat at the bedroom window and played with the little green legs and arms. This key-ring that had never meant much to me in the van – stashed away in the glove compartment, hardly ever thought about – now meant everything.

I looked out at the yard and tool shed, which seemed even more deserted with Duckman no longer climbing in and out of its window. He'd gone, just like he promised he would.

'You should come wi' me,' he'd said when we'd left the graveyard. 'Ah know someone who could get ye a job.'

'A job?'

'Aye, Nevis, surely ye know what a job is. It gets ye money.'

I looked at him blankly.

'Ye know,' he prompted, 'the papery stuff wi' faces an' numbers on it?'

'I know what money is,' I said.

'Thank fuck fer that.'

We were driving back to the farmhouse. I remember I started looking through the tapes in the glove compartment. There were twelve in total. I counted them. Duckman told me I could put one on.

'Have you got *Now 13*?'

He glanced across at me. 'No,' he said, flicking the end of his cigarette out the window. 'Were you even born when *Now 13* came out?'

'I was seven. I got it for my birthday.'

'Congratulations,' he said.

'I never listened to it.'

'How come?'

'Stereo broke.'

'Shit, man.' He sniffed. 'Life's a bitch.'

When Duckman pulled up next to Nigel Kerr's Land Rover he didn't switch off the engine, he kept it running. 'You're not coming in?' I asked him.

'No,' he said, 'ah'm goin', Nevis. Like ah told ye.' And then he reached behind my seat into the back of the car. 'Ah don't wear it anymore, so you have it.' And he handed me a black cap, its peak curved. 'Yer first fuckin' present given t' ye from someone *other* than Marshall. How does it feel?'

I gave a small smile. 'Thank you,' I said.

'Jus' summit to remember me by,' he shrugged. 'Now get oot ma car.'

I got out and stood watching as Duckman speed-reversed round so he was facing back down the track, and with one final nod, he left.

The cap suited me, I thought. I'd taken it to the bathroom and studied myself wearing it in the mirror. It fitted perfectly. I tucked my long hair behind my ears, studied the spot on my chin, the hair above my lip. 'Bum fluff,' Duckman called it. He told me I should shave.

'But I want to grow a beard,' I'd said.

'Then shave. The hair grows back thicker.'

Was that true?

I didn't tell Marshall about the cap from Duckman at first. I kept it under my pillow. It wasn't until that morning, standing by the window, staring out at the empty space where Duckman's car would normally have been parked, I decided that I should wear it. I suppose at the back of my mind I still had fairytales forming. The cap was like the second magical item the hero receives to aid him on his quest.

The dogs were lying in their kennels. Murdo awake and sniffing deep in amongst the straw. Red lying with head between paws. The mud in the yard after the night's cold air was solid, the brown had its sprinkling of frost. Where there had been muddy puddles a thin skin of ice covered them.

I studied the caravan in the field beyond the tool shed. I wondered whether I should go to him now. Wake him. I touched my cap and clutched the little frog key-ring in my hand as though I really was drawing strength from it. And as I clutched harder I imagined kissing my father – why not? In my dream that's what had woken me. That's how the fairytale ended. But in my dream my father had kissed back – together we'd broken the woman's spell. And while we kissed, the farmhouse had started to crumble around us, had started to crack and break like glass, shatter, smash; and the evil witch Elspeth screamed. We kissed all the more and the heat of our passion lifted us off the floor and we held each other as we hovered and spun, sparks flying. Elspeth's face began to melt, Ailsa began to wail and still we kissed and spun until fire flashed around us, tearing down the remains of the house, until there was nothing left. And still we kissed and held each other, until the fires cooled and the red embers turned to ash.

It begins with a kiss, I thought. And it ends with a kiss. That's how it should be. The hero wins his reward. They live happily ever after.

And I would have continued with my daydream if it hadn't been for the almighty shot that rang out and echoed from the woods, the treetops exploding with their crows.

'He's done it . . .' My hands were pressed flat against the windowpane as I stared. 'But he never does it . . .' I tried to calm myself. I felt torn as to whether I should run to him or stay where I was. What if he'd shot himself? His slumped body on the ground and the back of his head blown free. I felt sick. And then what if he hadn't? I could hardly run there and find him sobbing like he had been that morning. Either way it was better to stay. And on deciding this, enough time had passed and I already saw him at the fence on the outskirts of the wood, gun broken over his arm. I sighed with relief. He hadn't done it . . . he never does it. I watched him pause as he climbed over the stile and at first I thought he'd seen me standing at the bedroom window. But something else had caught his eye and made him stop. The bang of the caravan door as it opened and slammed shut; Elspeth, still in her pretty clothes of the night before, picking her way through the field and across the frozen yard towards the farmhouse. My father's face appearing at the window, his fingers pressed into the pane as he gazed after her, smiling.

36

SCENE: *The stage is split in two by a panel with a door in the middle. The left half of the stage is set up like a hallway, with a backdrop of old wallpaper and a painting of two deer running through a forest. A lamp on a wooden fold-down table is throwing a ghostly light onto the girl's face, who is sitting leaning against the door.*

On the other side of the panel, the door is blocked by a chair wedged underneath the doorknob. The stage is set out like a bedroom, double bed in one corner and a dresser with lots of colourful glass bottles and perfumes next to it. A boy sits at the window, straddling one leg in, one leg out over the sill. He is writing in a notebook, occasionally glancing out at the night sky and the moon. He is ignoring the girl who sits at the other side of the door talking at him.

GIRL: Ok, Nevis, I know yer in there and I know yer listenin' t' me so I'm just goin' t' speak. Ok? *(pause)* Nevis . . . ? *(pause. The girl reaches for the handle*

257

behind her and rattles it gently to make sure it's still locked before resuming her previous sitting position with a sigh) The thing is, Nevis, I want t' *help* you. I think you really need help. And well . . . now Duckman isn't here anymore ye haven't got any friends either, which can't be very nice. Can it? *(pause)* Nevis . . . ? *(pause. The girl presses her ear against the door)* What are ye doin' in there anyway? Are ye playin' with yerself? Ye know, my mate Sally reckons you get hairy palms if ye do that. And she says if boys do it too much their willies fall off. Did ye know that, Nevis? *(she giggles into her hand)* Nevis? *(she tries the handle again a little more irritably)* I know yer in there, Nevis! There's no point pretendin' yer not. *(she sighs and crosses her arms in a huff)* Ye know what *your* problem is, don't you? Yer scared of girls, probably because yev only ever lived with yer father in that stinkin' horrible van. That's right, isn't it? Yer scared o' me. An' yer scared o' ma mum. Yer scared of all girls. That's what my mate Sally says anyway. And she's older than me. She knows about Freud an' sex and she's got a boyfriend an' everythin'. She's smart and she says yer problems stem back t' yer childhood. *(pause. Ailsa rattles on the door once more)* Oh pleeeese, Nevis. Pleeease will ye talk t' me?

37

I was sitting with my legs straddling the windowsill, looking down into the yard, too far to jump, but there was a water pipe scaling the full length of the house. It seemed secure enough, bolted into the granite wall at regular intervals. I shook it and it didn't wobble.

'Nevis? I know yer in there, Nevis.'

Marshall was at work. Elspeth had gone with him. After witnessing her leaving the caravan that morning and my father staring after her with that silly smile spread across his face I was thrown into a fit of panic. It was like my fairytale was coming true. Elspeth really was casting some sort of horrible spell over Marshall and I was losing him. I felt him slipping away.

'Marshall.' I'd decided to confront him that after-noon. 'Marshall, can I talk to you?'

'What's the matter, Nevis?'

'I'm worried . . . about . . .' but the words wouldn't come out. What was I going to say? That Elspeth was some sort of witch and she was trying to steal him away from me? I knew it was ridiculous. I knew Elspeth wasn't *really* a witch. But there was something strange about her. She did have some sort of hold over my father.

'Is there something wrong, Nevis?'

'Nothing,' I said. 'It doesn't matter.'

I'd write him a letter. That's what I decided. And I'd already composed several by the time he went to work, but I'd torn them all out of my notepad and screwed them up into balls. *The truth*, I kept telling myself, *I must write the truth*. And I would spill my heart out onto the paper. *Marshall, I love you.*

> *. . . I love you, I love you, I love you.*
>
> *And it's ok. We shouldn't be ashamed. You can't help who you fall in love with. Remember? You said that to me. Do you remember?*

And then I'd rip it out the pad and screw it up.

> *Marshall, we have to leave. The farm is not good for us. She's trying to take you away from me. She's trying to tear us apart. Can't you see? Can't you feel it? You're so distant now. We hardly ever speak. I miss you, Marshall. I love you.*

'Nevis?' Ailsa just wouldn't leave me alone. I stared again at the pipe that led down to the yard. I could climb down it, I thought. I used to be good at climbing trees, even if there were no easy foot- and handholds, I could shimmy up skinny trunks or bear-hug my way up the thicker ones, squeezing my thigh muscles against the wood, shifting my hands up, arms tightening their hold. I could move up a tree like a caterpillar. I would climb with a book in my back pocket or a plastic bag tied to my belt if I wanted to carry up a bigger hardback. And then I would find a good nesting place, safe and secure, sit in amongst the branches and read.

'Nevvvis?'

I tore out some paper from my notepad, folded it in half and put it into my back pocket with a pen. I shuffled forward on the windowsill and stood up, one foot in, one foot out. I took hold of the pipe with my right hand and reached my right foot over so it was resting on a metal bracket. With my boots by the back door I would have to climb down in my socks. The wall felt damp from the day's rain. My heart started to thump, thump, thump. If I waited I wouldn't do it, I would just grow more and more scared. So I took a deep breath and put weight onto the bracket, gripping it with my toes, pressing my knee into the wall. Murdo started barking.

'Nevis?'

I slid out my other leg and then took hold of the pipe with both hands. I moved down slowly, almost sliding, tightly hugging the pipe in places while my knees and toes scraped against the wall. My heart still thump thumped sickeningly all the way, until it was safe enough to drop.

The mud in the yard was thick and wet; my feet disappeared into the sludge when I touched down and splashed up the back of my jeans. The stickiness was the only thing that stopped me from falling over. The yard light came on. Murdo still barked and wagged his tail. 'Shhh, Murdo!' I picked my way towards the kennels, stopping to pat both dogs on the head. 'Shhh! Quiet.' I had to hurry. I opened the back door, grabbed my boots and jacket and quickly splashed my way across the yard and over the gate into the field.

I had no real thought about going to the caravan other than that it would get me away from Ailsa. I could sit at the fold-away table for a while and work on the letter. I could leave it for him on his pillow. The image of Marshall with his arms around Elspeth floated back into my head. It had been floating in and out of my head all day, that and her leaving the caravan with my father's eyes and stupid grin following after her. I shook my head as though like an etch-a-sketch it would clear.

The caravan was messy. The table was folded down into a double bed. The covers heaped and ruffled as though Marshall had just thrown them back to get up and then left them like that. There were some half-eaten noodles on the side, fork still sticking out of the plastic pot. I enjoyed the mess of the bed and the smell of the cold noodles. It reminded me of the van.

My thoughts wandered back to Galbraith in his study,

talking about Proust and petites madeleines and tea. How our sensory experiences can later trigger memories. I let myself lie down and press my nose into the blankets, breathing in the smell of my father. I noticed I could only sniff one spot a couple of times before losing the scent. Every so often I lifted my head, breathed in the cool air and then returned my nose to the blankets. I moved onto the pillow, digging my hands underneath and holding my face into the soft cushion. That's when I found his wallet. My hand touched the soft leather. I took hold of it, pulled it out and stared at it blankly for a moment, just like when Duckman gave me the frog key-ring. Then I let out a laugh and pressed it to my nose, the smell of well-worn leather. So he did keep something from the van. He kept his wallet. I opened it.

There were three plastic cards and a five-pound note inside. Behind the cards there was a flat pocket. I jammed in my fingers and pulled out the small collection of papers. A few old receipts and a square card with a phone number on it: *Hamish Galbraith*, it said. It was while I was putting back everything I'd taken out I saw the cut in the lining.

A car pulled up into the yard. I heard my father get out and mumble something and I heard a man's voice I didn't recognise reply. Elspeth giggled. The car drove off. The gate to the field opened and then closed. Marshall and Elspeth walked through the grass, talking in lowered tones as they approached the caravan. I didn't move. Not even when Marshall had his foot on the step, his hand pushing open the door. I couldn't move.

'Nevis.'

Elspeth was right behind him. 'Oh dear, what's wrong?'

'Nevis, what's happened?' He moved towards me. 'Why aren't you wearing any shoes?' And then he stopped.

I couldn't take my eyes off her. Between thumb and forefinger I held the small square photograph of a woman. My chin, my eyes, long dark hair like mine. And on the back, written in pencil, my father's handwriting: Annie, I miss you. I love you. Come back.

38

'Have you got any photos, Mr Galbraith?'

'Do you mean family photos?'

'Yes.'

It was a Monday. The third hour of my third meeting with Galbraith. He was sitting in his armchair when I asked him about photos. He pointed to the bookcase to the right of the electric fire. 'Bottom shelf,' he said. 'That big black book on the end.'

I made a move to get it.

'I don't suppose you've remembered some of your lists?' Galbraith asked.

'Yes,' I said and I went to get the selection from my jacket in the hallway. I couldn't bring all of them. I hadn't wanted my father to see me taking all the paper and pads with me to my lesson – there were too many for just one homework assignment – so I'd picked out forty pages or so, curved them in half lengthways and tied them together with an elastic band so it could fit into my inside jacket pocket. At least if Marshall saw it I could tell him it was an essay and just hope he didn't ask to read it.

Galbraith rolled off the elastic band and rested the papers on his lap. 'Are you happy to look through those photos while I read? Or . . .' He didn't finish his sentence as I already had his photo album in my arms. I returned to my chair and sat down.

His wife's name was Grace. His sons' names were Calum and Thomas. I know because underneath the photographs there were labels. Grace and baby Calum at Fin's wedding, 1943. Calum and Thomas, cattle show, 1961. I looked at every photograph, studying each picture in detail – slowly working through the years. Sepia, black and white to colour. Each one seemed to have been placed carefully in chronological order. Galbraith, Grace, Calum and Thomas ageing with every turn of the page.

'You were alive in World War Two,' I said. I'd been through the album once and had gone back to the beginning. A young Galbraith in uniform standing to attention outside a front door.

Galbraith looked up from my lists. 'Yes,' he said.

'What did you do?'

'I was in the Royal Observer Corps. I worked nights at observation posts looking out for enemy aircraft.' He sat back in his armchair. 'You want to know some things about it?'

266

'Did you have to fight?'

'We were all fighting . . . in our own way.'

'But did you kill anyone?'

'No.'

I tried to imagine a young Galbraith at night, radio in hand, staring up at the sky streaked with spotlights, listening for the sound of airplane engines. 'I thought everyone had to fight,' I said. 'If you were healthy.'

'Not if you had other skills. Farming, for example. And shipbuilding. I worked at Hall Russell's shipyard in Aberdeen. Have you heard of it?'

'No.'

'It was bombed on the 12th of July 1940. I was only saved because my good friend Fin – you may have noticed some photos of him in there – rugby tackled me into the water.' Galbraith paused for a moment and I watched him silently recollect this memory. 'You never know how you are going to react in an emergency until you're faced with it,' he said. 'I saw those explosives drop from the planes and I stood paralysed to the spot, transfixed.'

I stared down at the album in my lap, at the pictures from Fin's wedding in 1943. There was a photo of just Fin and Galbraith, standing side-by-side, smart in their kilts and waistcoats and oil-slicked hair. I studied this man who saved a life. He was shorter than Galbraith and not as thickly built. He smiled perkily at the camera while Galbraith merely turned up the corners of his mouth. The other three wedding photos were the same: everyone beaming, but Galbraith straight-faced or forcing a smile.

'You didn't really want to smile in these pictures,' I said.

Galbraith eyed me quietly. 'You are very astute,' he said.

I waited for the explanation, but it didn't come. Instead Galbraith told me to look at the photograph in the bottom right corner, of Grace holding the baby Calum wrapped in a long shawl.

'He was only two months old in that picture. Before he was born my wife was an ARP warden. It was her job to patrol the streets at night and make sure there were no chinks of light showing from the windows. You know about the blackouts, right, Nevis? Some people used to say that even to smoke a cigarette outside would be enough to guide an enemy plane. So it was my wife's job to make sure everyone obeyed the blackout rules. And when the air raid sirens went off she'd help people get to the public shelters safely. She was very good at her job. And proud of it. But then she fell pregnant with Calum, and I insisted she left Aberdeen to stay with relatives, even though she'd have much rather carried on with her duties.' He smiled then. 'But even when she moved to the country she made sure she was always looking after the soldiers. Calling them in for tea or soup when they passed. She would write to me and tell me about it. They used to dote on Calum, these soldiers. One boy even made him a wooden pop gun – you know the kind – with the cork and string.'

'You remember a lot,' I said.

'In a way these are my wife's memories. What she told me in her letters. I never met the young soldier in question, even though he married a good friend of my wife's. He died fighting. I remember reading the letter from Grace telling me how her friend had received the telegram. Grace was quite distraught. She wrote saying the last time she'd seen the boy was when she was on her way to the store – she'd glanced in at their front window as she passed and saw him in uniform, sitting polishing his boots with a toothbrush. But she didn't stop to wave or talk and on her way home he'd left and she never saw him again. I'm not sure she ever forgave herself for that. She was so upset I went to visit her.' And then the expression on Galbraith's face changed, his eyes glossed over for a moment and he stared at nothing, just the air in front of him for the briefest second, before refocusing and looking back at me. He turned the corners of his lips up in a sort of forced smile. I pointed at it triumphantly.

'That's it,' I said. 'The smile. You're doing it again.'

Galbraith seemed taken aback at first, surprised, then thoughtful. He looked at me carefully. 'It's rude to point, Nevis,' he said.

I looked at my pointing finger. 'Is it?'

'Yes. When it comes to people. You should try to avoid it.'

So I lowered my hand to my side.

Galbraith sighed and pushed himself up from his chair. He walked across the room to the window and looked out into the garden. 'You know, Nevis, for a boy who has lived eleven years in a van, you can read people's faces very well. How is that?'

I shrugged, but Galbraith's back was turned towards me so he didn't see. 'I don't know,' I said. 'Maybe it's instinctive.' And then, without even thinking about it, as though the answer was always inside and waiting to come out, I discarded my previous 'I don't know' and said, 'I used to try and read what my father was writing through his facial expressions.'

'That's very interesting.' Galbraith turned his body slightly to look at me, his right hand holding the fingers of his left hand behind his back. 'And could you guess correctly?'

I thought back to my father bent over his notebooks writing and mumbling to himself, the various forms of frown etched across his forehead, the creases by the corners of his lips, his eyebrows sometimes raised, ears sometimes pricked. I always knew what mood he was in. And it wasn't just his facial expressions, but the way he held his pen, how much pressure he put on the page as he pressed in the ink, how fast the words flew out.

A thick frown, puckered forehead, you could count the lines, his eyes narrowed as he looked down at the page, his hand tight around the pen so it pressed into the lump on his middle finger. He'd be writing about a battle, I thought, a war between kingdoms, monsters fighting other wild beasts, blood and fire and death.

Or a slight smile and a light hold to the pen, the ink flowing fast over paper: a party, a jig, a barn dance with people laughing and drinking and holding each other as they waltzed around and smiled.

And then sometimes I would catch him just looking at me, but not really looking at me, it was an empty gaze. I could wave my hand in front of him and he wouldn't see. He was some other place in his head, some other world searching for words to put down on paper.

My father spoke more through his gestures and facial expressions then he did with his mouth. I knew when not to disturb him and when it was ok to ask a question. I knew when he was stuck over a word or idea or when he was having a good day writing. I knew if he was happy, sad, hot, cold. I knew when he had a headache – I recognised the headache frown. I could even pinpoint whereabouts, more frequently it clustered in the middle of his forehead and stretched out to his temples, but on the odd occasion I could see a heavy ache creep up from the base of his skull and spread out. A migraine. And I even knew how long it would be before he had to lie down and close his eyes.

Yes, if there was any slight discomfort, slight frustration, the slightest beginnings of an emotion on my father's face, I could read it. But could I guess correctly what he was writing about?

'Nevis?' Galbraith was still looking at me, still waiting for his answer. 'What *did* your father write about?'

'I don't know.' Maybe I said it a little too quickly.

'You don't know?'

I shrugged. 'I never read any of it.' I was trying to seem more casual.

Galbraith raised his eyebrows. 'What? None of it?'

I shrugged again. 'I wasn't allowed.'

'But surely you must have read *some* of it? Perhaps when Marshall wasn't looking? Maybe even when he was asleep?'

'No. I promised him I wouldn't.'

Galbraith nodded and then gave a little shrug. He was facing me; one hand hugging his elbow while the other twisted around his white pointed beard. 'Do you remember your first meeting with me, Nevis? When I told you under no uncertain circumstances should you read my notes? Do you remember that?'

'That was different.'

'Was it?' Galbraith was wrapping his index finger

deeper into his beard. 'Are you trying to tell me, Nevis, that you spent eleven years in the back of a van with a man who obsessively wrote day in, day out and *you*, an inquisitive young boy, didn't read any of it? Is that right?'

I stared down at the palms of my hands, opening and closing my fingers. I nodded.

Galbraith replied by clucking his tongue twice, not taking his eyes from me, then slowly moved back to his armchair and sat down. He picked up the story I'd given him earlier and waved it in the air. 'I forgot to compliment you, Nevis. Your writing is very good.'

I looked up at him quickly, surprised, and smiled a brief smile before looking away again.

'You're a good writer,' he continued. 'You have a natural talent. You should write more.'

'I have more,' I told him.

'More lists?'

'Yes.'

'Your memories?'

'Yes.'

'Maybe you should write a novel.'

'No.' I shook my head. 'Not fiction. I want to write the truth.'

'Ah yes, I almost forgot,' and Galbraith waved his finger in the air, 'your obsession with truth.' I shifted awkwardly in the armchair. Galbraith looked around the room at all his books. 'But perhaps you *should* consider your life and past as a novel, Nevis. Memory, after all, is not like a videotape recorder. You can't remember every little detail of everything you say and do. Only fragments. And then you flesh out the rest. Build a narrative around those snippets of fact so it makes sense.'

'You're beginning to sound like my father,' I said.

Galbraith smiled. 'You don't have to tell me anything you don't want to, Nevis. Everyone has reasons for keeping secrets about their life. I know because I have plenty. But at least with a novel you can disguise them.'

'You mean lie?' I said, crossly. 'Make things up because it looks better on paper? Now you really *are* sounding like my father.' The heat was in my face now. I could feel it burning. 'This isn't about what *you* want, or some other reader. This is about my memories, what's real and what's not. This is about . . .'

'*Truth?*' Galbraith finished my sentence off before I could, stopping me short. 'But what *is* truth?' He held up my lists. 'Your memories? Are they truth? True because . . . what? You say it is?' He smiled. 'And what about the truths that you don't say?'

We looked at each other. I was aware of my breathing, my heart had been racing and now I could feel it slowing again, back to its steady beat. I thought about Marshall and the way he'd hidden that photo of my mother in his wallet for years. I miss you. I love you. Come back, it said. I thought about his writing, the way he warned me never to read any of it: a writer's work is private, boy, until it's finished, he used to say. But of course I read it. Of course when he was sleeping I would pick up some pads and jotters and flick through these journals of ideas and thoughts. Stories, he called them. But they weren't stories. They were more like lists; like the lists that I write; records of everything that happened, everything that went wrong. Or just descriptions of her hair, her body, her smile. The way she spoke. The way she laughed. The way she stood on the steps to the garden on a bright day, held her face up to the sun and basked in it, breathed in deeply the smell of sweet grass and flowers and soil.

I looked at Galbraith who was sitting in his armchair, his hands clasped on his lap, his right thumb stroking the back of his left thumb, softly.

'You must never read my writing, boy,' he said. 'Do you promise?'

And I promised.

And then I broke my promise.

And ever since I've been wishing that I hadn't.

'I was never interested in what my father was actually writing about,' I told Galbraith then, which was the truth, I realised. It was more about the stories I could make up. The stories I could *pretend* he was writing. 'He wrote about love,' I said. 'About Annie, my mother. Everything he ever wrote was about Annie.' And I felt sick admitting it. And hurt. And jealous. And guilty because I knew I shouldn't have known.

Galbraith nodded. Perhaps he could tell I was upset, I don't know. He didn't press me for any more information. He let the quiet build between us. He glanced over my head to the window and then sighed a long and deep sigh. 'I'll tell you,' he said, 'a secret between you and me. Why not? I trust you.' He pointed at the photo album still open on my lap. 'You wanted to know why I wasn't smiling in those wedding photographs? Well, a few days previous to the wedding, Fin told me something was bothering him. Before the bombing at Hall Russell, he said, before he saved my life, he'd been having an affair with Grace, my wife. They'd been meeting up maybe once or twice a week while I was standing at my observation post. Fin was an ARP warden like her. They used to sleep together in the air raid shelters when the sirens weren't sounding.' Galbraith nodded quietly to himself as he spoke. 'And remember that soldier I told you about, Nevis? The one who crafted Calum a pop gun? Well, Grace begged me to come and visit her after her friend received the telegram only a month after he left saying he'd died in combat. I thought it was because she was so distraught. Another life lost. And someone she'd got to know quite well. But when I saw her I knew she was pregnant. She didn't say anything of course, but a mere seven months later she gave birth to a healthy baby boy. And she wanted to name him Thomas, after the soldier who'd died.'

'What did you do?' I asked.

'I agreed.' Galbraith turned up the corners of his mouth bravely. 'I quite like the name Thomas, don't you?'

'But why didn't you leave?'

'Surely you know the answer to that one, Nevis?'

I stared at the palms of my hands. My thoughts drifted back to the black and white photograph of my mother, the desperate words pencilled on the back; and I remembered the way Marshall agonised over his writing for hours, every sentence, every word, every syllable. It was all for her, I thought. It was all for Annie.

'Weren't you angry?' I asked.

'At first,' he replied.

'And then you just forgave them?'

Galbraith sort of smiled at this and then sighed as though the memories exhausted him. 'Isn't forgiveness one of the biggest elements of love?' he asked.

39

There was a knock on the door.

'Nevis, can I come in?'

I had to get off the bed to move the chair jammed underneath the door handle. My father entered hesitantly.

'What are you writing?' he asked, looking at the notepads on my bed.

'My homework,' I lied.

'Nevis, I think we need to talk.'

So that's how he was playing it. A direct attack, launch straight in so he didn't have to think about it, so he couldn't change his mind.

'What about?' I decided to play it stupid.

'Last night.'

'I don't want to talk about it,' I said. I went back to my bed and lay on my stomach. I picked up the pen I'd been using and turned over a fresh leaf in the pad so Marshall couldn't read what I'd just written. I pretended to work.

'What's your homework assignment about?' he asked.

'An essay on World War Two,' I told him. I'd already pre-empted the question. 'The civilians' war.'

'Sounds interesting.' He closed the door, moved the chair to the foot of the bed and sat down. 'Nevis . . .' he said again, 'we really need to talk.'

I remained silent.

'. . . about your mother.' He paused waiting for a reaction. When he received none he continued, 'I was wrong to withhold information from you. You should have known about her. I should have spoken to you about her, told you what she was like . . .'

'Why?'

'Because she's part of you.'

'No, she's not,' I said. I was starting to feel the bubble of anger I'd felt the night before return. 'She's got nothing to do with me.' I pressed the tip of my pen hard into the paper.

'Nevis . . .'

'What?'

Marshall sighed. 'The reason why we split up . . .'

'Don't you ever listen to me?' I turned on him fiercely. 'Didn't you just hear what I said?'

'All right, Nevis, calm down.'

'She's got nothing to do with me. I don't care, Marshall. She left . . . we carried on. We had a life together . . . she wasn't in it. So why would I suddenly start caring about what kind of a person she was now?'

'You seemed to care last night,' Marshall said quietly. 'You seemed upset.'

The tip of the pen was starting to rip the paper.

'She left me for another man,' he said. 'He was an artist, a stone sculptor ...'

'I know,' I interrupted, '... "renowned for chipping out grotesque images of women with penises and two men's heads for breasts." Am I right?'

Marshall's eyes widened.

'She couldn't get enough of it, could she, Marshall?' The anger kept spurring me on. '"She was all over him like a fly over shit". Wasn't that what you wrote?'

'When did you ... ?'

'She left us. She abandoned us. She didn't love us.' I slammed the pen into the notepad and tore down the page. 'The van was more a part of me than she was,' I said, 'but that didn't stop you burning it.' I got up, still clutching the pen in one hand and the paper in the other. I walked across to the dresser and pulled open the drawer, sliding it shut again with a thud, the colourful bottles on the top clinking and tinkling together. I moved back towards my father and pressed what I'd retrieved into his hand. 'This is what you really came to speak to me about, isn't it?' I asked. 'To get this back?'

'Annie,' he said, looking down into his palm at the curled, blackened corner, bubbled ink and melted – all that was left of the photograph of my mother.

'It's in the past now, Marshall,' I said. 'Forget about it.'

40

Guilt: I wonder if that's what my father felt when he set fire to the van, all our books, clothes, possessions, up in smoke. Because that's what I felt when I pressed the remains of that photograph in his hand. I felt sorry. There is nothing nice about vengeance. And yet the night before it'd been instinctive. I'd pushed past Marshall and Elspeth in the caravan, photograph still in hand, run back to the farmhouse, through the kitchen, up the stairs . . .

'Nevis!' Ailsa was still crouching by the door. 'I thought . . .' and she got to her feet. 'Why are you crying?'

I ran into the bathroom, slammed the door shut behind me and locked it. I started pacing, pacing, back and forth. I was breathing heavily. When I saw my reflection my cheeks were red and sticky with tears. My eyes were wet. I watched my face in the mirror. I watched the emotions spread and merge until I couldn't tell anymore what was anger, what was jealousy, what was heartbreak. And then I opened my mouth, dribble stretching from top lip to bottom, and wailed.

'Nevis?'

'Come away, Ailsa, quick.'

'Nevis, it's Marshall, let me explain.'

And then vengeance. That's when I felt it. There was a lighter in the bathroom. Elspeth used it to light her pretty little pink candles and incense when she was having a bath. I held the photograph over the flame and watched the corners curl, the inks melt and blotch and bubble, my mother's face blacken with the smoke that curled up from the fire and the fumes. I became light-headed. I dropped the photograph into the sink and steadied myself. I slowed my breathing. I closed my eyes.

And then guilt: giving back Marshall this photograph. It was the way he seemed to shrink when he saw it. The way his shoulders dropped. The way he whispered her name, 'Annie.' My father looked broken. I wanted to reach out and wrap my arms around him. 'But *I'm* here, I've always been here. *She* hasn't.' But I couldn't touch him. I left the room instead, thinking to myself, why couldn't he love me like that? Why couldn't he ever write about me?

41

I was supposed to be doing a test. Galbraith had set me
a chapter to read with some questions to answer afterwards, but I couldn't take my eyes off him. He was
reading my fairytale. I watched him closely, the way his
eyes moved over the lines, soaking in each word. He read
with a deep intensity as though the pages held him fast.
He stroked his beard and nipped its point between thumb
and forefinger. When he got to the final page, the last
paragraph, the concluding sentence, his eyes remained
glued to those final two words as though he couldn't
pull them away: THE END. Finally, slowly, he lifted his
head and looked at me.

'You're a good writer,' he said.

I must have been holding my breath because at last I
exhaled, long and deep. I smiled. I looked down at my
hands.

'Nevis?'

When I looked up again Galbraith wasn't smiling.
His eyes seemed wide and a brighter blue with concern,

he was frowning ever so slightly. He licked his lips and placed my story onto the coffee table. 'Nevis . . .' he drifted off. 'You're very close to your father, aren't you?'

The tone in his voice warned me not answer.

'Of course, it's only natural to be close to the one person you've grown up with.'

I was frowning.

'It's natural to be close to your father.' He was nodding encouragingly. 'But there is such a thing as "too close". Do you understand what I mean?'

'No.' I shook my head.

'Do you love him?'

'Yes.' That was an easy question.

'In what way?' he asked.

'Are there more ways than one?'

Galbraith fell silent. 'Yes, Nevis. There are many ways.' He turned back to the fairytale, to the very end page, and reread the kiss. 'Did this happen, Nevis?'

Everything about the way he asked me that question instructed me to lie.

'No.' I shook my head and shrugged.

'No?'

'None of it happened.'

'This is just a story?'

'Yes.'

'But what about memories? What about truth?'

'You told me to experiment with fiction.'

'But you love him?'

'Everyone is close to their father,' I said. 'You said so yourself.'

Galbraith clucked his tongue and looked at me. 'Nevis, do you have romantic or sexual feelings for your father?'

I frowned. I shrugged. I shook my head.

'And your father? Does he have romantic or sexual feelings towards you?'

Now I understand, I thought. While Galbraith stared into me, as though searching for the answer, I heard Marshall's voice: It must never happen again – he said. Do you understand? And I'd nodded even though I hadn't. But now . . . now I understood. Now I knew it wasn't about shame: it was about expectations, it was about social rules and regulations. It was about what the rest of the world perceived to be right and wrong. 'It's called incest,' Duckman had said. 'An' it's against the law. Ye know ye cannae splash aroon' in yer own gene pool.' Conforming. Obeying. Accepting without question. It wasn't about love. We weren't allowed to love.

'It's just a story,' I told Galbraith then, firmly. 'I made it up.'

Let me live alone in the closed confines of the back of a van any day, I thought. There is more freedom there than under the watchful eye of others.

42

I cut my hair. That night in the bathroom behind a locked door. I found a pair of scissors in the cabinet in amongst all the gels and creams and perfumes and make-up. They must have been the scissors my father had used on the day we arrived at the farm. He must have stood the way I was standing then, over the sink, staring at his face in the mirror. I took comfort in that fact. I even took a blade from the cabinet, soaped my chin and cheeks, and for the first time ever shaved the way he used to shave. I nicked myself twice. One on my chin and the other by my right ear, but all in all I was pleased with my work. My face felt clean and fresh and the soft tufty hair above my lip was gone. It grows back thicker when you shave, Duckman had told me.

And then I took hold of the scissors. At first I lifted my hair carefully in small clumps and cut a few centimetres from the root, letting the ends fall into the sink. The sound of the snip snip of the metal sliding against metal reminded me of Duckman and the day we decapitated weeds. I carried on cutting, speeding up the process by pulling most of my hair together into a side ponytail and hacking the end off. Yet still I must have been cutting and chopping and butchering my hair for well over an hour before eventually I stopped.

I stared at myself.

Often at the end of a fairytale the hero is transformed, given a new appearance, is made whole, handsome, dressed in new garments and then ascends to the throne, receives his prize, marries the young maiden, lives happily ever after.

It was not long before we had to leave the farm. A week at the most, Elspeth had said. For once she had brought back good news, along with the hundreds of boxes from town. She'd handed me a holdall. 'Fer yer things,' she said. 'An' if ye need any boxes . . .' she trailed off. She knew I didn't own anything. But I took the holdall, blue with red handles, and put my notebooks into it and my three t-shirts, some underwear, socks and spare pair of jeans. They weren't my jeans, they'd belonged to Duckman, as did one of the t-shirts. But I packed them anyway.

Elspeth and Ailsa began to methodically box up each room. Apart from the forbidden room. That remained locked. I sneaked round to have a look through the window and sure enough, Nigel Kerr still sat and silently stared at the grand piano – a mixture of both remembering the past and forgetting the present. While the rest

288

of the house bustled and breathed with activity, the music room remained quiet and still. Untouched.

There was nothing more for me to pack and so to remain out of everyone's way I kept myself locked in the bathroom, sat down on the toilet and reread my fairytale. 'Do you have romantic or sexual feelings for your father, Nevis?' I thought of Marshall by the corrugated iron bunker, his hand around his cock, pumping vigorously, his pelvis moving back and forward, back and forward and then the soft grunt and the long shot of white.

I should never have let Galbraith read the fairytale, I thought. I should have listened to Marshall. Other people don't understand.

'But it's not long now,' I told my new reflection, the haphazardly cut hair, my transformation. 'It's not long now before we have to leave.'

And then what? Where are we going? What are we doing? I'd packed my bag and yet had no idea. I took my black cap and pulled it down onto my head. I looked a bit like Duckman, I thought. The sides of the cap made my ears stick out a little. Although my face was long and his was more round. I wondered what I would look like if I got my ear pierced. A gold stud. I sniffed. I hawked up some phlegm at the back of my throat and then spat into the sink. I scratched the inside of my leg.

'Ah long fer the day ah can tell *you* t' shut the fuck up, Nevis,' I said out loud.

43

Through the thin horizontal strips of light I could see the white of Ailsa's socks and pale legs walk into the room, stop half way, swivel round slowly. I could hear her listening carefully.

'Nevis?'

I held my breath and crouched back into the smells of dirty washing. After a moment Ailsa must have decided I was not in the room and so left. I heard her retreating footsteps walk down the stairs. I breathed out heavily, a long sigh of relief, and pushed open the cupboard door. From downstairs I could hear Ailsa coo-call my name, 'Nevvvis', as she continued her search.

I stood in Duckman's slanted-roofed attic bedroom. Painted boy-blue walls, covered with posters and advertisements for alcohol, cigarettes, gigs. Empty bottles and cans of beer. An ashtray spilling its filthy black onto the carpet. Plates piled next to the bed with their leftover food dried hard like concrete. An empty piss-stained pint glass. Clothes scattered, crumpled in piles. These were all the things I'd been expecting to see. But Duckman's room was perfectly clean. Not a speck of dust on the grey carpet, no posters on the magnolia walls. The single bed was neatly made with matching plain green duvet and pillowcases. There was an ashtray, but it was empty. On the floor near the window there was a stainless steel pedal bin with a white label stuck to its side – LIFE – handwritten in capital letters. The bin was full of the ash and dead butts Duckman had smoked sitting at the window, looking out at the farm at night. On the chest of drawers there was a large mirror and next to it, a silver photograph frame – but the picture had been taken out. I wondered then if Duckman had cleaned the room before leaving, heaping together all his dirty clothes and dumping them in the large laundry bag in the cupboard. It was possible. My memory of Duckman somehow didn't fit with this clean bedroom.

I sat on the edge of his bed and opened the drawer of the side table. I was looking for a photograph. I wanted a picture of Duckman so I wouldn't forget. It's so easy to forget faces. Maybe that was the real reason Marshall kept the photograph of Annie. It wasn't because he was still in love with her; it was because faces are the first thing people forget. I didn't remind myself of the words on the back, or the way my father's face fell when he saw what I'd done. I told myself instead, like I'd told myself so many times in the past, that I hadn't read everything Marshall had written. What if there were other things? What if what I stumbled across were just diaries? A very large collection of private journals? It was possible. After all, I stopped reading my father's writing after a while and instead just made up the stories myself. 'He's not writing about her, he's writing about that couple sitting on the park bench feeding the birds. Or that woman pushing the pram with a wonky wheel. Or that homeless guy with a fat bulbous nose and warty skin, eating from the skips. That's what he's writing about.' Or the Kerrs. When I first arrived at the farm I really did convince myself that we were there so he could write about the family. Is it possible that you can lie to yourself so much that in the end you believe it?

In Duckman's drawer there was a long chain. I lifted it up with thumb and forefinger and stared at all the little key-rings attached: a basketball, a leather jacket, a tennis racket, a television set with a tiny face painted onto it, a little red blobby man with long and flexible arms, a soldier, a clipper lighter that actually sparked a tiny flame, a pistol, a packet of cigarettes, a small blue metal badge with the initials RFC. Hundreds of key-rings. I pulled out the plastic frog from my pocket and remembered the time Duckman had handed it to me. 'I used to collect key-rings,' he'd said. It really was like in my fairytale, Duckman presenting me with this magical item. 'That's all that's left,' he'd said. I dropped the chain back into the drawer and closed it, wondering all the while if I'd ever see him again.

I finally found a photograph in a shoebox underneath his bed. There were several, but I chose one of Duckman sitting on the roof of his car, feet resting on the door where the window had been wound right down. I recognised the grassy bank and trees by the river. He looked a little younger, but not much. He didn't smile or take notice of whoever was behind the camera; instead his face was turned thoughtfully towards the water. I wondered what he was thinking about. I slipped the picture into the back pocket of my jeans and returned the shoebox to its place under the bed.

It was better to stay in Duckman's room, I decided. I was sure Ailsa would give up her search and sit sulking in the kitchen or her bedroom for a while. She wouldn't look up here again. I hoped.

I lay down on the bed, suddenly aware that I could smell Duckman on the bedclothes. I placed my face flat against the soft pillows and breathed in. I missed him, I thought. I hadn't realised how much I would miss him. I hadn't realised how much I had changed since coming to the farm. Duckman had become a friend – my first – and it felt good. And I felt sad. It was only by lying on his bed and breathing in his smell I became so entirely aware of his absence. Lonely, I thought. This is what lonely feels like.

I slept.

When I woke up I was in the van, foetus-curled and cocooned in my sleeping bag, the sofa cushions beneath me, the fousty smell in my nostrils, the books, the clothes, the writing. I lay still for a moment, my face pressed against my father's blue woollen jumper, bunched up beneath me for a pillow. I didn't dare move for fear the image might shatter like glass, like something brittle and fragile. But if I didn't move, I thought, who's to say it wouldn't shatter anyway? And then I've wasted the dream, assuming it *was* a dream. For on the other hand this could be real, could it not? – the cushions beneath me felt real, soft, a little damp. And I could smell my father's odour interwoven in the wool of his jumper. I could reach out and touch the van walls. And so I did, my fingers soaking in the cold metal. Proof. Perhaps I'd just lived through one of those stories where after everything that happens the main character wakes up to find it had all been a dream. Beware the story that ends with waking up – my father used to say – it reveals a writer bored of writing. Always, always these mini pockets of wisdom. I often wondered whether they were a glimpse of Marshall Gow the writer or Marshall Gow the English teacher. Beware the poems about autumnal leaves. Beware the overwrought exclamation mark. Beware scenes with tears – on paper they seem contrived, too forced, melodramatic. Beware dream sequences.

I started to raise myself slowly onto my elbows. Everything was how I remembered it. The water container, the food chest, the camping gas cooker. Papers and jotters still hung from the van walls, the frying pan and pot on their hook. I crawled out of my sleeping bag and kneeled in amongst my memories. *There* was the book on the kings and queens of Scotland, *there* was the science encyclopaedia. Peeking out from underneath a pair of jeans I saw the corner of a little paperback book with a red cover, but when I pulled it free I noticed there was no title or author printed on its spine; and flicking through the pages they were blank. I frowned. I took hold of the book on kings and queens and looked through – there were pictures and there was writing, but when I tried to focus on the main body of text, or anything other than the title on each page, I couldn't read it. The words became blurred. I started to look closer at all the books that surrounded me, slowly realising that I couldn't read any of their titles apart from the few that really stuck out in my mind. And then I noticed the other inconsistencies, what sometimes seemed like strange tricks of light. I'd move my eyes around the van and there'd be a gap, a blur in the wall or an empty space of white – and I'd double-take – look back at the confused memory and try to fix it. Mostly that was easy, I'd just glance back at the gap and it wouldn't be there anymore. But other times I really had to delve deep into my mind and think *what was there?* *What can't I remember?* I'd pencil and paint the blank spaces with ideas until they seemed to fit. How easy it is to manipulate memory.

I got to my feet, bending forward so my head didn't hit the roof. I pulled back the grey cord curtain and climbed over into the front of the van, drawing the curtain closed behind me.

There was the perfumed cardboard tree swinging from the rear-view mirror, *there* was the rubbish strewn across the dashboard. I caught a glimpse of myself in the mirror clipped into the passenger's visor and then, as I remembered the time I'd sat with it in my back pocket and snapped it in two, a crack appeared in my reflection. I jumped at the sound and the split-second sight of my face breaking in two.

'Jesus Christ . . .' I tried to steady myself and calm my breathing. This could so easily become a nightmare, I thought. Where was Marshall? I turned around to face the closed curtain and watched as it started to draw itself aside unaided, like the red curtains at the beginning of the Punch and Judy show. And there he was, sitting centre stage on the sofa cushions, crouched with back bent over as he scribbled frantically into a notebook. The old Marshall Gow with beard and long ratty hair and dirty-looking clothes. My father.

'Marshall?'

'Shhh!' he said, holding the pen to his lips instead of a finger. 'I'm nearly finished.'

I watched. I waited. My father wrote page after page, falling into the words as they left his pen, pressing the ink into paper. I must have watched him for hours with baited breath. 'I'm nearly finished,' he said. 'You can read it when I've finished.' For days I watched. I waited. His beard grew longer. He became thinner. I would sleep and dream of eating, drinking, walking, reading. Once I even slept and dreamt I was dreaming, watching my father write and write and write.

'Marshall?'

He looked up. He smiled. 'It's finished, Nevis,' he said. 'It's finally finished.' But as he handed me the pages they burst into flames and burnt my hands. Shit! I threw them away and watched as the fire took to the sofa cushions and the books. Shit, Marshall, do something! But Marshall didn't do anything. He just sat and took long swigs from a bottle of whisky. It's for the best, Nevis – he said.

I woke from my dream within a dream, lying in the back of the van, cocooned in my sleeping bag, the sofa cushions beneath me. I lay still for a moment, my face pressed against the clothes bunched up under my head for a pillow. Everything was here. Just as I remembered. And then I saw him, my father, sleeping – head cocked back, breathing slowly, deeply – without any blankets over him.

'You'll get cold,' I whispered and put my arm over him. The sound of heavy pages thumping against pages. To arouse oneself sexually, the dictionary had said, or cause another person to be aroused by manual stimulation.

I kissed my father. I leant in and closed my eyes and pressed my lips against his. I could feel the coarse hair of his beard, taste the salt and pea soup and warm breath as I moved slowly, so slowly. And then a hand over my hand. I looked at my father and his eyes were open and staring straight at me.

'Nevis?' he whispered.

And then I felt the soft wet of his tongue slide into my mouth.

44

At first I didn't recognise where I was. The moonlight was coming in through the window, casting an eerie blue over the floor and deepening the shadows. I could hear an owl outside, coo-cooing – and then another owl reply. I sat up. I took a deep breath in and held it for a moment. I remembered my dream and felt my father's tongue still in my mouth. I closed my eyes. Exhaled slowly.

I have always been a dreamer – I've always had vivid and very real 'sleep adventures' as Marshall used to call them. He told me once dreams were a thing you could learn to control, although I'm not sure if I've ever managed to master my own. The trick, I believe, is to realise you are dreaming and yet remain asleep. A difficult thing to do, as most people on regaining any amount of consciousness will wake up. But it can be done. And when it is done a whole wealth of power is at your fingertips. Marshall would tell me of how he could go on the most fantastical quests, climb mountains, slay bears, ride atop a pterodactyl and soar the skies. He could control the weather, bring about a storm to drive away demons, take a deep breath and blow out a hurricane, a forest fire, a tsunami. Or better still, he could reverse time. A murderer could stalk him through the streets, sneak up on tiptoes, knife ready in hand. He could even strike and find his mark. But my father, in complete control, could rewind time to the moment just before, spinning around to rid the murderer of his weapon. No nightmare enemy could defeat him when he had this godlike magic at his fingertips.

I have never had this kind of control over my dreams. But I am good at remembering them, a skill in itself. And recently I've become more and more interested in their content, picking them apart, studying them. And this is why: if I dream so vividly, and I know that I do, with such intensity that I have no suspicion that what I'm experiencing isn't reality, then who's to say what is real and what is not? A dream is something that you wake from. And yet I've had dreams where I've dreamt of waking, only later to wake again – like that night, sleeping on Duckman's bed. And my dreams are not always threaded with the fantastical. Some are simply everyday moments: eating a meal with Marshall, walking through the woods, lying on the roof of the van. Some dreams aren't dreams but a moment of reliving a memory. But what if these dreams are distorting memories? Or what if the dream is representing repressed truths that I've somehow hidden from myself? Or what if I dream a moment that never happened, later to wake up and believe it was real? How am I supposed to know?

'Memory is not like a videotape recorder,' Galbraith had said. 'You can't remember every little detail of everything you say and do. Only fragments. And then you flesh out the rest. Build a narrative around those snippets of fact so it makes sense.' I thought about my lists and Galbraith waving them at me, mocking me. 'And these are true because . . . what? You say they are?'

I got up from Duckman's bed and walked to the window. The caravan light was on. Marshall was back from his late shift at the pub. I took off my baseball cap so I could press my forehead into the cold pane of glass and thought about the dream. My father. The kiss. It had felt so real.

Galbraith was right, I realised then. I needed confirmation. I needed Marshall to nod and say yes, Nevis, it was real. It did happen. Otherwise my memories were . . . what? They were nothing. They were worthless.

I left Duckman's room fast, hurried down the stairs onto the landing, then down into the hallway. I caught a glimpse of myself in the mirror, almost jumped. My face looked so different; my eyes darker and skin so much paler in the half-light that came in through the window. I touched my head where an uneven tuft of hair stuck out at an odd angle. And then from above me, through the ceiling, I heard Ailsa's bed creak, her soft footsteps pad across the floor. I moved into the kitchen quickly, closed the door gently behind me. And then into the gumboot room, again pulling the door shut. I put on my boots – I didn't bother with the laces – and moved silently out into the yard. I had to hurry, I thought. I didn't want Ailsa following me. This had to be private. Between me and Marshall.

The dogs were asleep. I could hear their heavy breathing. They didn't even raise their head when the back door light switched on. I jogged, light-footed, past the tool shed – turning when I was at the gate to the caravan field to look back at the farmhouse, checking the windows for movement. The bathroom light was on. Through the frosted glass I could see a shadow shift. I turned my back to it, put one foot on the crossbar of the gate and swung the other foot over.

It was then I heard it, sitting, straddling the wooden gate, the hollow thump, thump, thump coming from the caravan. It stopped. And then it began again. With every thump the caravan rocked slightly. Juddered. For a moment I just watched. I just listened. And then I dropped over into the field. Moved quickly towards the window, all steamed up apart from a small patch in the bottom right corner. I looked in. He was on top of her. His shirt was off and his trousers dropped around his knees, her skirt heaved back around her hips and her legs wrapped around him. I stood transfixed – like Galbraith must have done when the bombs dropped from their planes. When Fin told him about the affair with his wife. When he laid eyes on Grace, two months pregnant.

Sometimes now I wonder what my face would have looked like from the other side. Wide-eyed, open-mouthed, ghost-white skin.

And then I ran.

45

There are a few things that happened at the end that I think better to write about all at once. So I will. I did get to see Duckman again, the next morning in fact. Although when he returned to the farm I wasn't there. I was tucked up in a bed not my own. I remember waking up that day quite vividly, warm underneath the duvet with its pale floral design. I remember the feel and smell of the washing-powder-fresh sheets. I remember because I felt dirty beneath them.

The room I was in was small, rectangular, quite narrow. It could only fit the single bed I was lying on and next to it a small bedside table with a lamp. The walls were pale with a hint of pink. The ceiling was white. Above the bed was a window, which looked out into the back garden: a bird table on a small, square well-kept lawn. There were no gnomes, I'd noticed.

I had not woken up of my own accord but to the sound of ringing in the hallway from the telephone and then Mr Galbraith's voice answering. I could not hear his conversation. I was not trying to. I was in those first few blissful seconds of waking where everything was forgotten, followed too quickly by that sinking feeling of memories returning.

There was a quiet tap-tap on the door and Mr Galbraith came in.

'You're awake,' he said. 'Good.' And then he cleared his throat. 'I'm not expecting you to tell me why you ran away last night, Nevis. Not if you don't want to. But I'm afraid if it had anything to do with your father – a disagreement of some sort . . . or something else – then I have a confession that might not please you. He knows you're here. I left a message on his answering machine this morning and he's just called back.'

I looked away from the old man standing by the door.

'I hope you don't mind,' Galbraith continued quietly. 'I had to tell him you were safe.' He fell silent for a moment, as though thinking about what to say next. 'Are you hungry, Nevis?' he finally asked. 'Perhaps you should eat something before I take you back.'

'Back?' I looked at Galbraith urgently. 'I can't go back there,' I said. 'Please.'

'Nevis . . .'

'You don't understand,' I said and started to raise myself up into a sitting position. 'Mr Galbraith, I can't go back there.'

'Why not?'

'I can't tell you . . .'

He looked at me thoughtfully. 'What were you dreaming about last night, Nevis? Do you remember?'

'No,' I lied.

'Do you remember me waking you?'

I shook my head.

'Your father had some news, Nevis. Something happened last night at the farm. Do you know anything about it? Is that why you ran away?'

I must have looked frightened.

'Nevis . . .'

'It wasn't me.'

'It's ok, Nevis . . .'

I was starting to panic.

'Nevis, listen to me. Nobody's blaming you.' Galbraith was over at my side in a second, comforting me with one hand on my shoulder. 'Colin was up there with the police this morning. He's made a statement. Apparently Mr Kerr's been unstable for a long time. Since his wife died. It's not your fault, Nevis. You've not done anything wrong. It's ok.'

So you see, Duckman came back because his father finally did it. Pulled the trigger with the gun pressing into the roof of his mouth and not just pointing aimlessly towards the treetops. Duckman had missed the show he'd been waiting for. But perhaps he'd wanted to.

Perhaps that was the real reason he left, because he knew in the end his father was going to do it – kill himself – choose his dead wife over his living son.

The funeral was this morning. The church service followed by the burial in the afternoon. I didn't attend either. Instead I sat alone by the river and watched and waited. My father went, of course. I can picture clearly how he would have stood, his arm around Elspeth – comforting her while she sobbed, his hand pressed into the small of her back. I imagined her tears as part show for the private moment that she and Marshall could steal together – their intimacy briefly exposed as they held each other, acceptable when camouflaged by grief. How stupid I had been to not even see it until I saw it that night. Their bodies hot and wound tightly together.

And then I started to run.

That's what I told the police when they questioned me.

'I saw them together and then I ran.'

'So your running away had nothing to do with Nigel Kerr's suicide?'

'No,' I said. My statement tied in with the facts. Nigel Kerr had shot himself as the sun was still rising and by that time I was asleep in Mr Galbraith's spare bed. The two policemen nodded to each other and then the older one, a friendly man with black greying hair and matching moustache, smiled at me.

'There's just one thing that doesn't quite add up, son,' he said. 'Are you sure you're telling us everything?'

I've been looking at my hands a lot today. I've always thought in the past that when I'm sitting, thinking, staring, waiting, my hands are the best things to focus on. I like to look at the lines on my palms, open and close my long thin fingers or curl them into fists. I like the control. My hands are me. But today when I look at them I am distant, I feel numb. I don't recognise them. For the last few days it's been like this, my hands foreign to me.

I remember banging on Galbraith's door after running all that way. Exhausted. I didn't know what time it was, only that it was late and still dark. I was out of breath, my knees were grazed and bruised from falling and I'd twisted my ankle badly, so for the last mile or so I had to semi-jog with a limp. My lungs were painful at each intake of breath. I banged harder on Galbraith's door and then collapsed to my knees. I was so tired. And cold. I bowed my head and dribbled onto the step. That's what Galbraith – in dressing gown and striped pyjamas – opened the door to: a boy on his knees, shaking with tears and tiredness and fear.

'Nevis . . .' He took me in. 'What's happened, Nevis?'
'It wasn't me,' I told him.

'You're frozen stiff. Your nose is bleeding. Have you fallen?'

I lifted my hand to my nose and felt the dried crusted blood. Galbraith led me into the spare bedroom and went to get me a hot water bottle and a flannel for my face. I'd already fallen asleep by the time he returned, but he woke me up, softly shaking my shoulders and pressing the warm bottle against my chest, wiping at my nose with a warm wet cloth. 'Nevis, just tell me . . . has something happened? Is everything ok at the farm? Did *he* do this to you? Should I call the police?'

I shook my head weakly.

'Have you had an argument with your father?'

I winced from the words. 'He's not my father,' I forced myself to speak. 'Not any more.'

And with that Galbraith allowed me to sleep.

46

Duckman was still at the farm when Galbraith drove me back the next day. His blue Sierra was parked behind Nigel Kerr's Land Rover and next to it was a police car. I was nervous. Galbraith must have felt my fear or seen me swallow hard because he placed his hand over mine when we pulled in next to the Sierra.

'It'll be ok,' he said.

They were sitting around the kitchen table. Duckman kept his stare firmly fixed to the floor as Galbraith and I entered. Elspeth looked up with round watery eyes and black mascara-stained cheeks, she clutched her handkerchief tighter. My father, looking harrowed, stood up abruptly, but did not make to move towards me or open his mouth to say anything. He just stared. Ailsa was not in the room.

'Mr Gow, your son has been through quite an ordeal.' Galbraith was behind me and I felt his hands on my shoulders as he guided me further into the room.

'Yes, of course.' Elspeth took the cue, pushing her handkerchief bravely to one side. 'An' we've been so worried about ye . . .' She came over and hugged me, pressing my face into her bosom and holding me there. 'Why on earth did ye run off like that?' she asked. 'Ye silly boy. Ye coulda caught yer death.'

I struggled out of her grip and moved back against the wall. The look of disgust on my face did not go unnoticed. 'Don't touch me,' I told her.

'Nevis . . .'

'I'm serious,' I said. 'I don't want *anyone* to touch me.' And finally Duckman looked up to meet my gaze.

It was mid afternoon. The air was cold but clear, no sign of rain. Galbraith was inside with my father and Elspeth. Duckman and I stood outside with the dogs. They lay quietly for a change, sensing the solemn atmosphere. Even Murdo had his chin between his paws, looking up only briefly when we'd come through the back door, thumping his tail on the ground twice, and then lowering his head again.

Duckman took the roll-up cigarette from behind his ear, put it to his lips and lit it. 'Yev cut yer hair,' he said, not looking at me but at the muddy ground beneath his feet. I didn't answer. 'Why did ye cut it?'

'Where's Ailsa?'

He looked at me then for a second and then returned his eyes back to the mud. He blew a thin jet of smoke from between his teeth. 'Wi' the police,' he said.

'Why?' I must have sounded panicked. Duckman gave me a long questioning look.

'What's got intae you?'

'Nothing.'

'Then answer me this, why was Ailsa in the woods this mornin'?'

I frowned. I fidgeted. 'What do you mean?'

'She was there, Nevis. She saw him pull the trigger.' And he turned and kicked the wall with his boot. 'Fuck!' He spun back to look at me, pointing the burning cigarette at my face. 'Did you tell her?' he said.

'No.'

'Then why the fuck was she there? And why the *fuck* are you actin' so guilty?'

I was shaking my head.

'Ah trusted you.'

'I didn't tell her,' I said, still shaking my head. 'I promise, Duckman. I didn't tell her.'

He spat at the ground and turned away, taking a long and final drag on his cigarette before flicking it into the mud. 'Then why was she lookin' for you?' he asked, quietly. 'She said she was lookin' for you this mornin' . . . in the woods. That's why she was there. Why was she doin' that, Nevis? Was it some kinda fucked-up date?'

'No,' I said. 'I . . .' and the words stuck in my mouth. Why *had* she been looking for me?

47

'So you see, son, you say you started running *after* you witnessed . . .' The policeman coughed uncomfortably. '. . . what you witnessed in the caravan. But . . .' and he looked at his colleague for support. The younger, clean-shaven officer smiled at me.

'It's ok, Nevis. You're not in any trouble.'

'I'm not?'

He shook his head. 'Just take it easy and tell us what happened.'

We were sitting in the forbidden room – the old music room. It was odd being in there. It felt full of ghosts. The chimney whistled as the wind blew outside and occasionally a faint drift of ash fell into the empty fireplace. Along the mantelpiece there were framed photographs of the Kerrs smiling or working and one of Catherine at her black grand piano – which still stood proud but lonely at one end of the room, echoing notes ever so faintly. We were sitting at the other end, facing it, and I thought how in days gone by family and friends would have sat here and listened to Catherine play.

'We're not interrogating you,' the clean-shaven officer continued speaking. 'But we need the statements to tally, if you understand what I mean. For our records.' He paused and nodded encouragingly at me. I stared back at him, not saying a word and I noticed his smile turn into doubt and discomfort. He glanced at his colleague and then focused back onto me. 'Nevis?'

'I saw Ailsa,' I said. And both officers looked relieved. 'I ran back into the house and she was there. In the kitchen. She must've heard me sneak out.'

'What happened after that, Nevis?'

'She . . . comforted me.' It wasn't me, I thought. 'She calmed me down. I was upset.'

I'd run into the kitchen, I must have been crying. Ailsa had stood up from where she was sitting, waiting. 'Nevis, what's happened?' She ran over to me. She put her arms around me. 'What's happened?' And I pushed her away. Told her to get off. 'If you touch me again I'll fuckin' kill you,' I said. And yet somehow . . . somehow . . .

'She made me sit down. She brought me some water.'

The policemen were nodding.

It wasn't me. I see the bare white arse of my father and those grotesque wobbling thighs of her mother, the skirt pushed back to her hips, the rise and fall and heated

315

moans, nails on back and filthy red scratch marks. Marshall's face. Fuck! His eyes were locked shut, he refused to look at her. He didn't want to do it. The bastard didn't even want to do it. But I could see him inside her, he was sweating. He was trying to get whatever it was disgusting out of him, into her. 'You're a whore,' I screamed, 'you're a filthy, fucking shit pile.' She was beating his back. She was calling his name. She was holding his buttocks forcing him further, harder inside her. And from beneath me I heard Ailsa sob. It wasn't me. Her lip was bleeding. The red was smeared across her cheek, her eyes clamped shut, wet with tears and she sobbed and sobbed. She was saying something. My hands pinned her down. They weren't my hands. I was fucking her. It wasn't me. She was saying, '. . . please.'

'She kissed me,' I told the policemen and in the back of my head I could hear Galbraith's voice ask – and what about the truths you don't say, Nevis? 'She kissed me,' I repeated and felt her tongue inside my mouth. 'And then I ran.'

The policemen nodded. They smiled. They closed their notebooks.

'That'll be all, Nevis. Thank you.'

48

I don't know why Ailsa didn't tell the police the truth or why after I left her sobbing and alone on the kitchen floor she picked herself up, brushed herself down and came looking for me in the woods. That's when she stumbled across Nigel Kerr with the gun in his mouth. It's still unclear whether the shot went off and she began screaming – or whether she began screaming and then the shot went off.

None of it makes sense.

I need to try and slow this pace. In my head memories flash past, fast, rushing, and I can't make them out accurately. I get confused. Surely she would have said something? Surely she wouldn't have come looking for me afterwards? Surely I would have had a bruise across the knuckles where I'd hit her? There was blood on her lip, yet I don't remember striking out. In fact, I seem to remember kissing Ailsa again. But it wasn't Ailsa I was kissing, it was my father. And then I *was* my father and Ailsa was Elspeth. And then I was the boy in the car park and Ailsa was the drunken girl. Everything became disjointed. I panicked. I pulled away. I ran.

There must have been some sort of flow. Time is continuous after all – and yet I can't link one minute to the next. Everything becomes blurred from the moment I started running. When I try to put my mind to it, really force myself to remember, the only clear thing I can see is my father and Elspeth in the caravan – and then every so often a split-second flash of something else. Falling in the yard. The dogs barking. The back door slamming. Ailsa standing up. 'Nevis, what's happened?' She sat me down. She got me some water. I remember her holding the glass to my lips. I remember the wet in my mouth. 'Shhh, it's ok, Nevis. It's ok.' She was stroking my hair and whispering in my ear. 'You're ok now.' But even with my eyes shut I could see everything. Her wobbling thighs. Her heated moans. I squeezed my eyes tighter together. And then the boy pressing his girl up against the wall, 'Hold yersel' up, fer fuck sake.' That night in the car park by the skips. The girl's drunken head lolling. Her skirt pulled up around her hips. Her green skirt. My hand being taken and pressed against . . . his lips, my lips pressed against . . . her lips. Ailsa was kissing me. She had one hand on my shoulder and another hand on my thigh. I pulled away from her.

'No.'

'Nevis, calm down.'

Did I struggle? Did I try to push her away? None of it makes sense. Surely I would have struggled against her – in fact, I remember that. I remember sitting at the kitchen table and trying to pull away as she held me back by the shoulder. But something stopped me, something Ailsa said. 'Such a fuss over a wee kiss, Nevis . . . it's not like we've never done it before.'

'What?'

'You don't remember?'

And she told me about how she'd looked after me when I was ill, how she'd calmed me down when I had nightmares. She'd whispered in my ear – everything is going to be all right. She'd held my hand.

'You're lying.'

'No.'

She told me about the time I had such a horrible dream, I was thrashing and writing about on the bed, she couldn't calm me down. She was so frightened she had to leave. But before she left she dropped some perfume onto a handkerchief and placed it on the pillow next to my head in the hopes the smell would help me sleep easier.

'Do you remember?'

I remembered the handkerchief but didn't want to admit it. 'No,' I said.

She told me that when I slept she'd put her arm round me. Sometimes she'd kissed my eyelids . . . my cheeks.

'Only ever your eyelids and cheeks,' she said. 'But once – just once – I kissed you on the lips.'

And my body tensed. Every muscle in my body tightened as though resisting the idea. 'You shouldn't have done that,' I told her. 'If it's true you shouldn't have done that.'

'But you liked it.'

'No.'

'Then why did you kiss me back?'

I keep looking at my hands. I don't remember hitting her, yet there was blood: although, on closer inspection, it could have been my blood. 'Your nose is bleeding,' Galbraith had said. 'Have you fallen?' I don't remember falling on my face. I don't remember my nose bleeding at all, but my fingers found dried blood above my lip and in my nostrils. Proof. It could have happened in the kitchen. It could have happened during . . .

. . . and dripped onto her face.

'Please . . .' she was saying. '. . . please.'

Please stop? Please be careful? Please . . . gently please . . .

'Memory is not like a videotape recorder,' Galbraith had said. 'You can't remember every little detail of everything you say and do. Only fragments. And then you flesh out the rest. Build a narrative around those snippets of fact so it makes sense.'

But there is a way of making a memory more accurate, isn't there? If another person can agree that an event took place, then it's more likely to be true.

And yet Ailsa must have signed the statement, just as I had signed mine. *We kissed*, it said. *And then Nevis ran away*.

Nevis ran away because of a kiss.

I thought of my father.

Marshall didn't know I saw him with Elspeth that night in the caravan. And he didn't know about my confrontation with Ailsa. All he knew was what Galbraith had told him when he'd called that morning, leaving a message on the answering machine – Mr Gow, I have your son here. He's safe.

Marshall had played me back the message that night when we were sitting at the kitchen table. We were alone. Duckman was in his bedroom, packing away the rest of his belongings. Elspeth was with Ailsa. I'd crept past on my way to the bathroom earlier and I heard Elspeth humming to her daughter. I wanted to look in. I wanted to see if Ailsa had her eyes open and filled with the horror of the night before, but I didn't dare push the door further ajar. So I listened to Elspeth's quiet humming and hoped that Ailsa was asleep and forgetting.

'Why did you run away, Nevis?' Marshall was sitting

opposite me. He had his hands clasped in front of him on the table. For a while I watched him stroke his thumbs together. I didn't answer. 'I mean, where would you go? You don't know anyone.'

I know Galbraith, I thought. I know Duckman.

'Nevis?'

Without realising the tip of my finger had found the same deep scar cut into the table that I'd stared at on the first day we arrived at the farm. I was tracing it back and forth, feeling the groove against my skin. Marshall sighed. He rubbed his hands over his face.

'You know, I've run away before,' he said. 'Do you want to know why?' He didn't wait for an answer. 'Your mother, Nevis. I was trying to tell you before, the night after you found the photograph. Do you remember? But you were angry. You wouldn't listen.' He shook his head. 'Running away doesn't work. Trust me on that one. Your problems just follow you around.'

'They do if they're hidden in your wallet,' I said.

Marshall lowered his eyes.

'Do you still love her?'

'Nevis . . .'

'And Elspeth? What about Elspeth?'

For a moment Marshall looked surprised.

'And me? Do you love me?'

I watched him open and close his mouth silently. He looked away. 'There are different types of love, Nevis.'

'So I hear,' I said and pressed my finger harder into the table.

Duckman knocked before entering the kitchen, bag on his back and dragging a bin-liner of clothes behind him. He looked at me, then at Marshall, then back at me. 'Couldn't gi' us a hand, could ye?' Just like we planned. I got to my feet and followed Duckman into the hallway. 'You all right?' he whispered.

'No,' I told him.

Duckman picked up his stainless steel bin full of fag ends and ash with its little label LIFE peeling slightly at the corner. He handed it to me. Nodded. 'Let's jus' go, eh?'

I looked at him, then down at my feet.

'Nevis?' Duckman touched me on the shoulder. 'Are ye ready?'

The plan had been this: Duckman had a friend in Inverness who had a flat we could both stay at. We'd go there and 'sign on', Duckman had said – which seemed to mean we'd get free money because we didn't have a job. This didn't make any sense to me. Why work if you could get free money? But I listened anyway. Duckman seemed to know what he was talking about. He spoke about saving up, maybe even getting some 'inheritance', he said. 'And then we can hit the road. Live out the boot of ma car, sleep in tents, find work all over the country. Freedom. Pure freedom.' And me – sitting there listening, had nothing but everything that had happened running through my head. I had to get away. I couldn't be around Marshall after witnessing him with Elspeth. And I couldn't be around Ailsa after what I'd done. If I'd done it. Did I do it? So I nodded. I agreed. 'Let's go,' I said. But later that evening, standing in the hallway with Duckman, facing the front door, the plan had suddenly become all too real. And I thought back to Galbraith and his wife, always forgiving, always standing by her side without question, no matter what. Unconditional love. How could I leave?

And so when Duckman asked me, 'Nevis, are ye ready?' I said, 'no.'

We stared at each other.

'I can't do it.'

Duckman continued to look at me.

'I'm sorry.'

He shook his head.

'I can't do it,' I said again.

And he took back hold of the bin from my arms.

'I can't leave him,' I whispered urgently. 'You don't understand, Duckman. I promised.'

'Fine,' he said. And with his bag on his back, bin under his arm, dragging a black sack of clothes behind him, he moved towards the front door. It was on the tip of my tongue – the word 'wait'. But I didn't say it. I just watched as Duckman began to unlatch the door, and as he did so he said in a sort of sing-song voice, 'Marshall and Nevis hit the road in a beautiful white Transit van . . .' He opened the door wide and then turned to look at me. 'That's what yer hopin' for, right, Nevis? To drive away for a year an' a day to the land where the Bong-tree grows?'

I had no idea what he was talking about.

'Ye know reverse gear only really works in a vehicle, Nevis. It doesn't work at all with real life.' He wasn't smiling. He glared at me, then shook his head and moved off, dragging his bag out into the night. I heard his footsteps and then his voice in that same sing-song way, becoming more distant as he moved round the side of the house. 'And hand in hand in the back of a van, they danced by the light of the moon, the moon, the moon. They danced by the light of the moon.'

'Pure poetry,' I whispered after him.

49

I should write about the days that followed – the days that led right up to me sitting here now, bent up over my notepad just like Marshall used to bend and sweat over his. Although maybe there is little point in writing about the last seven days what with my time being solely committed to recording everything that's happened, to writing these lists and episodes and memories. But I should at least sketch the bare bones of what followed Duckman leaving.

At first I did not move from my spot in the hallway. I listened to Duckman's footsteps and then the car door open, eventually close, and the engine start up. I moved to the front door slowly, listening to the distant creak of the trees in the woods and the wind rustling branches, waiting for the sound of Duckman's car turning and bumping down the track. I stared out at the starless sky, for a moment completely absorbed in its infinite black. And then a chair-leg squeaked against the tiles in the kitchen behind me, and my father called my name, 'Nevis?'

Perhaps Duckman knew that I would run after him. Perhaps my actions are that predictable. He even left the door wide open for me so that the way was completely clear. But running away hasn't made me happy, just like Marshall warned me it wouldn't. And it hasn't made me feel free, as Duckman promised it would. I simply feel lost. And alone. Now I sleep on sofa cushions on the floor of someone's flat instead of in the van with my father, thinking every night 'what if, what if' and wondering if he's thinking the same thing.

This morning, before the funeral, Duckman had nudged me from my sleep with his foot.

'Wakey fuckin' wakey,' he said. 'Gettin' up?'

He told me as I pulled on my trousers and socks that I'd had nightmares again. He told me this every morning. 'Ah hear ye mutterin' and panickin' in yer sleep,' he said. 'Twistin' an' turnin' like yer wrestlin' a crocodile.'

'I don't remember,' I lied.

'No?' he said. 'Ye fuckin' sat bolt upright last night. Yer face sweatin'. Near gave me a heart attack. Ye don't remember that?'

I shook my head. I was sitting on the floor, pulling on my boots. 'I don't remember,' I said. Duckman crouched down so our faces were level and close. I could smell the nicotine on his breath. 'Nevis,' he said slowly. I wasn't looking at his eyes but at his yellow and black teeth. 'Yer shite at lyin',' he said. 'Did ye know that?' He didn't wait for an answer. He stood up again and stretched his arms and legs. 'Not that ah care o' course. Ye can lie all ye like. Ah jus' thought ye might like t' know that you were shite at it.' And he sniffed, scratched his crotch. 'T' be honest though, it's probably a good thing, eh? Ah mean, ah'm no sure ah want t' know all aboot yer weird fucked up psychological traumas. Best keep 'em to yerself, eh? Ye don't want t' burden me wi' shite like that. Ah got enough problems.'

A week after the event. A whole seven days. Sometimes I think that maybe it wouldn't have mattered what I'd done – I would have felt like it was a mistake. It's natural when choosing between two options to think 'what if ... what if ...' And that's what I've done every day since. Along with pouring out the past onto paper, ciphering through the days in the hopes it pulls everything together and makes sense. But it doesn't. I wake up each morning from yet another nightmare, scared of myself and my hands and what they can do. Forever confused and full of contradictory feelings. Hating Marshall and yet missing him completely. I had to see him again. I had to make sure. I told Duckman this morning I wanted to go back to the farm. 'Why fuck up yer fragile mind further?' he asked. But he didn't say no. He just shrugged and then locked himself in the bathroom for a long time. I heard him step into the shower; the water running, irregularly hitting the enamel bathtub, streaming from all the points on his body where it could no longer follow its contours: his elbows when his arms were bent, his fingertips, his chin, his cock. Water collects at these points and forms long drips, like taps not properly turned off. And then I heard his hand pushing the soap and water over his body, making it fall faster, striking the enamel harder. I was not thinking about Duckman. I was thinking about the sound. Analysing how it's formed. I wanted to remember the moment, sitting at that table, writing and waiting and listening to the sound of shower water running – because I was so close. Everything was gearing towards the end. And as I listened I started writing in my notepad about the night before, about how I watched Duckman iron his clothes. Black trousers, white shirt. Hole-free.

He laid a piece of clothing carefully over the table and pressed out the creases. Steam poured from the bottom of the iron every time he lifted it, made a wet sighing sound. And there was a little blue button on top that when pressed would squirt hot water.

Duckman caught me watching him. At first he looked at me fiercely, told me to fuck off, stop staring. So I did. I stared at my feet instead. Then Duckman cleared his throat and when he spoke his tone had softened. 'Come 'ere a minute.' I got to my feet and went to him. 'Don't s'pose you could finish off ma shirt?'

'I don't know how . . .'

'It's easy. Jus' take hold o' the iron, run it over the creases. Dinnae hold it still 'cause ye'll burn marks into the clothin'. Lift it every so often . . . aye, like that . . . and when that red light comes on ye need to let it heat up again. Leave it on the side until the light goes off. And mind t' keep an eye on the water level.' He pointed at the black lines underneath the handle and the transparent water gauge. 'Don't let it go below the line that says "min".' He caught my eye. He looked uncomfortable. I could see his neck and cheeks begin to redden slightly. He tried to shrug it off. 'It's easy, Nevis. A fuckin' child could do it,' but managed only to sound irritated.

'What do I do if the water level goes below the line?'

'Are ye serious?'

'What?'

'You fill it up, fer fuck sake. There's a hole right there.' He pointed.

'And what about the blue button?'

'Oh ah wouldna press that if ah were you. The whole fuckin' world will explode.'

I looked down at the shirt. I continued to move the iron over it. Perhaps he could see my own cheeks had flared red because he began to speak more softly. 'Ah

he might have even *been* it and if that was the case then how could I possibly leave him for good? My life would be meaningless. It would be a mess. I would be nothing.

Duckman asked me twice already before leaving this morning if I was sure I wanted to come along. Not to the funeral. I'd already told Duckman I wasn't going to the funeral. But to the farm, to see Marshall. Duckman seemed concerned. Ye look like shite – he kept saying – ye could stay at ma mate's flat and rest if ye wanted. Duckman's mate does not like me. He calls me that weird wee quiet fucker, always writing. And he never talks directly to me, preferring instead to talk through Duckman. 'Hey Duck, does your weird wee quiet fucker friend want a beer or does he just want t' write?' I didn't like the idea of staying in the flat without Duckman.

'He's gonnae be oot all day, Nevis. Ye'll have the place t' yersel'.'

'No,' I said. 'I need to see Marshall.'

'Why?'

'It's important. I need to make sure.'

'Of what?' Duckman crouched beside me, gripped my shoulder with his hand. 'If ye see him, ye know he'll try t' make ye stay, don't ye?' For a moment we stared at each other, so near I could see my reflection in his eyes, pale long face and close-cut hair. Still I didn't quite recognise myself. All week I'd been double-taking every glimpse I caught of my reflection. It wasn't just about getting used to having short hair. It was more than that. There was definitely something different about my face. It felt like I was looking at somebody vaguely familiar, but I couldn't quite remember who. Even then while Duckman stared into my eyes I wasn't looking back at him, but at myself . . . although not myself.

Perhaps this makes even less sense on paper, maybe I just sound crazy – but I felt split in two. There was me and then there was my reflection. And I had to choose between them. Or maybe somehow I had to make them one again.

'I need to make sure,' I repeated.

'Of what, Nevis?'

'That I'm choosing the right me.'

Duckman continued to hold my shoulder and stare at me. Then he let go, stood up, reached for his tobacco tin in his breast pocket. He started rolling a cigarette. 'As soon as ah get my inheritance ah'm ootta here,' he said.

'I know.'

'With or withoot you, Nevis.'

I paused. 'I need to see Marshall,' I said. 'He's got a piece to the puzzle.' I looked up at Duckman. 'And maybe even Ailsa too. If she's at the funeral, Duckman, you have to say to her that Nevis needs to know: did it happen. Yes or no.' Duckman stood stock-still looking down at me; feet shoulder-width apart, left hand cupping right elbow close to his body, cigarette between two fingers, inches from his face. He was like a monumental smoking statue. 'It's the twist,' I told him. 'If this really is the end then there needs to be a twist ... a revelation ... a transformation ... a change. There has to be development. There has to be a moment of clarity. Everything fitting into place, like a jigsaw. All questions answered. All knots carefully tied. Do you understand?'

Duckman flicked the ash from the tip of his cigarette.

'I need a moment of clarity,' I said again. 'I want things to make sense.'

Duckman shrugged. 'Fine.' He stubbed out his cigarette. 'So hurry up an' get yer little list of unanswered questions together. We're goin' soon.'

I didn't need to make a list. There was only one question. In the beginning there were more, but I knew they all paled into insignificance, like the moments I'd missed out and the memories that needed a trigger. The answers to those questions were irrelevant, they'd become clutter. I wanted to know what was real and what was not. Yes or no. The question that answers all other questions. The twist, the revelation, the transformation, the change. The truth. What an excellent dénouement.

50

I watched him through the caravan window, me on the outside looking in. He was packing a bag with his clothes and books. I noticed he packed the two mugs Elspeth had given us in the first week we arrived at the farm, the yellow one with chipped rim and the other with Edinburgh Castle on the front. Then I saw him stop, his hands resting inside the bag for a moment before removing the mugs again. Placing them on the table. There was not much to pack. My father had very few possessions. It was while he zipped shut the holdall I stepped up to the door and pushed down the handle. As I walked in I took off my cap. My father looked up.

He hadn't shaved. The hair on his chin was short and bristly. He looked unkempt, almost like the old Marshall, although he was smart in his hired suit, black tie and freshly pressed white shirt. His eyes seemed distant. When he saw me they began to focus and clear.

'Nevis,' he said. We stared at each other, me standing by the door, him holding onto the table as though steadying himself. 'You're back.' I eyed him carefully, trying to work out if Ailsa had changed her mind and said something. 'Where've you been?'

'It doesn't matter,' I said.

'It doesn't . . .' and his legs seemed to give way at the knees. He sat down quickly, elbows resting on the surface of the table, hands covering his eyes. 'I've been so worried,' he said. 'I thought I'd lost you. I thought you were gone for good.' And he started to shake. For a moment I had to look away and focus my attention on the metal sink, resisting the urge to run to him. 'Nevis, you can't leave me.' And I wondered then if what I was witnessing was a repeat of what my mother had witnessed eleven years ago. I looked back at my father.

'There's something I need to know,' I said – clearly and without emotion. 'About the van,' I added.

'No, Nevis.' His voice tried to regain some depth and authority.

'The day before we crashed . . .' Marshall still covered his eyes. '. . . I kissed you.'

'We need to forget about these things,' he said and moved his hands away to look at me firmly. 'Nevis, it's ok.'

'No,' I said.

'We have to move on. Just pretend it didn't happen.'

'But it did happen,' I said. 'I remember.'

Marshall turned his face away.

'But that's not all, is it? That's not everything. Yes or no, you have to tell me . . .' And I felt his lips press hard against mine, and his tongue slide into my mouth. 'You kissed me back, didn't you?'

Later I would remember this moment as time slowing down and stopping. Some memories are like that. You can hold them perfectly still, like a photograph, or manipulate time, slow it down, speed it up. I would always slow this moment down until it stopped completely. I even began to remember it in third person. I'd let myself climb out my body and walk around the caravan. I'd study my own face first, my eyes glassy, my mouth unsmiling, my haphazardly cut hair sticking out in all directions. I held my black cap at my side, my other hand clenched into a fist. I was squared up, like a cowboy ready to pull his gun. And my father sat opposite me, elbows on table, his hands still raised from when he'd been covering his eyes. I'd let myself get close to his face, so close I could smell his skin. Sometimes I even allowed myself to touch him, the hairs on his chin coarse against my fingers. This is how powerful a memory can be.

No, he said. No, Nevis, I did not.

51

I spent the rest of the day by the river, not far from where Duckman and I stretched out that tarpaulin. I sat on the bench and watched the water break against rocks on the riverbed, making the white in the rapid. The air was cold. My fingers were red raw and numb. I tried to write for a while and found my hand couldn't hold the pen properly. I had to grip it like a chisel and write with clenched fist. I wasn't writing anything in particular. Just what I could see: the green and yellow of the grassy bank, the molehills, brown bursts of soil. There were twisted twig-like plants at the water's edge. I don't know what they're called. In the spring and summer they look more alive, they go green, maybe even flower. But in the winter they turn skinny and dead-looking. The trees were skinny too, starved boughs, the branches bare and tangled with other branches from other trees, interlinking offshoots like cobwebs.

I sat and watched the river and watched the sky promise snow, clouding low and heavy above the brown and purple heathered hills that steeped up from nowhere and formed the valley.

I waited.

Eventually I saw him. Where the river bent round to the right and picked up speed, booming under the bridge, a black dot walking with two dogs just ahead. Within ten minutes Murdo and Red were sniffing around my feet, wagging their tails, licking at my hands and Duckman was walking down the path through the trees beside me. Murdo jumped up, his two paws on my lap, so I pushed him down, patted him on the head. 'Sit,' I said. He barked and moved off to join Red at the edge of the embankment, drinking the river water.

Duckman did not say anything as he approached. He just silently joined me on the bench and we were both quiet and watched the river and the dogs for a while. I wondered who would be the first to speak. I wondered if it should be me, but I didn't know what to say and I didn't want to be the one who broke the silence. Eventually I looked at him.

'Apparently it's ma fault,' he said.

I looked back at my hands.

'They don't say it to ma face mind, but behind doors. Ah heard them this mornin'. Apparently he did it 'cause ah left. But that's no the case; he was gonnae do it anyway. *You* know that, don't ye, Nevis?'

I nodded.

Duckman looked at me, straightfaced. 'Ailsa wasnae at the service,' he said. 'She's gone back t' Aberdeen. Ah overheard Elspeth sayin' she's no very well. She's in shock.'

'Oh.'

'Ah guess ye would be if ye witness someone shoot 'emsel' in the gob, eh?' He spat into the grass. 'Ah guess it also means ye'll no have the answer t' yer question.'

'Perhaps it's better that way,' I said. I was thinking back to my father's resilient 'no' and wishing – not even that it'd been a 'yes' – but for silence. Silence would've been better than denial.

I was pressing my thumbnail deep into a notch I found in the bench, just underneath my right leg. Duckman was sitting next to me looking thoughtfully at the river. I felt the dirt build up under my nail, but I kept digging into the notch anyway. Duckman looked at me briefly then back at the river.

'Ye know, Nevis, ah think yer supposed t' ask me aboot the service.'

'Am I?'

'It's the done thing.'

'In that case, I won't,' I said.

That seemed to amuse Duckman because he smiled.

'Do you hate him?' I asked instead. 'Your father. For killing himself.'

Duckman did not take his eyes from the river. He just

shrugged. But I noticed how the tension had gone. What-ever oozed from Duckman before – the death of his mother, his forgotten sister, the potential suicide of his father – none of it was there anymore.

'Ah don't know, Nevis,' he said. 'Ah don't really feel anythin'. Just sorta . . . empty.' He looked at me. 'What aboot you? Did ye get yer moment o' clarity?'

I looked down at my feet.

'Did you get yer twist? Yer revelation? The pieces t' yer weird wee jigsaw?'

'No,' I told him and I felt almost bitter. There are too many things now that make little or no sense. How can I be so sure that something happened – to the point where I can feel everything again the minute I cast my mind back, not just emotions, but physical touch, and yet I'm told it didn't happen. It didn't exist. It wasn't real. Ailsa signed her statement, with no mention of anything more than a kiss, yet I was inside her – I *know* I was inside her – how can someone mistake such a thing? Duckman's denial at the river that he touched my leg, his insistence that I must've been dreaming yet I'm certain of my complete consciousness. And my father returning my affection. That night when he woke up and my lips were pressed against his. He kissed me back. I know he did. I can feel it. I can feel it. All over again. Can a mind really make up things like that? And so vividly? If so, how am I ever going to know what is real, what is truth? It hardly makes any sense to continue with lists and questions that cannot be confirmed or answered. 'Nothing makes any sense,' I said.

He sighed. Spat. 'Well maybe you were askin' the wrong questions.' He looked at me. 'Ye know, life doesnae have t' be so cryptic, Nevis. All this bollocks aboot "choosin' me's" and grand revelations. We're no livin' in a fuckin' poem. There's no prettily wrapped package you can tie all this intae: "and they all lived happily ever after. The end." Ah know that's what yer tryin' t' do. But ye can't. It's too messy. It's nuclear. You're born and then – boom – a mushroom cloud. It cannae be contained.'

I smiled. I thought of my father. 'With such a poetic tongue in your head, Duckman,' I said, 'perhaps you should be a writer yourself.'

'Fuck off, Nevis, don't be a wanker.'

I stopped smiling.

'Just ask yersel' this, it's quite simple: do ye wanna stay or do you wanna go?' He stared at me. He waited for an answer. But I was silent. I was looking at the river. Stay or go. What was worse? To watch Marshall clumsily act out the role of the socially acceptable father? To pretend everything was how it should be between us? To forget the past and begin – not just a whole new chapter – but an entirely different book, where the van and our past and the kiss didn't exist. Or do I leave?

We've changed, I thought. *I've* changed. Perhaps that was one of the reasons I knew I'd come to the end. A character has to go through some sort of development – they have to be different at the end from how they were at the beginning. And I'm different now. I can feel it. I turned to Duckman then, who was still watching me closely, waiting for my answer, and I said, 'I'm scared.'

Duckman looked away. 'Ye'll soon enough learn how t' hold yer own hand, Nevis and no rely on someone t' hold it for ye. Ah've managed.'

And even though I felt sick and torn and completely clueless, I said, 'Let's go.' And Duckman smiled when he looked back up at me. Nodded. 'Good decision,' he said. He got to his feet and called to the dogs. He started walking towards the trees, turning after a moment when he realised I wasn't following. I was still sitting on the bench. I had my cold hands shoved deep into my jacket pockets and my fingers had touched upon the spindly limbs of the frog key-ring.

'Are ye comin'?' Duckman called back to me from over by the trees.

I said nothing but got to my feet and started walking slowly after him, my fingers still feeling their way around the key-ring. And then I stopped. Took it out. Held it in my palm. I could hear Marshall inside my head. It's Kermit, he said, from *Sesame Street* – and I moved his little green hands so they were covering his eyes.

This is an important part, I thought. A good ending. Marshall never did describe how to write a good ending. You have to start with a bang, he said, grip people by the throat and shake them hard like you're never going to let them go. But how do you end? I walk to the edge of the embankment, extend my arm, fingers loosely holding that little green body. Ready to let go.

And I let go.

Acknowledgements

I want to thank all the tutors and students at Bath Spa University who read the manuscript in its early stages and gave me good feedback and advice, in particular Gerard Woodward and Tessa Hadley, both brilliant mentors. And thank you Will Francis, my excellent agent, Carole Welch, my editor, Ruth Tross, assistant editor, and everyone involved at Sceptre for all your hard work, commitment and enthusiasm. And thank you Freddie (Carla) Senior for somehow managing to live with me (and my mood-swings) while I was writing most of this. You too gave me sound advice and excellent criticism. More importantly, you were an awesome friend. And lastly, thank you so much to everyone at Coleford Mill, without whom I would never have finished this novel when I did. I have never met a more kind and generous family. Thank you.